ALPHONSE

ALPHONSE

A Novel

by
Carl Sever

Published by SparkPress, a BookSparks imprint,
A division of SparkPoint Studio, LLC
Tempe, Arizona, USA, 85281
www.gosparkpress.com

Published 2017
Printed in the United States of America
ISBN: 978-1-943006-24-3 (pbk)
ISBN: 978-1-943006-25-0 (e-bk)

Library of Congress Control Number: 2017937856

Cover design © Julie Metz, Ltd./metzdesign.com
Book design by Stacey Aaronson

This is a work of fiction. Names, characters, places, and incidents either are the product of the author's imagination or are used fictitiously. Any resemblance to actual persons, living or dead, is entirely coincidental.

Dedicated to my son, Devin and my daughter, Stephanie

I

FRANCIS: EARLY SUMMER, 1959

———

CHAPTER ONE

The Canal

THE CANAL WALKED STRAIGHT THROUGH TOWN WITHOUT a sound, or anger, or hurry. Two concrete culverts beneath the five main streets of town were more than adequate, for even in the worst of rains it never flooded. Along the banks, patches of chickweed would peek through the rocks by the first of May. And, if an old man or a boy were patient enough, and if he poised above a culvert long enough in early June, he could, if lucky, witness a dark cloud of infant catfish swirling close to the cement for safety and comfort. The two thousand miniatures would disappear by July, and just a few would grow to prosper as blue cats west of town, where the canal would finally be forgotten by most.

Carved out in the early 1800s, the canal floated barges drawn by oxen. Back then, it was the principal means of transporting goods shipped down from the Great Lakes and moved inland to Dayton and Fort Wayne. On into the 1900s it eventually gave way to steam locomotives that linked Buffalo to Cleveland, Toledo to Chicago.

St. Joseph, an Indiana town of five thousand Germans, flourished thanks to the canal, and within a decade of the town's founding, its Main Street paralleled this vital link. A mile and a bit west of town the canal connected with the Little Auglaize, which ultimately joined Five Span before flowing into the Ohio River in the south.

Waste water and sewer lines emptied into the canal so by the time it left the town limits it was little more than an open sewer. If one would've waded the confluence, his boots would've brought to the surface thick, black goo, and there grew a powerful stench where it joined the Little Auglaize.

But in my thirteenth summer, I was oblivious to the smell. In my sheltered mind, the canal was the Euphrates, the Little Auglaize the Tigress, merging here to form the fertile Mesopotamia. On these banks, a boy could conjure adventure and beasts; his fantasies could swell toward epic.

Back then, we spoke reverently of this spot, referring to it in near whispers as "The End." Little did I know that I'd venture to The End but once that summer, that it would be far into autumn before I would return to my boyhood hideaway.

It was the summer of '59, and school had been out just a few days. Zach, my older brother by a year, and his best friend Jack Rupert, had been horsing around in the garage when I lunged off our back porch. The screen door smacked shut just as I landed on the sidewalk. When I whipped into the garage to get ready, Zach snarled, "God F'n damn, Francis! You're always late."

"I'm all set. Dug the worms last night."

Timidly, I ventured a quick, "Hey, Rupert . . ." but it didn't work. Rupert only grinned while he casually bounced the basketball against the garage floor.

Not often, but every so often, Zach allowed me to share his friend. I thought of him simply as Rupe, the nickname my brother called him, though I never would've dreamt of calling him that to his face.

In two shakes, we tore from the garage that Friday with freedom pulsing through our bodies, unbounded possibility pounding against the pedals of our bikes. Bringing along my fishing stuff and my faithful cane pole, I did my best to keep up, whipping down the stony alley behind our house, and on the way became convinced that a giant blue cat awaited me at The End after my slow torturous winter.

Rupe wasn't crazy about fishing like me, and he found it absolutely paramount that morning to bring along a basketball. I suppose the first thing you have to know about St. Joseph High School is that it was famous statewide for its basketball teams, and it was a rare season when they didn't make it at least to the regional tournament. So it's not surprising that a basketball was brought along as part of the tackle that first summer foray on the first of June.

Threading a night crawler on a hook, I tossed my offering to the grayish water. Boy, did I get a kick out of fishing. Others thought me silly while I'd wait hours for a simple hint from my bobber. But heck, I didn't care; somewhere in the gunk was a huge catfish waiting to bite.

I'm sure Zach was only teasing when he smirked, "Ain't no fish in there, Francis . . . it's a shithole!"

"But the canal's wide here." I tried my best to defend The End. "And it's deep on the other side. Louie said—"

"That ole goat, he's crazier 'n Alphonse!"

Zach spun the ball on a finger and shot a wink at Rupe.

Well, that morning Zach and Rupe started messing around, faking left, tucking the ball in a crook, zooming all around . . . dang, basketball at The End for cryin' out loud. True thespians, they counted down through the climax of the game. The crowd went wild of course, and both were carried on the backs of teammates as all heroes must be.

By eleven o'clock their foreheads glistened with sweat, and their panting couldn't conceal their intense fantasy, having their pictures in the newspaper or seen in a giant poster hung on display down at the First National Bank. I was watching from the bank, and secretly rooting for my brother, when the ball ricocheted from an elbow and went sailing into the canal. Splatting down, it bobbed not far from my cork.

"Hey, Frank," yelled Rupe. "A little help!"

Geeze . . . Rupe needed my help—didn't even call me Francis. I waded in. The sickly warm water came up to my thighs. After flipping the ball up to Rupe, I waded back, and maybe it's one of those markers in life that become permanent, but even now I can still see my brother's nasty look with that impatient frown etched on his face. Anyway, I sure liked tossing that ball back to Rupe.

I had no sooner wound on a fresh worm and tossed it back than my cork began ticking sideways. Carp bite like that . . . better wait. If it ain't a carp, it might be a stupid sunfish, probably too small to pull my cork under. Hope it's a blue gill. You can eat 'em if they're big enough. I jerked my pole up sharply, and a really nice blue gill emerged from the soup, shuttered its tiny flanks against the ground while its gills fluttered and searched for water. I cupped the little bugger in my hand. Its gills were blue, and it had that black spot on its cheek, but the belly was a deep yellow, and the iridescent blue running down its sides gave way to purple close to its tail. Its eyes were orange. Just imagine, from a sewer, a moonbeam gasped for oxygen in my hand.

"Look, Zach!"

Guess it was awful small, and I didn't really blame him for ignoring me. I marveled at it only briefly. Too small for a stringer, it was fun anyway, and I threw it back. I'm not quite sure, but I think that little blue gill was the only fish I caught that entire summer.

Soon after, the sky grew dark and pressed down heavy against our first summer fun. A wicked flash of lightning sent us scrambling to our bikes, and while thunder rolled over the town, we jetted from the dirt trail out onto the gravel road. As usual my brother led the way, while Rupe powered from behind with the basketball. Barely keeping up, I was gripping the butt of my cane pole against the handlebars when everything felt upside down. It was as if the canal itself was falling from the sky as curtains of driving rain smacked us full force.

It's hard to think about that time without reflecting on the town and its religion that invaded every fiber of my young body. Had I been a bird, perhaps a pigeon nesting in the steeple, I might've been able to understand how completely St. Joseph church dominated all, colored everything, and how far it cast its dark shadow across the Indiana countryside.

Even the grain elevator, the place where the hopes of our farmers beat, was dwarfed by the immensity of St. Joseph church. Brick paved streets sectioned the town into identical blocks, and in every direction, the streets intersected others at right angles. All in short order led to the wide welcoming steps of our Midwestern Vatican. The immense gold cross atop the steeple reassured the faithful and called out to the stranger; the four twenty-foot wide clocks, one each for the four directions, measured out time for the farmer on his tractor, the housewife hanging laundry in the back yard, the man delivering milk in the darkness of early morning.

Ever since I was a pup, my summers of emancipation from school came with working alongside Zach, diligently plowing head-first into the chores of the church that Monsignor Brennon doled out to its chief maintenance man, Edgar Sadler.

Edgar Sadler was our dad.

My brother and I used iron hooks to pull clinkers from the boilers and wheeled them in tin tubs up the ramp. We sanded smooth the carvings in student desks and applied coats of varnish, polished terrazzo floors with machines twice our weight, and at least once a week, ran long wire brushes down the flues above the boilers. From each flue, the brush spat out soot that coated our faces and ringed our nostrils and mouths with dark gray ash. These were our summers back then, and never did it occur to us that it could be any other way.

CHAPTER TWO

The Mysterious Death of
Mrs. Cunningham

IT MIGHT'VE BEEN TINY, BUT THAT BLUE GILL WAS STILL A
great start to my summer. Yet the day after our excursion to
The End, everything got all screwy.

I'd never paid much attention to the newspaper. I know
my brother didn't, but it was a headline on the front page of
the *St. Joseph Herald* that abruptly steered my thirteenth
year way off course: MRS. CUNNINGHAM FOUND
DEAD, PSITTACOSIS FEARED. Even if I'd read it myself, it wouldn't have made much sense. But the parishioners
had, and when one of its flock succumbs under strange cir-
cumstances, its mystery infects all, and in unison the folks
in town demanded answers.

Few in our town had ever heard of the disease, and Dr.
Webber had only seen a couple cases in all his forty-one
years of practice. But within a day the town's gossip had
found clues, and within two days, speculation about the
mysterious illness had mushroomed to a doom that ripped
through the parish like something detonated.

The very day after the headline, Dr. Webber regretted

naming the presumed disease and knew he should've reported only that Mrs. Cunningham died of natural causes. Details grew distorted, anger swelled, and the day before the funeral, a committee was formed to make a formal demand to Monsignor Brennon.

The fact that Mrs. Cunningham was a pillar in the parish had everything to do with it. Just sixty-nine, healthy and blessed with the vitality to initiate and oversee charities, she moved through the parish with a gentle face and kind words. So when the doctor cited psittacosis, and the town learned that it was a disease of the lungs caused by exposure to birds, more specifically pigeons, the good folks of St. Joseph grew wary and panicked about the pigeons that nested in the high reaches of the church's steeple. Quickly, their anxiety found voice, and they pondered who among them would be next.

For as long as parishioners had sauntered along the walks encircling their grand cathedral, pigeon droppings had been a fact of life. The birds thrived high in their steeple, and no amount of daily sweeping or scraping could erase the fact of where they nested. Until Mrs. Cunningham's unexpected death, no one gave the pigeons a second thought beyond fanning away the smell that occasionally wafted down past the choir to insult the faithful as they sang in their pews.

But within three days, the Victoria Crowned Pigeon replaced one of the seven biblical pestilences. A thick coat of uneasiness blanketed the parishioners at Sunday's High Mass. Blanch Pohlman, Mrs. Cunningham's dearest friend, sat isolated, her shoulders rounded, her gray face hanging low over the hymnal in her lap, space strangely vacant on either side. In the stillness before Mass, others, too, sat apart, finding unusual room on the pew for a purse or a squirming toddler. The usual nudges and musings were gone; smiles and nods were made at a distance.

The Monsignor was baffled; he was determined to find a way of reassuring his parishioners that their own demise was far from imminent, that all would soon return to normal.

Zach was already nodding off next to Dad, but I was on the aisle sitting next to Mom in my usual spot, so I had a good look at Monsignor Brennon when he marched from the sacristy and climbed the four steps to his podium.

Towering above us, he stood erect and steady at the podium. I could see his deeply pleated cassock draped to the floor, hiding his shoes, see purple piping running down his black sleeves to the cuffs, see the lacing that decorated the edges of his white surplice. The sash around his waist was gold and braided with large brown beads. An antique gold cross was emblazoned on his chest, glittering in the light from the stained-glass windows. I could tell that what he wanted to say was awfully important, but I couldn't recall him ever taking so long before beginning to speak.

I suppose he was an inch or two above six feet, and though he was thin, nobody would ever call him skinny. His face was sharp, almost severe, his nose and lips thin, his deep-set eyes dark and secretive. The ragged scar that ran the length of his jaw was deep red, almost purple, and oddly, seemed to fit naturally with his brooding eyes. I was always curious about that scar but never had the nerve to ask. To me way back then, he could've been the president of the United States, all powerful, knowing everything, always right. And I know I wasn't the only one who looked upon him that way, for he dominated the town so thoroughly that the townsfolk simply called him, THE Monsignor.

I thought it weird that his message was so short: He would redouble efforts to scrape clean the walkways and promised an end to the smell. I didn't know it yet, but on these guarantees, my summer would spin into dark and strange territory.

The V. C. pigeons had roosted in the church since it was consecrated in 1852, and in that time over a century of pigeon poop had accumulated in the bell tower. It was over a foot deep in places. And so, the Monsignor blamed the bell tower; it instantly became the insidious place that grew and incubated disease, the place that had surely cut short Mrs. Cunningham's life, and the place where the congregation believed their own mortality might soon be measured. The Monsignor was confident that his few minor adjustments would quell the parishioners' fears. Little did he know.

And it was outside right after Mass when it was decreed. Dad told me that I, along with Father Yossarian, were assigned the job of excavating the bell tower from the century's pigeon guano.

———

IT DIDN'T TAKE LONG FOR me to understand how completely different my summer was about to become, how strangely my days would be strung out. They'd begin at eight sharp and most often would extend well into the evening. First off, a diligent scraping of the sidewalks around and approaching the church was paramount. The night's accumulation simply had to go first. Between church services, my job was to sweep the aisles, rearrange and organize the materials in the racks, and be Alphonse's right hand man. I was never very clear about Alphonse's job, but he was always around, child-happy to do the messy jobs for which my Dad never found time.

I'd always felt a mysterious unspoken bond with Alphonse, yet it took 'til that autumn before I got a true glimpse into the heart of the old hobo and began to understand the wisdom of the fool. But that was just me. Everyone else believed Alphonse was off his rocker, one of those old geezers who'd fallen off the tracks once too often, and tilted a few degrees off kilter. I don't know how he kept pulling it off, but the man could find a way to make the simplest thing complicated, all the while grinning this stupid grin when there was absolutely nothing humorous.

I thought he must've been damn near a hundred years old. He was skinny as a reed; his beard, if ya wanna call it that, was scraggly at best, and he had the habit of chewing his stogies to the nubbins. The brown juice seeping from his mouth was so common it could've been called a feature. Like the southern man he was, he'd stuff his pant legs in his boots, and when it was scorching hot and he worked outside, he'd wear his bibs without a shirt, relishing in the fact that it pissed the hell out of the Monsignor.

He seemed to be always doing something weird, but in

that first week he did something that made no sense and confused me. It was lunch time, and from where I sat eating my sandwich in the shade, I could glance over to the school playground and watch my brother and Rupe goofing around on the basketball court. I was minding my own business when Alphonse called me over to give him a hand.

Well . . . Alphonse didn't exactly call me over. He bellowed loud enough that had there been a Mass in session, they would've had to cancel the sacrament on the spot. I took off running, rounded the corner, and sped toward the causeway that connects the rectory to the church sacristy. Alphonse, saw in hand, was perched in a maple tree that overhung the walkway. Sawed branches lay scattered beneath the tree, and a garden hose was running, soaking the ground beneath him. He didn't seem to want anything or need help. He just smiled down and said, "Howdy do, Francis." Confused, I could only stand there like a sore wart. Then I saw it.

And I wasn't the only one who saw it. Traffic had been whizzing down Second Street but was now backed up by the red light. Drivers honked their horns, jeering and hooting through their open windows. The Monsignor had pushed aside his window curtain to see what all the commotion was about. His crooked jaw instantly hinged open as he watched Alphonse continue to saw away.

Alphonse had perched himself far out on the limb and was sawing close to the trunk. The man was sitting on the limb he was cutting off! And happy as a damn clam, ta boot! He was whistling and grinning, and his legs were dangling carefree ten feet or so above the ground. The more the limb sagged, the lower our collective jaws hung open. The moment stretched, filling with the sound of slow cracking.

For me, the climax of the whole deal wasn't when Alphonse plunged to the ground alongside his limb; it was the exquisite look on his face when he thudded to the soggy ground below. Alphonse had the look of total surprise, as if he had no clue that there was anything wrong with his pruning skills. I simply didn't get.

Alphonse was sprawled out in the mud, clearly pretending to be in shock, but I was worried. It was a crunching fall, and he had to've broken something. I crouched low by his side to see if I could help.

"Alphonse!"

"Did ya see it?" He tugged my sleeve. "See the whole thin'?"

"Half the town saw it. Where ya hurt?"

He peeled himself up, leaned on an elbow and grabbed my arm hard.

"Was the Monsignor lookin'?"

"Saw him peeking out his window."

"The bastard watched me?"

"Yeah . . . I guess so."

With a face like he was about to die, Alphonse struggled to sit up straight; he exaggerated swinging his arms wide to wring the kinks out of his back, then groaned like a mule, loud enough to be heard on Second Street. And get this: he winked at me.

"Help me up, Francis. Go slow, make it look like I'm bad, real bad."

"You landed smack dab on your head!"

"We need ta go slow." Alphonse reached across and latched onto my shoulder. "Gotta stand."

With his groans chiming in as background, and the theatrics he thought necessary, the process of getting Alphonse to his feet took minutes, to the delight of the Second Street crowd. Alphonse played up wobbling on noodle legs while I just stood there watching and wiping my muddy hands on my jeans.

"'peciative Francis."

I stared at the soaked ground.

"You planned this whole thing?"

"Mean like I knew I was gonna fall?"

Dang, was I ever confused. How can anybody plan to be surprised?

"Geeze, Alphonse . . ."

"The Monsignor thinks I'm sneakin'." He managed to fish out a stogie and stuff it in his mouth. "The bastard thinks I ain't crazy."

"What ya just did is crazy in my book."

"Best lean on ya some more. Ya sure he watched the whole shebang?"

"Ain't like a class play."

"Hell if it ain't! Now let's take 'er real slow. Thought I might have a sit with ya while ya eat yer lunch. Course if ya don't mind listenin' ta my babble."

"S'pose not."

We hobbled to the shade, Alphonse eased down to his butt, crossed his legs, and relaxed his back against the tree. He folded his arms with his hands behind his head.

"Been lookin' things over Francis. With all this fool scare about pigeons, looks ta me like yer gonna be in for a shit-ass summer."

I never imagined how right he'd be.

CHAPTER THREE

The Bell Tower

I WAS IN THE TALL WEEDS THAT FIRST WEEK. THERE WERE daily Masses in the morning, at noon, and an evening Mass for some of the farmers, and it was drilled into me that any alteration in the schedule would send the parishioners into a tizzy. From the beginning, because the Monsignor was adamant that nothing should disrupt this schedule, my cleaning the bell tower couldn't begin 'til late. He insisted that the banging above the choir, and the dust from crushing the slabs of crap into tubs, must all wait until after the last Mass, when his Church was closed for business.

My partner in this job, Father Yossarian, had come from Hungary. He was a short, round man, about thirty, balding in weird spots. His wide, friendly smile flashed when his broken English and guttural accent let him down. I suppose he looked upon himself as handicapped with his language wanting, and to make up for this deficit he cheerfully took on any task the Monsignor demanded of him.

While Father Yossarian was eager to begin cleaning the bell tower, I cringed at the thought and was pissed with the way my summer was shaping up. Zach would be doing his regular work in the boiler room with Dad, lucky him, while

I'd be isolated in the bell tower with Father Yossarian for God knows how long, hauling out pigeon crap.

I had climbed the rickety steps up from the choir loft to the bell tower lotsa times before, but that was when I was just a kid. I remember watching my dad's attempt to fix the immense clocks in the steeple. While he banged in iron shims under the worn-out machine, I'd gaze out the turrets and wonder at the tiny cars and the tiny people scurrying along the sidewalks lined with little bitty trees. Back then I never paid much mind to the pigeons cooing high overhead and was simply grateful to sit and gawk for a while as my dad clanged away on the clock.

That first evening, after the last of the farmers had gone, Father Yossarian and I got our first go around of what was entailed. I remember being grumpy about my new job and having to work late, so I didn't fully appreciate that Father Yossarian had taken a strong liking to me, and that he relished our work together into the late evenings of June. He'd pry up an eight-inch slab, I'd crack it in a wash tub, then he'd lower it by rope down to the choir loft. He'd scurry down the stairs and empty the tub, then return just as quickly, his face always filled with a smile.

Round-trip after round-trip, then he stopped abruptly and clapped me on the back saying, "So, what you think now, Francis?"

"This is gonna take forever." I wiped the sweat from my forehead with a sleeve.

"Not forever." He motioned toward the far corner where he'd concocted a table out of some heavy planking. "You bring sandwich? You hungry?"

At the table, the Father waited for me to pull my bologna sandwich from a bag. Watching me, eyes eager in his puffing round face, he asked me with all the importance he could muster, "You like music, Francis?"

Up there in the bell tower with all that pigeon crap, I thought the question was weird and out of place. I'm sure my look was stupid when I peeped, "Guess so."

He didn't seem to notice my sour mood, and stated emphatically, "Boys your age like music."

"Ain't ya going to eat?"

The Father twisted the key on his sardines.

"Music is good, Francis. What you listen to?"

Wadding my sack into a tight ball, I sputtered, "S'pose Roy Orbison is nice."

"You like him?"

"Guess so . . . he has real dark glasses."

"Do your friends like him?"

"Yep . . ." I stared at the deck. It looked like acres. "We sure got a lot of scraping to do."

The Father wiped his mouth with a hankie, put his things away, then flashed his toothy smile. "We should have music for our work."

"What about the Monsignor?"

He rolled his eyes and waved his hands as if to dismiss my worries. But we never did have music up there, though I don't know if that was because neither of us had a radio or because Father Yossarian knew I was right about the Monsignor.

We pried, scraped, and lowered tub after tub down and out, day after day. Seemed odd, but under all that guano, the deck planking looked brand new, like even the finest grains had somehow been preserved beneath the heavy coating of pigeon filth. And so we'd become archeologists of sorts, excavating boards that had been laid down a century before, and had we the science, we would've been able to recognize the seasons by examining the different colored layers of guano and spreading them apart on a table like a calendar.

After what seemed like an eternity to me—late June—we found ourselves sweating together in the far corner of the bell tower, where the guano was well over a foot thick.

We were down to our last section when I made a monumental discovery that in hindsight, ultimately saved me, protected me throughout the rest of my thirteenth summer. The finest tones of color and touch of texture were etched in my brain, and, if I had the skill of an artist, I could paint even now an exact replica of what I found.

It was late, and we were sweating with the energy of having the end in sight. Father Yossarian had only been away a minute or two when I pried up a foot-thick slab.

As I hoisted it into a tub, it suddenly split apart. Not crumbling, but splitting laterally, revealing an oddity that you might find in a museum or a science lab: a perfectly preserved pigeon squab. The tiny statue of feathers in the odorless guano told a story, and for me, it read like a ledger.

For a hundred years, the crimson of the chick's feet, the ivory of its bill, even the iridescent purple around its throat remained unfaded by death. Holding it in my hands, the infant pigeon spoke history, and alone in the bell tower, I conjured the story of how it must've died. I understood instantly that it'd hatched with its wings terribly wrong.

Teasing out the nubbin of its malformed wing, I knew the squab would never fly, never take its place in the sky alongside siblings winging to the farmer's field to feast on grain, never have the strength of its parents to rise high in the steeple and coo till morning. Born wrong, born unlike its brothers, I wondered if its parents flung it from their nest out of disgust, or let it starve from neglect before it tumbled to the deck never knowing their guano would encase and preserve it for a boy to discover a century later.

I was kneeling on the deck as though about to be blessed in sacrament, when Father Yossarian rushed in and gazed over my shoulder. That was the only time I ever witnessed the good man without his wonderful smile. His round face flushed and his mouth formed a silent "Oh" as he stared down at the treasure in my hands. I remember that he didn't look away; I remember he stood rigid and motionless as if he were waiting for the Earth to split open and swallow whole the church with us inside. Right then and there, I needed a pat on the back, but none was offered, and I didn't ask.

Confused, scared, I turned and extended my hands toward him with the squab.

Suddenly, his hand shot out and his fingers pressed silence to his lips. In smooth movements I never knew he possessed, he carefully lifted the squab from my hands and wrapped it in a hankie he'd taken from his pocket. After folding in the ends, he rolled it neatly into a tight small bundle. Without a word, he left me kneeling there. I still recall the sound of the creaking stairs as he descended to the choir loft.

Everything turned suddenly strange. Something significant in the Father had changed, but I had no idea what or why. The rest of that evening he was silent. He worked with a vengeance, ruthlessly jamming the remaining slabs into the tubs and staunchly refusing to look at me. I couldn't understand the reason for his bizarre behavior or fathom the manner in which he treated the little bundle of feathers. The way he had carefully carried it, holding it away from his body, spoke of reverence, yet at the same time, his actions said he was afraid; it was something evil, something to be reviled.

It was sunset when we lowered the last tub down and toted it to the wide trash bin behind the church. Father Yossarian's face showed no joy for having completed a job well done. There were no pats on the back or congratulations that we'd worked hard together and plowed our way through to the end. Instead, he turned his head slowly, searching the corners and viewing the wide expanse of deck boards that now lay exposed, shiny and reborn. He took it all in, then left without saying a word, without ever looking back in my direction.

I stayed on a while longer, uncertain what I'd done to upset Father Yossarian so thoroughly. He looked frightened about something, and I knew from his face that it must be something really bad.

After I'd given the floor another sweep for good measure, I sat at the Father's table and stared out the turrets at the late evening sky. I couldn't get the thought of that pigeon child from my brain; the idea that it could never fly with its siblings wouldn't go away.

The sun was low and its light angled golden through the bell tower, sparkling the dust that still hung in the soft, pastel air. Above me the great bells hung dormant over the new deck, and higher still in the blackness, the pigeons cooed in the stillness.

CHAPTER FOUR

Mr. Baumgartner

ISOLATED FOR NEARLY ALL OF JUNE WITH FATHER YOSSARIAN, I'd been so focused on doing that crappy job that I'd lost the real reason for doing the work at all. That we'd been watched, that our progress throughout the cleaning had been gauged, became obvious the day after we were done. Shortly after noon things were happening in the bell tower. I was sorting through the hymnals in the pews about that time when I saw the Monsignor and some bigwig stroll through the church and disappear behind the door leading up to the choir.

Mr. Baumgartner, head of the parish council, was next on the scene. He was a huge man with a bright, red face. He charged his way from the vestibule, then pounded up the stairs to the choir loft. When my dad crooked a finger at me to follow him and the others to the loft, I knew the thing about Mrs. Cunningham's death and the pigeons wasn't going away so easily, and the concerns about how to forge ahead were going to be figured out in the bell tower on the brand spankin' newly-cleaned deck.

With the enormous German bells as witness, the Monsignor began.

"I'm sure you're not aware Mr. Baumgartner, but yesterday at this time, you would've been standing on a foot of pigeon droppings." The Monsignor gloated, smiled as though he'd done the work himself. "I'd say that's accurate wouldn't you, Francis?"

Taken by surprise, I could only chirp, "Yessir."

The Monsignor began a slow stroll, his hidden shoes clicking against the deck.

"Mr. Baumgartner, certainly you must know Edgar's son. He's a precious . . . I mean wonderfully good worker. He's worked terribly hard the past three weeks scraping and hauling out the filth. I'd say he did a pretty darn good job."

"Edgar's boy?" Mr. Baumgartner seemed distracted. His eyes kept pivoting around, checking out the turrets, trying to see high in the steeple. It was as if he were measuring the place. "What's your name, son?"

I cleared my throat and squeaked, "Francis."

"Well, Francis, looks like a bang-up job. Lot of work for a boy your age."

I didn't know what to say, and my voice didn't seem to work anyway.

The Monsignor paused and smiled thinly. "Mr. Baumgartner, you called this meeting?"

"So the floor's been scraped, Monsignor." Mr. Baumgartner's voice was gravelly. "We still have pigeons, and they'll crap tonight."

The Monsignor resumed his methodical pace. Holy moly, if the Monsignor didn't look like Dracula . . . if it weren't for the sound of his shoes clicking with each step, I would've sworn he was floating across the deck, scanning for weakness.

"I appreciate your candor, Mr. Baumgartner. Have you or the council come up with any ideas?"

"A couple." Mr. Baumgartner quickly scanned the bell tower then pointed a stubby finger up toward the darkness of the steeple. "I'm telling you, Monsignor, none of us on the council have forgotten what Dr. Webber said about these damn pigeons! We're for using poison."

"Poison?" The Monsignor stopped in mid-stride, glowering at the huge man. "If you think the smell of pigeons is scaring everyone, imagine the smell of rotting birds. No, there'll be no poison in my church."

"It's going to take more than this." Baumgartner dismissed the deck with an angry wave. "Something's got to be done, and soon. You're the last person I need to remind about Mrs. Cunningham's contribution, and what she meant to this parish. And it's a damn shot more than money."

From where I waited in the back, I could tell Mr. Baumgartner was steaming. Sweat beaded his forehead. He took a few quick steps closer to the Monsignor, then turned and stomped back toward the turrets.

With his hands anchored to his waist, the Monsignor's steady eyes tracked the man. He appeared content seeing Mr. Baumgartner struggle.

"Mr. Baumgartner, I'm certain you understand my position on using poison."

"Have it your way." Baumgartner gestured at the open turrets. "It wouldn't take much to net these off. Snare a couple dozen birds, and they'll catch on."

"Let me get this straight, Mr. Baumgartner. You want to drape netting around these turrets?" The Monsignor took giant steps toward the turrets and arced his full arm to suggest the entire church steeple. "These birds will just nest in another spire. We have twelve. Net all of them, and my church will be shrouded like death. It'll look like a tomb." He scoffed. "Is that what you had in mind, Mr. Baumgartner?"

"I'll not have you talking down to me!" He raised his head and pointed his red face directly at the Monsignor. Tilting his chin up, his attempt to regain composure was weak. "At the very least we should board up these main turrets."

"Like an abandoned warehouse?"

Baumgartner tugged at his tie, his breathing suddenly becoming heavy and rapid.

"You have the answers, fine. So what do you propose I take back to the council?"

"I'd like to hear from Edgar first."

My dad was an angry forty-year-old man. Handicapped, legally blind, he'd always looked upon himself as a center, almost as if his near blindness gave him the right to barge through his days without any regard to authority, without ever considering that his bark to an innocent request was out of line. Yet now, out in the open with the others waiting for his comments, he was reticent, uncomfortable with the parish elder and his Monsignor. He never turned his clouded eyes to the group but kept his gaze firmly fixed on the deck.

"Francis here has spent the better part of the month cleaning this floor. You should've seen him trudge home after working late. All in all, I think he did a good job. Like the Monsignor said, the crap was awful thick up here. Maybe . . . I don't know . . . maybe with the bell tower cleaned now, and if Francis keeps the sidewalks clean . . . say twice a day . . . this whole big scare about the birds will go away on its own. Everybody's worry will die on the vine. I'm thinking we should just bide our time." He peeked up briefly. "It's a thought."

Dad's modest idea wasn't good enough for Mr. Baumgartner. The elder's face grew red then redder still. His eyes bulged suddenly, like he was scared, while his big hand tore away at the tie around his neck. I thought he was about to explode.

But he didn't say anything. He just clawed at his shirt collar, then leaned sideways and grabbed his arm before crashing down face first. Later, I heard Doc Webber say he was dead before he hit the deck.

If the Monsignor's devoted were worried about pigeons before, Mr. Baumgartner's death in the steeple surely raked alive the urgency for the Monsignor to do something more radical, even though his death had nothing to do with his lungs, pigeons, or psittacosis. The town's folk focused solely on the fact that he died in the bell tower, and the parish pigeons—not a massive heart attack after climbing the steep stairs—were every bit the culprit for his death as for Mrs. Cunningham's.

But Monsignor Brennon's decision held firm, and as Dad had predicted, talk of pigeons and death gradually quieted. People resigned themselves to doing nothing as they waited for another parishioner to fall, believing that the scourge could rise again at any time. A few muttered to their neighbors that the parishes of Fort Wayne and Decatur had pigeons, and you didn't hear them crying that the end was near. Others reasoned that if the birds had nested there for a hundred years, maybe it was the divine will of the Lord.

So on into July nothing concrete was ventured and all the pragmatic solutions had been vetoed by the Monsignor. But every time a parishioner crunched his shoe against the sidewalk or got a whiff of residual pigeon smell from above during Mass, doubt crept in.

———

A THIRD OF MY SUMMER vacation had vanished. The great pigeon scare of St. Joseph lay dormant, and though my work with Father Yossarian was over, a monotonous routine weighed over me like a thick woolen blanket where I could only see darkness, where I could only wait.

I had to sweep the walkways, not just around the church, but now around the entire school complex by midmorning. Cleaning the church and its lavatories, and the relentless organization of the pews, kept me hopping herky-jerky. Instead of a steady block of time, my summer job was spread out dodging Masses, weddings, and funerals, my days ending with me not arriving at my house until it was nearly dark.

One Friday after the last Mass, just before I could head up the stairs to sweep the bell tower, something happened that scared the willies out of me. The few Mass-goers had left, the Monsignor was up front out of sight in the sacristy, and I was nearly done with gathering the trash from the pews and putting the hymnals back in place, when bam! just like that! Two sacred Hosts fell from the pages of a hymnal to the floor, one of them glancing off my bare hand. Jumping back in reflex, grabbing my hand like I'd touched a burner, I screamed out in terror. I couldn't move.

Charging down from the sacristy, the Monsignor stooped in front of me and clutched my shaking shoulders.

"Francis! Are you all right?"

"I touched one!"

"What?"

"I touched a Host with my bare hand! What'll happen? I know it was a mortal sin, I'm sure of it!"

"Slow down."

His grip on my shoulders tightened.

"They just fell out!"

"Hosts?"

"In the hymnal . . . I swear it was an accident."

He released me and leaned down to pluck the two wafers from the floor.

"Well, now." He smiled gently down at me. "It appears we have a second grader that isn't fond of the taste."

"Some kid used his fingers 'n' hid 'em there?"

The Monsignor held my shoulder softly.

"And he won't go to hell either. If you're young and didn't mean to touch the Host, Francis, it isn't a sin. Our Lord knows it was an accident."

He knelt in the aisle and offered the Hosts in his hand.

"Would you like to touch them?"

"With my bare hand?"

"I'm the Lord's servant. He would never allow me to lead you into sin. It's all right." He urged with his eyes. "You can touch both of them, Francis."

I remember my crooked finger quivered as I slowly reached forward and felt the wafers.

CHAPTER FIVE

The Fishing Derby

AFTER WORKING IN THE CHURCH ALL OF JUNE, AND DEALing with the endless pigeon crap in the bell tower, the Fourth of July couldn't come quick enough. My Fourth of Julys were always the best, always magical. Right off, I had no duties at the church, and my dad never demanded that I work the normal stuff in the boiler room. And, especially this year, I didn't have to scrape the walkways or do anything else resembling going near the bell tower.

I've always gotten a hoot out of fishing ever since our neighbor, Louie, gave me one of his old cane poles. Wasn't much. He threw in some hooks and a bobber, but the thing that was special, the thing that ignited my fishing passion, was that he told me the secret of where I might catch a giant catfish. Louie had fished The End when he was a kid. Heck, the summer before, I had plenty of time to really scout out The End, and while Zach took up basketball, I messed around on the banks and planned how I'd land a whale.

St. Joseph always planned a great celebration for the Fourth—tents, games, clowns, and cotton candy all happened at the municipal park where the little kids could swim for free. The whole day was loaded with fun, smells, things to see, and of course there were the fireworks at dusk. I never had money for cotton candy or to play those games, but that's okay. For me, the highlight of the day wasn't any of that stuff; it was St. Joseph's annual fishing derby!

The canal ran next to the park where all the tents were, where moms and dads milled about with their kids. On this special day, a quarter mile section of the canal was roped off. On the ends, screens were staked across the water to the bottom. Sometime the night before, a truck hauled in a thousand catfish, one with a metal tag crimped to its fin. The lucky kid who caught the tagged fish won a brand-new Schwinn bicycle. I'd peeked; it was a green cruiser.

I had my worms, my pole, a sandwich I'd made, water in a Mason jar, and the crawdads Louie told me about. And, oh boy! Everything was ready. Kids half my age, most with their dads, crowded close to my left, and some teenagers I didn't know were loud and messin' around to my right. Why they didn't take the start of the derby more seriously I'll never know. And on the far bank a ton of kids were shoved and elbowed into position by their parents.

But get this . . . I had the whole shebang figured out! Pushing my 'Y' prop into the soft ground, I saw tire tracks in the mud close to the water. The way I had it figured is that the tracks must've been made the night before when the hatchery truck stocked the canal. Holy moly 'n I got the clue fair 'n square!

Even before the horn blew the start, I was having my

best day ever. Heck, there was no church, and I could give a hill o' beans if the whole town got sick from pigeons. But dang was I nervous, and did I ever want to win. I knew Dad would be awfully proud if I got the new bike, and I figured even Zach would want to borrow it sometime. I barely heard the starting horn and took little notice of the hundreds of whipping poles and miles of baited lines being tossed to the canal.

The sudden flurry over, kids settled down on their butts while dads crossed arms over chests, each anxiously waiting for a nibble. Down the way, a little guy whined that it was too hot and wanted a soda pop. I could hear an annoying brat demand to know when he'd catch a fish. Not long after, at the far end by the screen, a kid caught a sunfish and there were cheers.

But this was only background noise, and my total focus locked straight ahead as I sat ready on my haunches and eyed my cork.

Suddenly there was no more noise, no whining kids. There was no mistaking; my bobber scooted sideways. Gotta be a cat!

Not sure how I did it with my hands shaking to beat the band, but I ran the silver tip of my stringer through its gills and out its mouth, then splashed my first cat into the drink. It had to be over a foot.

Another crawdad!

Gotta hurry!

On both sides, parents hurried kids over to get a glimpse of what a real fish looked like. I'd raise my stringer only a tad. That was all right, but I couldn't let anyone see what bait I was using. Hunched far over, I stabbed another crawdad on my hook and tossed my line back.

Eventually things calmed down, and they returned to their spots buoyed by the excitement of their own chance to win the bike. But the sweet spot belonged to me, and I sat by myself grinning that I had the perfect ammunition.

I had no sooner rested my pole in the 'Y' when another bite behaved like the first. Gotta watch out . . . others'll catch on . . . gotta act like you're the best ole fisherman in these parts and it ain't a big deal. The fish was on the stringer before anyone noticed. Two cats in less than an hour. My mind galloped with the possibility. But the tagged one? Tossing my rig back, I was in business again when low and behold, Zach came over. Dang, in the middle of everything, he just waltzed right over and plopped down next to me.

"Hey Francis . . ."

I motioned for him to lean closer. Scrunched down, I slid the stringer up on the bank briefly to give him a peek. God, I felt good.

"Christ Francis! Ya usin' firecrackers?"

"Secret bait Louie told me about. Catch the next one. We'll make a team!"

"Gotta meet Rupe." Zach's twisted his head, taking in the whole derby scene. "God F'n damn if you ain't a fisherman."

Boy, I liked him sayin' that.

I was sorta glad Zach didn't hang around for my third big bite. Plain as day, I knew I had the honey hole when I hooked another. I tried to be cool, play it real nonchalant if you know what I mean, but the fish was a monster and way stronger. I know I should've seen it coming, but with cats on the stringer, the groups on both sides had gradually eased closer to my spot.

While I did my best to control the beast, and it was obvious that I'd have to bring him in straight to the bank, my cat had other plans. Dang! In no time the fish had weaved a couple lines together, then a dozen, and those to my right started tugging against those to my left, and across the canal a dad had launched his kid's spinner into the mix. The dad had no sooner shoved the pole in his son's hand than the rod was yanked into the drink. Wow, if I didn't have a hairy mess on my hands. Eventually my side won, and the kid's rod, along with a bail of string, was finally pulled ashore. Even though the cat was gone and there was nothing to fight over, you should've heard the squabbling.

Some man, a cigarette hanging from his mouth and barking like a sergeant, pulled out a knife from a case on his belt.

"Boys, this'll be the end o' it!"

We all just stood there and watched while he cut off our lines, wadded them in a ball, and threw the mess up the bank. And just like the horn had gone off again, the derby started over. Speed was the key and poles were restrung. Hooks and bobbers came next, and baits were heaved back to the spot where I'd hooked my last one.

Louie's pole didn't come with spare line, so I moved higher on the bank to watch. Far down the way by the culvert, a dad cheered, even applauded as his stupid kid caught fish after fish. Even from where I sat, I could tell they were just measly sunfish—weren't real fish at all.

Don't know who won the bicycle; I know it wasn't me.

If I'd had extra line, maybe if those guys hadn't horned in on my spot, I might've won the prize. Heck, it was my spot and I had the crawdads. But after sitting in that scorching sun for a while, I no longer cared; I had on a stringer two of the biggest fish I ever caught.

By mid-afternoon the skillet heat had driven off most, and after I ate my bologna, I, too, decided that my derby was over. I was heading away from the tents and candy with my cats dangling on a stringer by my leg, when out of the blue I got an idea.

I'd ventured cross town to Alphonse's shack ever since I could ride my bike, but I never brought him anything neat. So right then and there, I headed that way, and it felt good to plop my fish on his picnic table. Should've seen his eyes pop when he took a gander at them. He liked most of my story and said that cats make for right fine table fare; said he'd fry them up and we'd have fish sandwiches for lunch on Monday.

That was the end of my fishing derby, but my Fourth of July wasn't over. I got to the football stadium early so I could sit at the very top to watch the fireworks. All set, people packing in, I was trying to locate my brother and Rupe when Alphonse climbed the bleachers and sat himself right down beside me and held out two candy apples, one for him, one for me. Should've seen him; the more he gnawed, the more candy hung from his whiskers.

"Haven't had a candy apple in forever." I relished the taste. "It's sorta nice having one with ya, Alphonse."

"Sorta? It's goddamn gentlemanly of me."

"Got some in your whiskers."

"Have it planned that way for later."

I've always gotten a kick outta seein' the fireworks, but with him watching with me . . . well, it made me feel important.

The shindig didn't last all that long—maybe a half hour—and while the folks were wandering away, we stayed to hang around and jabber.

"In my day, Francis, I noodled fish. I was a damn good noodler if ya wanna know the truth. When I wanted to use a pole, which was almost never, I used dough balls." He tried seriousness, but ended up with a big grin. "None of this crazy crawdad stuff."

"Louie told me about the crawdads."

"Looks ta me like ya woulda won that bike fair 'n square."

"Shoulda seen that bike, Alphonse!"

"She's a damn dirty shame."

"It was a Schwinn and bright green!"

"Next year I'll fix ya up with some dough balls."

"Can't be better 'n crawdads."

"I know fishin', Francis." He poked me on the chest. "Dough balls."

The lights were still on in the stadium, but everyone had gone. Alphonse slowly pulled himself to his feet. After we'd clomped down the bleachers, I stalled by the banister overlooking the field.

"Alphonse, do you have any sisters?"

"Nope." Alphonse suddenly turned serious and eyed me. "Why in tarnation did ya ask me that?"

"Just wondering?"

"Wonderin' what?"

Instantly, I became defensive.

"What it'd be like having a girl in the family is all."

Alphonse parked an elbow on the banister, then leaned forward, studying me straight on.

"S'pose havin' a sister would be all right." His eyes nailed me in place. "Now ya listen. I know Zach doesn't always have time for ya, that's just the way brothers do 'er sometimes. But trade Zach fer a sister? Nah."

"I didn't exactly mean that."

"What, with him goin' inta high school this year, might feel like he's left ya all alone."

"Don't take it wrong, Alphonse. It's just that sometimes, it'd be nice to hang around with someone besides you."

A slight giggle escaped from Alphonse's mouth.

"Reckon that's right, but yer brother ain't as far away as ya think."

"Ain't mad, are ya?"

"Hell no."

Out of nowhere, he suddenly put me in a headlock. Man, was he quick for an old man. For a few minutes we horsed around under the stadium lights until he started panting and I got the nerve to sock him hard in the leg.

II

THE SUMMER OF '59

CHAPTER SIX

The Sleep Walk

As it turned out, the summer of '59 remained scorching hot and there were those in St. Joseph that swore that this was the hottest summer they could ever remember. And so with his wonderful Fourth of July behind him, Francis had no choice but to beat out his days at a methodical pace. On those Friday evenings when he arrived home late, he'd find clean clothes just inside the back door, then rush unseen to take a long bath. After the tub drained, he refilled it for another long scrub. With fresh clothes, he'd eat alone at the kitchen table, then mosey off upstairs to the bed he shared with his brother.

It'd been a Wednesday and he'd been lunching in the shade on the church grounds, when he spied his brother and Rupe across the way on the school playground. He couldn't be positive, but he thought Rupe was pointing his direction and arguing with Zach. Were they talking about him? What did he do wrong this time?

Lunch over, he headed for the janitor's closet in the vestibule to retrieve the mop and bucket he'd need for cleaning the church restrooms.

The door was wide open. He stared at it, puzzled. Why would the Monsignor or anyone else leave the door open in the middle of the day?

He was backing out the door with the mop bucket when he saw a note with his name on the shelf. Beside it was a 30-yard spool of green-striped fishing line. His forehead wrinkled as he flipped the note over and over with his fingers, reading and re-reading the message: FRANCIS, DON'T WORK LATE.

Finally, he wadded the note and carefully placed it in the bottom of the trash can.

He'd found a similar note the week before, but then the door had been locked. He'd thrown that note away, too, confused by what it meant, no idea who wrote it.

Dang, this fishing line is brand new and came from Montgomery Ward, he thought.

He picked it up, glanced over his shoulder, then quickly set the spool back on the shelf and backed out the door with the mop bucket.

It was quarter 'til five that Wednesday, near quitting time for most, and over an hour before a few devoted would straggle in to the evening Mass. Francis was scraping the sidewalk outside the altar boys' entrance when Alphonse grabbed him on the shoulder from behind. Startled, Francis whipped around.

"Alphonse! Scared the bejeebies outta me!"

"Gettin' me a bad feelin', Francis."

"About what?" Francis had never seen Alphonse so grim. His loony mask, the look that everyone interpreted as proof of his being "touched in the head," was gone.

"That asshole Monsignor. Has he been actin' weird 'round ya?" Alphonse wasn't jittery or nervous, but he was fired up, grinding his boot in the dirt, kicking the bits of pigeon shit left on the sidewalk. "I mean doin' or sayin' strange shit to ya?"

"Don't pay much attention to him."

"The bastard paid a visit to yer Pa this afternoon. Seems the prick ain't fond of our little visits, like maybe I ain't such a good influence on ya."

"Why would he think that?"

Alphonse craned around, scanning the church grounds.

"Why ya so worked up about the Monsignor?"

"Me 'n that bastard go way back, Francis, back ta before when Zach was born."

"But why—"

"According to yer Pa, the bastard says I can't be trusted. Told yer Pa that he was suspicious about the two of us havin' our chit-chats."

"Suspicious?"

"Yup." Alphonse worked his stogie into a soggy mess. "Reckon I'm a wild card."

Impatient, Francis swiped the sweat from his forehead. "What exactly are you talkin' about?" He gave the walk a couple quick scrapes.

"She's mighty complicated. That Monsignor's one ugly man." He spat his stogie to the lawn. "And just thinkin' about the S.O.B. gets my brain ta boilin'."

"You've always had it in for him."

"Have every right ta be. Me bein' a crazy weirdo all this time, nobody gives me a second thought, and I've been free ta see things 'n hear stuff. I've been watchin' the way the bastard's been treatin' ya."

"Treatin' me?"

Worry creased Alphonse's face, his eyes growing wide and watery.

"The way he stands back and watches ya since ya cleaned out that goddamn bell tower. I see 'im just watchin' from his office window."

"Why would he do that?"

Alphonse was about to speak, but stopped and grew pensive for a few moments.

"Never mind. Just don't like the way the world's spinnin' these days. He was a son-a-bitch the first time I ever laid eyes on 'im. Reckon a leopard can't ever change his spots. Want ya ta remember Francis, if times get bad for ya, I mean real bad . . . you come find me 'n it don't matter what or when."

Alphonse scratched his beard and stared out across the church lawn.

"Don't know how she happened, Francis. But there was a time when I'd deal with shitty days just by sittin' in a box-car and listenin' to the clickety-clack." He searched his bibs for another stogie, but found none. "Well anyway, right now I'd like ta just sit on my ass and watch the wind play in them elms." Tugging Francis on the shoulder, he turned him to view the expansive lawn. "Over there, I'd like ta watch the blackbirds come in fer the night and hear 'em squabble in the trees."

HE DIDN'T THINK HE WAS taking any longer than normal that Friday evening, but at the sharp rap on the door, Francis pulled the plug in the bathtub.

"You think you're the only one needing the bathroom!"

"Almost done, Mom!"

The bathroom had no window, almost no space to move about, and Francis had his fresh clothes in the bowl of the sink. Over his wet body, he threw on his clothes as the tub drain still gurgled. She shoved open the door.

"From now on you'll get fifteen minutes! And you'll check with the rest of us before you start."

"But . . ." He jammed his feet in his sneakers. "Okay."

After balling up his dirty clothes, he slunk through the kitchen toward the laundry room.

The living room was dreary. An end table flanked the lounging chairs, both stained and worn badly on the arms. At the far end against the wall, their brown couch sat on the faded carpet, threadbare by the door. Despite the room's four windows, the space never filled with brightness, and even on bright summer afternoons, the huge trees out front never allowed sunshine inside.

Sara sank into her chair and pulled a sock that needed darning over a light bulb. Sara was German. Tall and thick-boned, her face and manner spoke of her fatigue. Still though, her eyes were clear and they held determination, a fierce drive that said she'd suffer anything if it moved her family forward. The paisley print of her housecoat had long since faded, and the once colorful slippers she wore showed their years. The wisps of hair curling and falling over her face, she tucked mechanically behind her ears, and it seemed that the more she mended the more she pursed her lips tightly together.

Pensive for a long while, she suddenly looked up beyond the needle at her husband and grumbled, "That boy's gotta start thinking of others."

Edgar raised his heavy eyelids. "He's fine. He's had a long day."

Edgar's hair was wavy, almost black, and he hunched in his chair that evening as though preparing for doom. He was a big man, muscled heavily in the shoulders and back. His hands gripped loosely the chair's arms. Appearing dirty, fingernails outlined in soot, his hands were huge. His years of tearing down motors and pumps, and his endless shoveling of coal in the boilers, had stained his hands permanently. His fingers were callused, overly fat, and it wouldn't be an exaggeration to say they looked like sausages. Sitting so, there was more than fatigue in his cloudy eyes; there was worry.

"And what's to show for it?" Sara jabbed the needle against the bulb. "The three of you've been working longer this summer than ever, and where's it gotten us?"

Edgar carefully set his glasses on a table, then grabbed the newspaper in his lap and smacked it to the stack by his chair. His coal-stained fingers clenched.

"Not tonight, Sara."

"Then when?"

"We're doing all right."

She pointed her threaded needle. "We deserve better than this."

Erupting from his chair and thumping toward the window, he growled, "We've been through it a thousand times." He stared outside at the blurry street lamp. "Maybe this is all we deserve. Hell, I'm damn near blind!"

"I'm tired of hearin' that excuse." She muttered at the mending in her lap, "A janitor."

Edgar whipped around. "That's right! A damn janitor! Can you even say 'maintenance man'? How about 'chief maintenance man'?"

"A title." She shook her head, but didn't look up. "We've been stuck in the same place for how long?"

"You forget when we moved here, I had no choice. You forget we were in an awful bad way . . . thank God for the Monsignor willing to go out on a limb. That man could've been thrown in jail for hiring an unlicensed man to operate those boilers. Let alone a blind one!"

"Even priests change. Where's his help now?"

Edgar stomped back to his chair. For that matter, Edgar stomped everywhere. Heading to and from work, going downtown for hardware or a haircut, his walking was more of a pounding. He'd pound down Second Street never seeing a thing; he'd pound past neighbors never hearing their "Good Morning." It didn't matter how short or long; he'd pound with his head hanging down nearly to his chest.

"If things had turned out different, for sure as hell I wouldn't be in this spot. Maybe if . . . good God, lady! You want me to be unblind!"

"All I see is right now. I've watched both my sons working for a church that should be fair and caring. And they've never made a dime."

"Their work's my affair!"

"I should just keep my eyes shut? It's wrong, Edgar. You know it, and I know it."

Edgar raked his face with his hands and dug at his eyes.

"Maybe this fall, after this damn pigeon mess is behind, I'll talk with the Monsignor. Zach's starting high school. Maybe the church can afford to pay him a little."

He aimed a sideways glance at his wife and snapped open the *Herald*.

"Now I don't wanna hear another damn word."

———

As July became August, the Monsignor and the pigeons remained in a standoff, and while Francis floundered in the monotony of his work, he was unaware of the fiery discussions between the church council and the Monsignor, and he had no clue that his mom and dad were suffering with money issues. To top it off, he was unable to get a grip on why his brother, who hadn't even started high school yet, would rather hang out with Rupe than him. He floated alone, only marginally aware that it was the last month of his summer vacation.

Sometime mid-July, the Monsignor began climbing the rickety stairs up to the bell tower with Francis every Friday. The Monsignor had explained to Edgar that his weekly inspection was necessary to ensure that the bell tower would not revert to the horrendous state it'd been for most of the century. Francis thought little of this, and had come to look upon the Monsignor's week's end inspection as normal.

It had been the second Friday in August, when the Monsignor changed the routine and delayed their bell tower inspection. Francis had been sitting in a back pew mindlessly looking at the pictures in a song book. His face was blank. He didn't blink. Appearing out of nowhere, the Monsignor had moved silently to stand beside him. Francis jerked up suddenly and sensed instantly that there was something strange about the Monsignor, an odd look in his eyes, a difference in the way he spoke.

"My my, Francis, the church has never looked better, and you've finished early. I'm sorry, but we'll have to wait a bit longer for the bell tower. I simply must finish writing the most glorious letter."

He smiled down gently, standing erect above Francis.

"You've been such a blessing all summer. I won't be long."

Though starting later than normal, sweeping clean the bell tower was as it had been for the last month. Scraping the brittle filth off the floor took little time, and sweeping, even thoroughly the recesses of the corners, took little more than half an hour all told.

Francis had just emptied the dustpan and hung it on a nail when the Monsignor moved close to rejoin him. Francis understood the ritual and held out his hand. The Monsignor thumbed a dime to Francis's palm, and with it Francis understood that he was to light a votive at the feet of the Virgin Mary before he left.

With the votive's flame flickering orange against his face, he knelt at the Virgin's feet, a mere speck kneeling silently beneath the church's high arching ceiling. His head lowered; it began again: in his hand, he cupped the pigeon child.

In colored detail, he recalled when the foot-thick slab split horizontally, revealing the preserved pigeon squab—its crimson feet, its ivory bill, its malformed wings. His mind sailed into the mystery of how it must've died.

A bit after nine, he rose from the kneeler and walked slowly down the center aisle, the votive still burning as the brass door clicked shut at his back.

———

THE MONSIGNOR'S SERMON AT SUNDAY'S Mass was particularly long-winded. Up front, Edgar and Sara sat attentive, but at one point Zach nodded so sharply that his forehead hit his dad's shoulder. Francis endured by studying the details in the stained-glass windows above the altar. At last, the service ended. The Monsignor had no sooner disappeared into the sacristy before Zach tore off, hoping to catch a glimpse of Janet when she came out with her parents.

Outside the church, Francis wandered away while Edgar and Sara meandered slowly home, both silent, both troubled in their separate worlds.

For Edgar, Sunday afternoons were his time, time to work uninterrupted in his shed. This Sunday, it was a time to screw the hardware on the small maple cabinet he'd been trying for weeks to fix. It was getting late when his wife's angry voice from the kitchen screeched loud enough to be heard in the shed.

"You're late, Francis! That was three hours ago!"

"But Mom, Louie said crawdads stay soft only a few days."

"You were down at the creek all this time catchin' crawdads?"

"I was gonna catch crawdads . . ."

"Your feet aren't wet! So where'd you go after church?"

"Reckon I went to the canal . . . I guess."

"Either you did or you didn't!"

"But . . ."

"Wake up! It's going to rain. Those tomatoes need a good hoeing."

"I can do the hoeing lickity split."

"Like you knew to do it right after Mass?"

————

DESCENDING DEEP INTO AUGUST, THE days for Francis dissolved steadily away. Not so long ago he was confused about where an hour had gone, then two, but now whole afternoons vanished without understanding how; days floated away without his ever knowing where. All the while, blaring reprimands of others tumbled through his brain.

What's wrong with you?

Pay attention!

You listening?

Francis! You're always late!

And Francis would wonder where was his fantasy of catfish bigger than his leg, where were his dreams of being like Zach and making his dad proud?

Loss built on time lost, and while his yawning need for

notice ballooned, he was certain he'd become invisible. Gone was the summer's fishing derby and its magic, lost was his memory of The End and the careful watch of his bobber.

Francis lay fast asleep that next Friday, alone in bed, sweltering in the muggy night air. Just before midnight, he got up, descended the steep staircase, then swiftly stripped off all his clothes and dropped them on the porch as he left through the front door. He headed straight down Second Street toward the church. After a vain attempt to open the brass front door, he retreated down Second Street, then through the porch again—not pausing at his clothes where they lay in a heap—and crawled back into bed.

That same night, Zach had stayed out late, cattin' around with Rupe. Their single mission was to stroll nonchalantly along the streets of town and, if lucky, see a couple girls doing the same. For Zach, one girl in particular.

"Look!" Rupert jabbed Zach in the ribs. "Is that Janet?"

"Where?" Zach's head swiveled. "Where the F you talking about?"

"Jesus, Zach! She's with Schmidt in that car."

"Damn . . . son of a damn bitch."

Zach slumped, hearing the car radio fade away.

"That's F'n shitty, Zach."

"Like I give a shit, Rupe!"

It was shortly after midnight when Zach and Rupert witnessed the unthinkable. They scurried to hide in the trees. Before them, they could only watch in bewilderment, the image grooved painfully into their brains, as Francis stood naked on the steps of the church, trying the front door.

Had a church elder witnessed Francis sleepwalking, he surely would have whispered, "What's wrong with that boy?" Another would've insisted that "Edgar oughtta whip some sense into that kid." At the very least, most in town would've averted their gaze and thought, "How awfully odd, never seen the likes of that."

By the time Zach finally made it home, his mind was in turmoil—he should've been jealous about Janet, should've been ready to have it out with Schmidt. Instead, the image of his naked brother on the church steps continued looping through his brain. What did it mean? Christ, what should he do?

He stepped quietly onto the porch stairs and froze. Edgar sat hunched in his aluminum chair, motionless like a statue silhouetted in the moonlight.

Shit, this's all I need, thought Zach. *It can't be that late.*

Zach stared straight ahead, waiting for the tirade.

"Explain." Edgar's voice tightened.

Zach cleared his throat. "Just cattin' around with Rupe . . . feelin' our oats, I reckon."

"Francis."

"Oh!" He wasn't in trouble, yet there was no relief. "Don't know what ta say, Dad." He extended his palms, pleading innocence. "Kinda spooks me."

"Anybody see him?"

"I don't know . . . I didn't—"

"Think!" Edgar slammed his fist against the armrest. "It's damn important! Where'd he go?"

"Tried the church door, then down Second and back here."

"Past Jettinghoff's?"

"Reckon so."

"That old man up?"

"Not sure, Dad."

"Anybody else?"

"Caught a glimpse of somebody leaving down the church steps. Whoever it was, was probably gone before Francis got there."

Sara, wrapped in a faded robe, stepped out to the porch.

"What's all the commotion?" She pointed a finger at Zach. "Why aren't you in bed?"

"Everything's all right, Sara. Havin' a talk with Zach is all."

"At this hour?"

"About done. Go back to bed, Sara."

She sighed, then silently retreated into the dark house.

"He done it before?" Edgar kept his voice low, almost a whisper.

"First time I ever saw anything like it . . . Rupe neither."

Edgar stood up so fast his chair banged against the back wall.

"Jesus! So now he'll tell his Pa?"

"Nah . . . he's in the same boat as . . . wouldn't worry."

"God almighty. Naked." They stood for a long moment in the dark. Locusts screeched in the elms out front. Finally, Edgar asked, "He tried to get in the church?"

"He climbed the stairs and pulled the handle. Wasn't like he was trying to break in or anything."

"With that street light blaring down?"

"What can I say, Dad?"

In a flash, Edgar grabbed Francis's pajamas, stormed

inside, and stomped up the narrow stairs to the bedroom. Linoleum squeaked loudly under the weight of the two giant steps it took to cross the room.

Francis lay face down on top of the faded quilt. His months of working outdoors had tanned his face and hands dark, while his body remained white, appearing as if it'd been held by his hands and dipped in ivory paint. He was breathing softly. Edgar whipped the pajamas across Francis so hard they snapped.

Francis cried out and sat bolt upright, his eyes opened wide.

Edgar snarled, "Get dressed!" He turned quickly away and stormed down the stairs, pushing past Zach.

Zach hesitated by the edge of the bed he and Francis shared. He couldn't look at his brother.

Francis's voice quaked.

"Zach . . . why did Dad . . . what?" He reached out and felt the pajamas, then grabbed the quilt and pulled it in tightly.

"What's happening, Zach?"

Zach said nothing. Francis struggled into his pajamas under the quilt.

In stages, Zach laid down on the edge of the bed as far from Francis as he could.

"What's wrong, Zach? Aren't you gonna put on your pajamas?"

Zach never undressed nor did he slip under the bedding, and that night, he wet the bed for the first time of his life.

CHAPTER SEVEN

In the Cold, Unveiling Light

DESPITE THE FACT THAT ALPHONSE HAD SCROUNGED THE materials from God knows where, his shack was relatively perpendicular. It was a black and white affair, fourteen feet by twenty or so. Water droplets poised against the black tar paper nailed to the sides, and the corrugated tin roof had been bent along the edge, allowing rain to flow away from the cinder blocks at the base. The low front door hinged on the soles of two tennis shoes screwed to the gray planks. And while his west window was opaque plastic, the larger east window was glass. The stoop had two warped steps, and an awning angled over the tiny porch. Though most of the letters on the awning were faded, it still was legible: "Tri-County Hardware."

An outhouse gawked out back in the tall weeds. It had no door. A wooden walkway rose a few inches above the bare ground, skirting the shack and extending to the picnic table out front. Not cluttering the front or the sides, an incredible assortment of stuff was piled at the rear of the shack. A student desk, a wheelbarrow, enough cardboard that it had to be bailed with twine, an old basketball rim, a mound of miscellaneous throw-aways from the church, all this and more was stacked with an order known only to Alphonse.

Less than the length of a football field or so from the shack, two sets of freight tracks curved out of sight toward Vandellia, nine miles to the south.

The light drizzle would become rain, but not for a while. Alphonse sat hunched over his picnic table, a checkers game in progress. Two black kings occupied the back row. His chin rested on his fist while he tapped a red game piece against the board.

Tilting his face toward the looming sky, a touch of a smile wrinkled his old face as he took note of Butch wandering up from the marsh.

His dog had one brown eye, the other so light blue that it hinted of being albino, perhaps blind. He was oddly tall and lanky for a dog. His legs were wet to the knees, and as he meandered forward, his hind quarters didn't follow square ahead. His stash, stained yellowish brown, curled down from his muzzle, and his face was nicked and scarred, saying this ole boy had been around. Sniffing things over only briefly, Butch gingerly settled beneath the picnic table.

Alphonse reached down, giving Butch a quick scratch behind the ears.

"Makin' the rounds, eh?"

Sighing, Alphonse let the game piece drop from his hand, then scooped them all in a box. "Lunch break's 'bout over Butch. Seen any rats taday?"

Butch shook his head and yawned widely.

"Don't s'pose I could teach ya ta deal cards, could I?"

Beyond the curving rails came a faint train whistle.

Alphonse waited and listened, and as the sound grew stronger, his face brightened and he straightened his back. Butch ignored the growing vibration in the ground that shook the water free from the shack's siding. A long train, its caboose still hidden, crawled past, the power of the diesel pounding against the shack. Popping to his feet, Alphonse stuffed both arms beneath his bibs, and from where he stood, he eyed the huge engine spewing black smoke into the thick, drizzling air.

He spoke softly. "Now they're all diesels."

His mutterings grew harsh. "Things ain't the way it used ta be, Butch. People ain't the way they used ta be."

He shoved the game board in its box.

"Don't like it, not one damn bit. Next thing ya know, they'll have us eatin' off o' damn china."

As the sound of the freight faded north, Alphonse took a quick scan of the sky and was moving toward the door when Zach zoomed in on his bike. Zach's short curly hair dripped like the weather.

His mouth hanging slightly open with surprise, Alphonse motioned for Zach to hustle.

"Zach! C'mon 'n git in here outta the wet."

"In a hurry, Alphonse," scowled Zach. "Dad wants ya to get that motor from Watney. Said he needed it yesterday."

"Jesus H. Christ, Zach!" The wrinkled old face beamed. "Ya ain't been 'round here in a coon's age."

Alphonse gave him a quick tug on the arm to head inside, but Zach pulled back and stayed on his bike.

"Guess yer gettin' touchy. Hell's fire, Zach, when ya were just a baby . . ."

"Ain't a kid anymore," said Zach, cutting him off.

Alphonse's face sank.

"Hope ya know I'm rootin' fer ya ta make varsity. Been watchin' 'n yer gettin' damn good with that basketball.' "

Uncomfortable with the compliment, Zach looked away and quickly scanned the shack and picnic table, while tapping his feet anxiously against the pedals.

"Gotta get back. Don't forget that motor."

Not waiting for a reply, he tore toward Franklin.

Alphonse watched Zach until he'd disappeared, then grabbed a coat from inside and headed down First Street toward the junkyard. He'd just entered the place when Watney charged up and sneered, "Tell Edgar I'm tired a sittin' on his damn parts!"

Watney was a big man in his fifties, burly, too, with a wild beard and black hair curling up from the neck of his stained T-shirt. When he spoke, he lipped a cigar in cadence with his words.

Halting abruptly, he leaned against a white stove rusting in the drizzle, arms folded across his huge chest as if blocking entry. "Edgar pulls this same shit every time."

"Hold on, junk man!" Alphonse bristled. "Ain't takin' yer crap. Just need that motor."

"Got two o' his friggin' motors." He jabbed a finger toward a covered work bench. "And a damn pump."

Impatient, Alphonse's face grew darker like the weather. "Just the half horse."

"I'm supposed ta just sit on his other crap?"

"I'd recommend it."

"I run a damn business here." Watney groused and took

a swift kick at the ground. "Tell Edgar he needs to pick up his other crap."

"Gotta problem, talk ta him."

"Sends you or his snot-nosed kids."

Alphonse took a quick step forward, waving a threatening finger. Rain coated the hobo's face. "Careful, Watney. Edgar's boys are mighty special ta me."

"I could give a damn." Watney hoisted a tagged motor from the work bench. "Tell that prick he can shove the other motor and the pump up his ass."

Alphonse screwed on a wry smile. "Ya mean Edgar or the Monsignor?"

"Wise-ass. How ya get off playin' a stupid idiot all the time, then come in here bein' a wise-ass? You got a damn screw loose, I'll tell you that."

"Been brought ta my attention."

Watney shoved the motor at Alphonse and snorted. "The way I see it, is you just fell off a freight one day and ended up bein' a blind man's flunky. You ain't nothin' but a burned-out bum."

"Best get it straight, junk man." Alphonse grabbed the motor. "I ain't never been a bum."

———

MOST EVENINGS, IF IT WAS pleasant, Alphonse walked the freight rails far beyond town. Butch insisted on tagging along, although he always fell behind and complained. His complaints were justified, for Alphonse didn't walk so much as march, and his marching was just shy of a jog. He would pound mile after mile, his head bent down, sometimes south toward Vandellia, other times toward Jennings. The lights of St. Joseph would grow faint at his back, and often during the summer months he'd not return to his shack until it was pitch dark and late at night. Perhaps it was hobo instinct, maybe his decades of familiarity, but he cruised down the rails in total darkness without a stumble or a catch while the frogs of summer grunted from nearby ponds.

Gradually over that summer though, his nightly jaunts began to warp. Alphonse would pop from the rail bed, hook a left down Second to where it intersected with Pierce Street, and make a jog over to the sprawling Church complex. Over the weeks, he'd become aware that as he drew close, his body tightened, his senses heightened. He grew alert to anything unusual, anything not as it should be.

In his pocket, he carried a master key that Edgar had forgotten about, a key that unlocked everything, the smallest closet, the doors to classrooms, even the entry at the top of the back stairs used by altar boys when they assisted at masses.

Along the basketball courts outside the high school, around the back to the grade school, then up the broad steps to the church itself, the heavy brass door yielding to the master key, a quick circuit through and out again; he patrolled in an ever-tightening circle that seemed always to end near the street light that flooded the church façade with cold, unveiling light.

In the harsh light, his face appeared carved, lines etched deeply around his narrowed eyes. He crossed the street to

Beckman's, Butch close behind, was turning toward the shack he called home when he witnessed the unspeakable.

Francis, naked as a baby, was tugging on the great doors. His skin glowed ghost-white beneath the street lamp. Alphonse suddenly couldn't breathe, and in that eternity, there were no sounds, no movement beyond Francis's slow pull on the doors.

His fruitless tugs over, Francis shuffled down the steps and slowly made his way down Second toward home.

Alphonse shook his head violently then hustled across Pierce Street, Butch limping quietly behind. He hung in the shadows and tracked Francis to his home.

"I shoulda . . ." he muttered bitterly as he watched Francis climb the steps to the porch. "Nothin' matters anymore. Damage is already done."

He waited to be sure Francis was safely inside.

Gathering himself finally, he headed toward his shack, continuing to mutter, "Christ, Butch . . . what'll we do now?"

CHAPTER EIGHT

The Loony Bird in the Causeway

SINCE JULY, ALL HIS SATURDAYS WERE IDENTICAL TO Francis. This one wouldn't be any different from the one last week or next week. The vows of joy that were exchanged at weddings in the morning floated with the goodbyes sobbed at funerals in the afternoon. But this Saturday there was an abbreviated Mass schedule and no cleaning the bell tower, so his routine should've left time to wander the canal with his cane pole or to mess around on his bike away from home and the chores of the church.

But anymore, Francis seldom rode his bike, and his thoughts of fishing The End were rare while he muddled through his summer days simply doing what he was told.

So early that Saturday morning, despite the previous night's confusion with his dad and his brother's odd behavior, Francis clawed with his scraper at the pigeon droppings on the cement causeway just outside the sacristy. His hightop All Stars were powdery with dust, his patched jeans were too short and hung loose from his waist, and his faded blue T-shirt with its barely discernable "St. Joseph Blue Jays" was already drenched with sweat. With his scraping making a tremendous racket and his brain numb, his scraper suddenly plowed into Alphonse's boot.

"Already workin' like a damn fool, Francis."

"Alphonse! What're you doing here?" Francis gave his scraper a couple quick jabs.

"Couldn't sleep." Winking. Thoughtfully, Alphonse wiped the brown juice from his chin. "Yer Edgar's boy all right."

"What's that supposed to mean?"

"Work . . . just work and nothin' but work."

Francis kicked his sneakers together. Their pigeon filth puffed in the air.

"Still gotta lot to do."

"It's Saturday, for Christ's sake! Got yer whole life ta work like a dog. Ya might try doin' somethin' fun."

Suddenly deep in thought, Francis paused.

"Well . . . maybe I just will."

Alphonse surveyed the walk and steps, then grimaced at the sacristy door.

"Best learn ta relax. Can't have much more ta do."

"After this . . . I know the restrooms are a mess in the vestibule."

"Give ya hand. Want me ta run the scraper?"

"Nah . . . just got these steps left." Wiping the sweat from his forehead with the back of his hand, Francis's face remained bland, his eyes dull. "This is more important than all the other places combined."

"Reckon, ya been schooled."

Francis was clawing his scraper against the stairs again when Alphonse suddenly reached over and held the scraper still.

"Hopin' we might have us a little talk."

Francis scowled. "Thought we were."

"Won't be long 'n you'll be done with that damn bell tower."

"Yep."

"Figure next Friday'll be the end o' it."

"Guess so . . . school ain't that far away."

"Let's have us a sit." Alphonse gestured down to the steps. "Hell, yer damn near done out here."

Francis scanned around, his face and manner cautious as if he were about to break some rule. He lowered and sat tentatively next to his friend.

"Say, Francis, last night . . . last night me 'n Butch were takin' a stroll 'n saw the church lights on. Hell," Alphonse watched for a reaction. "Think it might a been after nine."

Francis cracked his scraper against the steps. "So?"

"Damn shit ass schedule. What'd ya do after gittin' home so late?"

"Reckon I went to bed early. Boy, was I bushed."

"Ya just hauled off 'n went ta bed?"

"This is what you wanted to talk about?"

"Just curious." Alphonse cleared his throat. "Been thinkin' . . . doesn't seem ta me that it should take all that long ta sweep the bell tower 'n git the job done."

"It doesn't."

"Sure takes ya a long time ta get outta there."

"Yeah, guess so."

Alphonse chewed his stogie thoughtfully.

"Over two hours for that pissant job?" Alphonse tried to be cavalier. "Friday nights are fer chasin' girls."

"Geeze, Alphonse."

Francis popped to his feet and started banging his scraper. He stopped abruptly, his face suddenly tight with seriousness.

"Alphonse, you remember that baby pigeon I told you about? Well, up in the bell tower I start thinking about it . . . 'n before I can shake a stick, it's real late."

Alphonse slowly pulled himself to his feet, his face pale, his eyes focused faraway in concentration.

"Ya just git ta thinkin' about that squab?"

"Pretty weird, ain't it?"

At the rattle of the rectory door closing, Alphonse spun around.

The Monsignor glared at him. "You have no business being here."

Alphonse slowly eased in front of Francis.

"Just havin' a chat with Francis. Ain't a mortal sin."

"Your life's a mortal sin." The Monsignor's dark eyes knifed. "Move aside."

"Now Pope, I could do that if I wanted to, I surely could."

"Insolent fool. Edgar's the only reason you're still here."

"Sure takes a load off my mind."

The Monsignor flicked away the comment with a flippant wave, then smiled generously toward Francis, who'd inched out from behind Alphonse.

"Francis, I can't tell you how much I appreciate you paying special attention to the causeway this morning. This, and after working late last night, well . . ." He seemed to savor his words. "I simply don't know how I would've gotten by without you all summer."

The Monsignor moved forward, gently patting Francis on the shoulder.

"Keep yer dirty mitts off this boy!" Alphonse's face flashed red as he tried shoving the hand away. He wasn't fast enough.

Ignoring Alphonse, the Monsignor kept his gaze fixed on Francis, smiled down benevolently, then rested his hand lightly on Francis's shoulder.

"We have only the ten o'clock wedding today. With school about to start, I'm sure a nice Saturday break'll feel awfully good. You deserve it, Francis."

"Goddamn it! I know what's goin' on!"

Grinning conspiratorially at Francis, the Monsignor made a "loony-bird" sign against his temple as he nodded toward Alphonse, then moved smoothly up the stairs and into the sacristy.

Francis stared down at the swaying robe until the door clicked closed behind the Monsignor. Alphonse, trembling, forced himself to speak calmly. "Francis—"

But then he could say no more.

For long moments, Francis stood still and silent, his tan face twisting with confusion, his round eyes filled with a worry he didn't understand. Slowly turning, scanning all about, it was as if he were inventorying his world, the massive church, the school at his back, the traffic rolling down Second, the scraper he just now discovered in his grip. Across the way, he watched the grackles settle in the trees. Then, as if to break a spell, he cracked the scraper loudly against the last of the cement steps.

CHAPTER NINE

The Great German Bells

AROUND THREE O'CLOCK THAT SAME AFTERNOON, FRANCIS slouched on his back steps tormenting ants with a stick. He could hear his mom rattling around in the kitchen, and he thought his dad must've wandered off to yap with a neighbor. Since he'd gotten home from work, he'd seen his brother only briefly, and figured he must be messing around with Rupert as usual. One at a time, he smeared the ants on the walk with his stick, then watched in wonder as those specks of life evaporated against the hot cement.

Can't just sit here all day, he thought.

He flung his stick at the garden. *Heck . . . I'm doin' somethin'*, he thought to himself.

With sudden purpose, he popped to his feet and briskly rounded the corner of the garage. Inside, an ancient jalopy, rusted beyond repair and devoid of gas and functioning tires—a relic from a previous church tenant—filled most of the space. Against the wall, leaned his bike. It was dusty, the chrome on the handlebars had rusted off in spots, and one of its pedals was bent down from some long-ago crash. He was about to hop on and jet out when his brother yelled, "Get the F outta here!" through the jalopy's open window. Francis whipped around.

"Whatcha . . ."

"And hurry the hell up!"

"What—?"

Zach pushed his head out the jalopy's window and barked, "None of yer damned business!"

A girl's head quickly raised up next to Zach's shoulder.

"Hey, Clinker." She exaggerated clearing her throat. "I mean, Francis . . . everybody calls you Clinker though, right? Remember me?"

"Janet." His voice, barely a whisper.

Janet patted her hair back in place and beamed. "We were in arithmetic last year."

Zach leaned out and spat.

"You're supposed to do the gardenin'. The old man'll kill ya."

"He ain't around."

"It's yer hide."

"Thought you'd be with Rupert."

"Get lost!"

"Watcha doin' in that piece of junk, doesn't even run?"

Zach rolled his eyes, let out a whoosh of breath, then his lips pressed tightly together.

"Get lost, idiot! This is private!"

Francis pumped his bike with vengeance down the alley, ripped past the church, never slowing to catch his breath until after he'd screamed down Fourth and made it to City Park. He dropped his bike to the ground and perched himself atop a picnic table, elbows pressed on his knees, head propped on his fists. After a bit his panting slowed.

Zach always gets what he wants . . .

Big hero . . .

She was in my class, not his.

───────

THAT ENTIRE WEEKEND, ZACH COULD find nothing to pull himself from the haunting image of his brother's sleepwalking, not Rupert and basketball, not his rendezvous with Janet in the garage. He was still jaundiced on Monday and it seemed to him that his dad barked out orders by the dozen. Zach had been wheeling a cart of clinkers up the ramp when Rupert caught up to him.

Rupert's grin was so wide it pushed back his ears.

"How's it goin', Clink?"

Zach didn't bother turning around when he grumbled, "Been workin'."

Rupert's enthusiasm was as if he'd not seen his friend in years.

"Must've gotten somewhere with Janet."

Grunting the cart up the ramp, Zach ignored the comment.

"Jesus . . ." Rupert kept pace and eyed him. "What's eatin' you?"

"Nothin'."

"So, what time ya off?"

"Any damn time I want."

"Bullshit."

Rupert followed outside and watched Zach empty the

tub in the barrel. A cloud of ash billowed up. Zach banged the tub against the blacktop and hissed, "You tell yer old man?"

"Tell him what?"

"You F'n know!"

"What're you talking . . ."

Zach cut him off. "You know damn well what!"

"You mean Friday night? C'mon, you know I wouldn't say anything."

Zach was in Rupert's face. "If yer lyin' . . ."

Rupe took a step back, shaking his head. "Ain't a big deal."

"Ta hell it ain't!" Zach grabbed Rupert's shirt. "This ever gits out—"

"Damn, Zach!" Rupert clawed the grip from his chest. "Ease off!"

"He ain't your brother!" Zach took a deep breath. "It's already been a couple days, 'n I still can't get it outta my head . . . Francis like that on the church steps."

"Maybe . . . hell, Zach, maybe ya just need to hang out with him a little, maybe have a conversation with the guy."

"Just see to it that ya keep yer trap shut."

Zach grabbed up the tub and was about to head back inside, but Rupert blocked him with an arm. "When's the last time you had a real talk with Francis? I'm serious, Zach. He needs more 'n just Alphonse."

"Alphonse can have 'im."

"Ya can't just leave it like that."

"We got nothin' in common anymore."

"Ain't right. Francis is closer to Alphonse than his own brother."

Zach let a slight sigh escape. "Got that right," he said in low tones, clenching his teeth.

"Damn, Zach. Sounds like you're jealous of Francis getting all the attention from Alphonse."

"That's F'n bullshit!"

"You always said Alphonse was a big part of the family."

Zach tried pushing past Rupert.

"So what if Francis was F'n weird." Rupert snorted and smiled, then patted Zach on the back. "How about asking 'im if he wants to play some hoops sometime?"

"You crazy? Francis couldn't hit the broad side of a barn."

"Never know. He might just surprise ya."

"B-ball? Really?"

"Why not?"

Zach suddenly wilted.

"The other night, Rupe . . . doesn't it give ya the creeps?"

"Let it go, Zach. Just a little B-ball with Frank."

"Can't even talk to him. And now with . . ."

"Christ, Zach! I'm marchin' my ass over to the church 'n arranging the whole god damn thing."

ONE DAY IN THE LAST week before school would start, Francis waited on the church steps for people to file out, waited for them to walk sobbing to their cars and then to the cemetery. He worked his face into a gigantic smile, then quickly made it angry, with deep, forced lines. He tried on another wide grin, then relaxed his face to bland.

Meandering up the walk, Alphonse lugged a greasy pump. He plopped down on the steps next to Francis, his face drawn, haggard.

"Guess where yer Dad's got me headin'?"

"Junkyard."

"I couldn't give even one shit fer that Watney." He studied Francis for a moment. "Takin' in a pump 'n he'll have me leavin' with two . . . 'n probably a motor."

Alphonse forced a smile. "Ya seem outta sorts the last couple days."

"Just working."

"Nah . . . I mean yer lookin' like ya got somethin' on yer mind."

"Got school coming up is all."

"Won't be all that bad. You'll be kissin' this shitty job adios."

"Yep."

"S'pose it's time." Alphonse moved to get up.

"Sometimes . . ."

"Sometimes, what?" Alphonse quickly settled back down.

"Nothin' really."

"A chat with you will be a hell shot better 'n listenin' ta Watney. What's gnawin' at ya?"

"Everythin'. Nothin'." He ground his sneaker against the step. "I don't know."

"Hell Francis, that ain't no different 'n me half the time."

"Been a weird summer, Alphonse. All started with these dang pigeons."

"But ya made it through." He patted Francis on the knee. "And Friday'll be the end o' it. If nothin' else will, bein' done with that damn bell tower oughtta put a smile on yer face."

Francis frowned but didn't say anything for a while. Eventually, he turned to face Alphonse.

"Remember last Saturday morning, Alphonse? When I was scraping the causeway, and you were there?"

"What about it?"

"Guess—Shoulda seen your face when you saw the Monsignor. Everything about you changed. You must really hate him cause yer whole body scrunched almost to a ball. Your voice scared me."

"Sorry, ya know I didn't mean to." His hands suddenly became fists. "But I can feel my hair standin' on end just thinkin' 'bout 'im. Have ya seen that son-a-bitch walkin' 'round here happier 'n a pup in a red wagon? That bastard's got somethin' cookin'."

"Kinda weird hearing you talk like that about a priest."

"Well . . ." Alphonse blinked slowly. "Reckon it does. It's like this, Francis. I knew 'im before he was a priest— knew 'im even before I met your ma 'n pa. He's probably been a sick bastard since the day he was born. He might be your monsignor 'n boss, but he can't be trusted to ever tell ya the truth."

"But if you can't trust a monsignor, then . . ."

"Ain't never been religious like you folks, but religion can't ever disguise who you really are down deep. Goin' ta church ain't that much different 'n drinkin' liquor."

Francis chewed on that for a long moment, then seemed to make up his mind about something.

"Alphonse, I need to talk to you about something important."

"I'm a listener."

"I think Zach hates me. He won't talk to me, he won't even look at me . . .'n I think it's getting worse."

Alphonse rubbed his ragged beard. "Brothers are like that from time ta time."

"It's kinda like he's disgusted to be around me."

"When did this all start?"

"Last Saturday, all of a sudden like."

Alphonse sighed, shaking his head slowly. "He'll ferget all about it in time."

"Forget about what?"

Alphonse paused, scrambling for the right words. "Whatever's eatin' at 'im."

"I see ya watching him play basketball all the time."

"Right proud of 'im. I was there when he was brought inta the world." He looked up, but his mind was focused elsewhere, to a former time. "Hell, like I always told ya, kinda feel like he's part mine."

"Heard Dad tell the story a hundred times, you helping them outta that freight yard."

"You boys are damn near all growed up now, but I won't ever forget that night." He shook his head at the wonder of it. "Zach's startin' high school 'n gonna make varsity."

"You don't know that," Francis protested.

"Can't wait to see 'im put on that uniform."

Alphonse slapped Francis on the back. "Ya think we should get back at it?"

"Gotta do the restrooms pronto, and we've just been sitting here yapping away."

"Yappin' away ain't always bad. And if ya ain't careful, ya

just might be gettin' better at it. 'preciate ya keepin' me from that asshole Watney as long as ya did."

––––––

THERE WERE A FEW TIMES on the calendar—Christmas, the Fourth of July—that brought the good folks of St. Joseph closer together, and the days before the start of a new school year ranked as high as the holidays. The town buzzed with hope and gossip: Think the 'Blue Jays' will make it to regionals this year? Maybe my little Davy will get along just fine in first grade. If Lucy doesn't get in his homeroom, she says she'll go nuts. Sister Mary might make a wonderful principal, compared to last year's disappointment.

The summer had been baking hot, and the children thought it too long as they waited anxiously to learn of their new teachers and prayed that the friendships of last year would not have been forgotten.

Francis had just finished sweeping the aisles and making every pew proper and complete. It was already late as he sat in the far back, waiting for the Monsignor and this last night inspection to begin. The evening light through the stained glass streamed in blues, greens, and yellows, and splashed the reds of Christ's hands against the elegant stone wall that held the Stations of the Cross.

High above in the steeple, the great cathedral bells hung dormant. Cast in Germany and imported in the late 1800s, they'd tolled to the countryside and had enthralled the souls of St. Joseph for decades. But St. Joseph's congregation had not heard their magnificent bells for a dozen years; the last peals sounded when Father Brennon was consecrated Monsignor. The decades of dust and pigeon filth had been cleaned away, yet the bells remained mute.

Showered in soft colors, Francis waited. His mind elsewhere, he didn't notice the Monsignor rushing down the aisle, didn't raise his head.

Hovering close in the aisle, the Monsignor licked his lips before speaking.

"As usual, everything looks wonderful, Francis."

"What? Oh . . . sorry."

"Tonight shouldn't take long. This'll most likely be our last inspection."

The Monsignor pointed beyond the communion rail, a satisfied grin stretching his scar until it seemed nearly to disappear in the fading light.

"I'm sure you've been curious about what I've got hidden by the altar?"

"Maybe, a little."

"It's a surprise for the congregation. This Sunday I'll unveil it at High Mass. Would you like to take a peek?"

In the dissolving color, Francis sat motionless.

"Not interested? I have some wonderful announcements this Sunday as well."

Francis didn't answer, but only stared at the shafts of color playing on the far distant wall.

The Monsignor leaned down and studied Francis.

"Perhaps we should have a little talk."

The Monsignor knelt in the aisle on one knee.

"Remember back in June, when you found the holy Hosts?"

"Yes."

"You were afraid. I explained that a servant of the Lord could never lead you into sin. Remember?"

"Yes."

"You believe what I said?"

"Guess so."

The Monsignor rested his hand softly on Francis's shoulder. "I never told you, but the council wanted me to hire a new man to do your job. Sweep up the pigeon dirt and make sure the bell tower never returns to the ruin it was. I didn't listen. This silly pigeon worry has been kept in check because you've done a remarkable job all summer."

"Always try my best."

"You do. I understand you're going through some big changes, and I just want you to know that our Lord leads each of us down different paths."

Grays and the deep shadows of late evening criss-crossed and crept in from the corners, coating over the last of the pastel colors. Hidden lights surrounding the altar were angled upward, illuminating the twelve marble apos-tles standing cold and mute as they guarded the garish tab-ernacle of gold. The pews were empty of sinners praying for solutions; the vacant confessionals held no forgiveness, and the great volume of the church grew dark and dismal be-yond the communion rail.

The Monsignor shifted his hand to under Francis's arm and gently urged Francis to his feet. Locking his eyes to the Monsignor's swaying cassock, Francis held his head down as he followed the Monsignor to the door leading up to the choir loft and beyond.

High in the steeple above the bell tower, pigeons moaned softly, while a naked light bulb glowed through the dingy air.

At the table that Father Yossarian had cobbled together back in June, Francis was bent over at the waist, eyes closed, holding still. The Monsignor's surplice and cassock lay folded neatly on the table.

The Monsignor's breath quickened as he moved silently. He was about to kneel alongside Francis when, without warning, his world exploded with confusion. It was like a flash of lightning from a starry night sky, it was like being hit full force by some unseen power. Cold brass shattered the stillness, and the building sound swallowed whole the bell tower, Francis, and the Monsignor. Hundreds of beating wings knifed through the turrets as the charging sound reverberated and pounded, devouring the quiet.

This night, the great German Bells had been reborn.

The Monsignor's face turned ashen as tidal waves of sound smothered and bound his trembling body with hoops of steel. He staggered, stepping into his cassock; his body quaked violently, and it was all he could do.

He screamed, "Enough!" and rammed his fists in his pockets.

Yet through all the confusion and tremendous noise, Francis was unable to focus, unable to pull himself from the deep far away place that had always sheltered him, from the pigeon child that had always protected him.

In full panic, the Monsignor half-dragged Francis down the steps past the choir and out the front of the church. At last outside in the cool night air, he desperately gulped a huge breath. As Francis finally turned to face him, the Monsignor gazed into the pale young face, into the confused young eyes. Eye to eye for a brief second, the Monsignor suddenly began trembling and averted his gaze. He turned Francis around, then gently pushed the boy in the direction of Second Street before slipping around the corner and into the darkness.

It was 9:11 that Friday night when old man Jettinghoff abruptly stopped rocking on his front porch to listen to the bells, when a confused Mrs. Miller way over on Fourth Street stepped into her slippers and flipped on her bedroom light. And, it wasn't until a few hours before dawn that the pigeons returned to roost in the steeple.

CHAPTER TEN

The Monsignor

HOURS AFTER MIDNIGHT THAT SAME NIGHT, IN THE STERILE glow of the street lamp, a dark figure skirted the corner of the church's stone façade and climbed the stairs to the brass door on the left. The silhouette paused briefly to unlock the door, then slipped inside, locking the door behind him.

Sixteen ornate pillars, eight on a side, rose over fifty feet to support the domed, gold leaf ceiling. The oak pews, parallel and vacant, had for a hundred years been bolted into a pattern not unlike a military formation. The stone sculptures of the Stations of the Cross adorned both walls up to the communion rail, while the twelve chiseled apostles stood silently above the altar as if to bear witness in the dim light.

The hunched figure moved slowly through the black shadows, the hem of his black cassock sweeping the polished floor, the click of his footfall measuring the time and distance to a pew adjacent to the confessionals. He kept his hands tucked tightly within the pouch of his cassock as he eased into the pew. He sat quietly a long time before carefully pulling a holstered pistol from the folds of his cassock.

The holster's brown leather was faintly shiny, with scuff marks along its edges.

Bewildered in some distant world, he sat absolutely still, disoriented and confused. His tangled black hair, his wrinkled surplus and cassock scuffed with dirt at the knees, all made it obvious that the Monsignor had had a horrendous night. Darkness rimmed his cold eyes, his gaunt face was pale and even the scar on his jaw seemed insignificant compared to the look of desperation on his drawn face.

In due time, he watched his hand unbuckle the holster strap and withdraw the Walther P-38 pistol. Staring down at his trembling hand, he watched the slight wobble in the gun. He pressed its barrel against his thigh, pinning it to steady its shaking. He closed his eyes and tried for minutes to slow his breathing. Eventually, the color in his face began to return, and the jagged scar on his jaw grew dark and purple as if it had a pulse.

POZNAN, POLAND

1943

THE COMPOUND, A HUNDRED SQUARE kilometers of countryside near Poznan, Poland was encircled by a ten-foot high wire fence. A placard hung above the steel gated entrance: UHLAN CAVALRY FIFTEENTH REGIMENT. Random patches of bramble and dense woods and trenches cut at odd places, in odd angles, deep enough to conceal a man, broke up the otherwise uniform brown landscape.

Black pennants adorned with red swastikas alternating with white and red pennants flapped above an expansive lifeless field. The wooden barracks squatting beyond the manure dotted field were dwarfed by fourteen barns and massive hay mounds that heaped over the corrals.

This was the place for the Polish Cavalry, the place where tactics were taught and maneuvers memorized.

Twenty uniformed soldiers sat at attention atop their mounts, their backs to the woods. Rotmistrz Janicki, "Captain of Horse," with his medallions sparkling in the late day sun, pranced in front of his unit on a magnificent horse. Nineteen hands tall, deeply muscled with barely restrained power, the horse accentuated Janicki's unusually short stature.

Janicki halted, facing his unit directly, and shouted, "The greatest victory of the Uhlan Fifteenth Regiment!"

The soldiers bellowed in unison, "Battle of Komarowo!"

He scrutinized the line, searching for defects, eyeing decorum. Near the end of the line, Lieutenant Brennon's skittish horse pawed at the ground and reared its head wildly.

The veins in Janicki's neck swelled as he shouted, "Szeregowiec Brennon!"

"Yes, Sir!"

"Even your mount feels your weakness!"

Young Brennon looked squarely ahead, his dark eyes steady.

"Dismount!"

"Yes, sir!"

"Szeregowiec Brennon! Your mount deserves better

than the likes of you. Beating this poor animal with a crop would've gotten your horse shot and put this entire unit in peril. Poland can ill afford to lose this animal. Hand over your reins. You'll walk to the barracks."

Brennon led his horse the thirty paces. With his shoulders squared, he stood at rigid attention and handed the reins up to his captain.

Janicki saluted the others.

"Unit dismissed."

For some time, Brennon refused to move, glaring at his unit casually trotting away. Stone-faced, he marched the five kilometers back and entered the barn where he knew his captain waited. Brennon's horse had already been forked hay, and its tack hung correctly in place on the wall. In the stall at the far end, Janicki was grooming his mount and listening for Brennon.

"Szeregowiec Brennon! What do you have to say for yourself?"

"Whatever you want me to say . . . sir," said Brennon, approaching quickly, his tone dangerously close to insolent.

Janicki flung the brush to a corner. His horse shifted nervously in the tight stall.

"You're unfit for this unit! Remove your saber."

Brennon unhooked the weapon from his belt.

"You stalled my horse?"

"After what your mount's been through, it's the least I can do."

"Captain?"

"Your piss-poor horsemanship. If you can't follow orders, if you're not prepared, you'll be killed, along with your unit."

The captain tugged at his tunic, straightening his uniform.

"You've been a shit soldier since you arrived. Why the hell are you even here?"

"Conscription. I wasn't given a choice."

"You listen! Every man has a duty to defend his country."

The horse shifted skittishly, its eyes white and wild. Janicki reached up to calm it. "Even my mount despises you."

"And I have no fondness for horses." Brennon clenched his fists by his side. "I was ten when my father was mowed down riding one of these beasts. Killed by a self-propelled gun made of steel like our TKDs. In Lithuania." Brennon's cynical voice knifed through the air. "Your so-called 'greatest victory at Komarowo.' Riding a horse is suicide against a TKD."

"I don't give a damn about your father!"

"So it's my patriotic duty to ride a horse to my grave?"

"You could die a worse death."

"I'm supposed to just hop on my trusty steed with a saber? You're a fool if you think we can defend Poland by playing cowboy with Hitler."

Janicki thrust a hand in his uniform's pocket and yanked out a small paper-bound book. Its front cover pictured Adolph Hitler, mustachioed with cold eyes in a face devoid of emotion. A red banner across the bottom highlighted the title, "Mein Kampf."

"Moja Walka!" Janicki spat. "This shit was under your bunk!" In a flash, he took a quick step forward and slapped the book against Brennon's face. "First a coward, now a traitor!" He threw the book down and ground it into the stall's manure with his boot.

Recoiling, Brennon regained his composure almost instantly and sneered, "You yourself preached that you must understand your enemy. Ever listen to Hitler's broadcasts on the radio?"

"Propaganda hardens lies into steel! I could have you shot."

"For understanding the enemy?"

Janicki's face contorted in fury. "For a sickly coward who reads Hitler!"

"You're just a little endowed small man on a giant horse. You look stupid sitting up there in your toy uniform."

"Traitor!" Janicki screamed. Slamming his elbow against the horse's flank was an accident as he cocked his arm ready to punch Brennon.

The horse suddenly crazed and bucked, its legs kicking wildly. Brennon threw up his arms and tried ducking out of the way, but he was too slow. One hoof grazed his arm, but the other crashed squarely against his jaw, knocking him face down in the stall. He lay stunned, sprawled out, horse manure plastering his hair.

Blood oozed from his mouth that flopped uselessly open, and the splintered jaw bone protruded through his cheek.

"Dishonorably discharged!" Janicki quaked.

Brennon tried propping himself on an elbow, but fell back down.

"Live with this disgrace for the rest of your life," Janicki spat down at Brennon. "And with your ugly jaw as a reminder, you weak bastard!"

Long After Midnight

THE MONSIGNOR'S EYES WERE SEALED tightly.

Crashing through his memory of Poland, the great German bells thundered in his head. Pounding again and again, the tremendous sound devoured everything, smothered all reason.

Two . . . three . . .

Francis, so young, so perfect.

Those eyes, wide, trusting eyes.

Pigeons!

Four . . .

Clashing brass.

The bells, five . . .

Grotesque.

Pigeons!

Everywhere.

Forgive me . . .

Talons.

Beaks.

Drilling.

Cursed.

Impossible.

Raptors.

Pigeons!

Carnivores.

Wake up.

Forgive me Father . . .

Everywhere.

Hair.

Skull.

Scalp.

Brains.

Wake up.

Feasting.

Blood.

Pain.

A thousand arrows . . .

Forgive me Father for I have sinned. My last confession . . .

Doom.

Six . . .

Seven . . .

Eight . . .

His head snapped up sharply. He braced his arms against the pew to steady his shaking while his eyes gradually cleared, focused, and located bearings.

The pistol . . .

Swiftly—Coward! No one must ever know—he shoved it back in his pocket. After settling and closing his eyes briefly, he made a protracted and precise sign of the cross on his chest.

He rose abruptly from the pew and walked swiftly beyond the communion rail to the altar, then halted and studied the pulpit. In the weak light, in the quiet of his magnificent church, he climbed the four steps and positioned himself at the podium.

A benevolent, gentle smile radiated from his face as he looked out over his imagined flock. The faithful crowded every pew; even in the far back, they wedged in, craning to see, straining to hear. His words swirled high among the apostles, wound through every aisle, and were absorbed in a thousand ears like a healing tonic. Women put hands to their faces; men, with their jaws ajar, leaned forward to savor every word. With an ever-widening, peaceful smile, the Monsignor arced his arm far out and blessed his flock.

He suddenly knew then the way out, what he'd do, and no one would ever know.

Sweeping gracefully into the sacristy, he stood at the counter with note pad and pen, and wrote,

Dear Mr. Bockman,
Please accept my apology for this late request. As you are
no doubt aware, our wonderful bells tolled last evening
for the first time since I was consecrated monsignor. As
part of many wonderful announcements I wish to
convey this Sunday, I was hoping to include our bells to
mark this most glorious day. Unfortunately, I
accidentally set them off more than a tad ahead of
schedule.
Could you please include in your late Saturday paper
my small explanation that you'll find attached?
Sincerely,
Monsignor Brennon

CHAPTER ELEVEN

Francis and the Calling

SCAFFOLDING ENCASED THE BELL TOWER LIKE A SKELETON, yet after only a few days, the beginnings of louvered panels shutting off the turrets could be seen, and with the construction, the Monsignor became certain that at last this would close the chapter on his pigeon nightmare. And, with the new school year about to begin, Francis rejoined Zach, working again alongside his brother while St. Joseph parish made ready for the students' return.

Schedules were set and revised, duties were doled out, and nuns with lists in hand would plead for attention from Edgar. It had been this way ever since Zach and Francis could remember, and year after year, Edgar rattled out orders to his sons. The brothers came to relish these days, understanding that they held knowledge that their fellow students desperately sought, and in those days before the start of school, Zach and Francis achieved a small degree of notoriety.

Buzzing back and forth with supplies, speeding through hallways and wheeling desks down corridors past bustling teachers, they were privy to nearly everything vital to the anxious and excited students.

What homeroom am I in?

Is that battle ax my English teacher?

Zach, is Karen in my science class?

Nuns conferred in hallways, and parents comforted six-year-olds while running their fingers down the rosters taped by the classroom doors.

Alphonse alone seemed unaffected by the frenetic pace to get things done. Perhaps he stayed separate simply because he'd always enjoyed being above the clamor in order to observe, his ears always tuned to the goings on. Yet even amid the flurry of extra work, he was unable to overcome his need to dig at the Monsignor whenever he could. Ever since he followed the Sadlers to St. Joseph over a decade ago, he relished watching the Monsignor scratch his head in bewilderment—and, more than once, shake his fist in outright anger—at his shenanigans. But this year, Alphonse understood that his exploding fear and deepening hatred toward the Monsignor would need to be dealt with by much more than his silly games.

Amid the chaos that Wednesday, Alphonse had been nonchalantly sweeping the hallways. The nuns shook their heads in dismay as Alphonse chewed on his stogie and pushed his four-foot wide mop down the halls. With his hands in his pockets, his expression carefree, almost jovial, he marched with giddy enthusiasm past the classrooms, the mop handle propped firmly against his chest. Rounding a corner to begin another swath, he paused, leaned to the side, and spoke softly to a short pudgy nun carrying an armful of Crayola boxes, "Ya know, women come and go talkin' of Michelangelo." Her gaunt face, squished by the horseshoe frame of her veil, scowled in an odd combination of impatience and confusion. Completing the pass at the end, Alphonse caught a glimpse of his reflection in a window. Stalling, his carefree expression suddenly gone, he looked back at his reflection, then shook his head with disgust and shook his mop with vengeance.

In another wing, Francis charged down the hallway with a box tucked under his arm.

Sweat collected on his face, and he shuddered at the unexpected and deep chill slicing through his body. He was wiping his forehead with his already sweaty sleeve when Sister Loyola leaned through her classroom door and cornered him.

"Oh, bless you, Francis! Did the office send new erasers?"

"Probably in here." He gave the box a little shake.

"Please bring those supplies in here?" She ushered Francis into her room. "I've been meaning to talk to you."

The sister was a large woman, tall, with long arms that waved like a conductor when she talked. Her neck appeared exceptionally long, and supported her head that appeared way too small for such a big body. Her veil hung loosely alongside her long and happy face.

"Lots to do, Sister."

"I don't know what we sisters would do without you and your brother." Her waving arm punctuated her speech. "Busy, busy, busy."

"Reckon it's that time, all right." He teetered unsteadily as he placed the box on the desk at the front of the room.

"Are you all right?" she said eyeing him with concern.

"I'm okay." He wiped his face again.

"I'm not so sure. Better rest for a minute."

"Dad's got a ton of stuff for me to do."

"I'm sure he does." As if there wasn't enough room in her body to contain the news, her cheeks puffed out and her twinkling eyes grew wide. "But what I wanted to talk to you about is important, Francis."

Francis sat on his hands and held still, trying to ignore the shaking in his legs.

"I promised the Monsignor that I'd have this talk with you." She settled herself in the chair beside him.

"You know, Francis, I've been teaching here since before you started first grade. I've watched you develop into a sensitive young man. The Monsignor told me what a wonderful boy you've been all summer. You should've seen his face when he said how fond he was of you, that you performed whatever was asked of you beautifully."

Francis managed only a short peep.

"He was the first to mention it, but we've all been noticing. Francis, we believe you have a Calling."

Francis blinked rapidly with sweat in his eyes. "A what?"

"We believe the Lord is calling you for a higher purpose. We all agree that you should begin thinking very seriously about the seminary."

He rubbed at the sweat collecting on the back of his neck.

"You mean like become a priest?"

"Yes, a priest."

He let the idea marinate a moment.

"But . . . why would I wanna do that?"

"Because you have a gift."

"No girlfriend?" He cringed; his body shuddered.

"You're being silly." She chuckled. "Of course you can have girl friends, and you always have a choice. But with your calling, it leaves little room for a girlfriend like your brother and the others in high school." She beamed at him. "This is a beautiful time in your life, Francis."

He slumped forward, cradling his sweaty head in his hands.

"What's wrong, Francis?"

"Just got lots ta do."

"Of course you do, but I think you should take it easy for awhile. Should I find your father?"

"Oh, no. No."

"Well, we have the whole year to think these things over. But for now, don't take our little talk lightly. Francis, you do have a gift."

————

ESCAPING FROM SISTER LOYOLA AND her talk of gifts, Francis retreated to an obscure corner of the school basement. He pressed his back into the coolness of the tiled wall, then slowly slid down to the dank floor.

He was burning up yet shivering. After trying to get back on his shaky legs, he had no choice but to ease down prone against the hard floor. The cool cement felt good against his scalding face. He was lying face down with his hands beneath his chin, his side wedged tightly against the wall, when Alphonse found him.

"Francis?" Alphonse, his eyes wide with sudden worry,

quickly knelt alongside. He scanned for a twisted back, anything bleeding, any hint of an injury.

He gently touched Francis's forehead, then slowly pulled back, resting his hands on his knees like a Buddha.

He spoke quickly, but softly.

"Francis, did ya fall?"

"Hot."

"Yer head's colder 'n a witch's tit."

Francis's voice shook. "Gotta . . . get back to work." He tried raising himself up on an elbow.

Alphonse blocked him with a hand.

"Hold still."

"But . . ."

"Jezu-peet . . . yer Dad can live without ya fer a few damn minutes."

Francis shivered uncontrollably, his teeth chattering.

"Christ almighty, yer teeth are clickin'. I'm gettin' yer pa."

"I should at least—"

"Stay put!"

"Edgar!" Alphonse stormed into the boiler room. "Francis is awful sick!"

"What?" Edgar twisted a wrench on a steam valve, watching gurgling water evaporate instantly against the hot metal.

"He's damn near passed out!"

"Hands are full. Bring him here."

"Damn it, Edgar!" He spat his stogie in the trash and instantly raked the juice from his chin. "Good God, man! It's just a damn leak! Hurry."

Edgar studied the valve for a moment then scowled at Alphonse. "Christ—"

EDGAR GINGERLY CARRIED FRANCIS TO the wheelbarrow and wheeled him up the ramp to the outside. He let out an exhausted breath, looked back down the ramp, then held out his arms as if Alphonse could grant him more time.

"I got 'im, Edgar," said Alphonse, grabbing the handles.

"Just get him home. Tell Sara I should be home by five."

Francis grimaced; Alphonse grunted as they bumped across Second Street.

"Have ya there in no time, Francis." Sweat trickled down his weathered face.

Francis groaned.

At the curb, Alphonse reversed to pull the wheelbarrow backward up and over.

"Sorry . . . 'bout the rough ride." Alphonse's voice rose with each bump. "Ya doin' all right? Where ya hurtin' now?"

"Hip." Francis's reply was barely audible.

"Did ya fall?"

Francis pressed his colorless lips tight.

"We made it! We're goin' in the front door."

Alphonse scooped him up and shoved open the door with his boot, muttering, "Ya got me scared ta shit, Francis."

Francis squirmed in his grip and moaned.

"Ya should be headin' ta the doc's now . . . damn."

Alphonse lowered him gently to a kitchen chair. Francis leaned back on one hip with the leg out straight.

The back door banged as Sara came through, balancing a clothes basket on her hip. She gasped and dropped the basket when she saw Francis's tortured face.

"What happened?"

"Hurt my hip."

"He's on fire, Sara." Alphonse, his eyes quivering, his feet shuffling, said in a panic, "Damn if he ain't sicker 'n shit."

She felt Francis's forehead.

"Francis, is your stomach okay?"

"I found 'im nearly passed out. Says his hip's smartin' like a son-a-bitch."

"You carried him from school?"

"Wheelbarrow." Alphonse nodded toward the front door.

"Edgar know?"

"Said to bring him here, he'd be home in a couple hours." Alphonse tugged at his beard. "Sara, this boy needs the doc, pronto!"

"Doc Webber's not cheap."

"Sara, I ain't ever seen anythin' keep Francis from doin' his work."

She leaned down for a closer look.

"It's your hip, Francis?"

"Sorry, Mom."

"Alphonse, would you run to the rectory and ask the Monsignor if he could drive us to Doc Webber's?"

Alphonse took a step back, his eyes fluttering with sudden dilemma.

"Me 'n that man . . ."

"It's Francis, Alphonse."

"Hell, Sara, ain't but seven or eight blocks. I could wheel 'im there in two shakes!"

She rested her hand against her son's forehead. "You up for another ride, Francis?"

"It'll be all right. Just give me a little bit, Mom."

"No. I don't like the looks of this." Sara stood, her mind made up. "The wheelbarrow, Alphonse."

———

FRANCIS WAS IN THE ETHER about what was happening to him, about what Doc Webber's verdict was. In pain, delirious, he remembered only snippets of the conversation the doctor had with his parents.

Edgar rubbed his hands together. His work clothes were smeared with grease; coal dust darkened his face and hands.

"How bad is it, Doc?"

Doc Webber raised a hand to stall Edgar. He took his time listening to Francis's heart through the stethoscope, then gently rolled him on his back and listened again.

"Will he be all right?" Sara clutched her rosary. Edgar patted her on the shoulder.

"I can't be certain, won't really know for a few days, but I think we're damn lucky."

"Don't feel very lucky now," Sara said quietly.

"It looks like the infection and inflammation has settled in his hip. For now, it appears that it hasn't affected his heart. Rheumatic heart fever is awfully dangerous."

Edgar stammered, "Rheumatic heart fever?"

Doc Webber nodded. "RHF. Nasty disease."

Sara took a deep breath before asking, "Was it something he ate?"

"No. The problem's bacteria . . . had he complained of a sore throat?"

Edgar and Sara shared blank looks.

"Say anything to you, Sara?"

"You know how he keeps to himself."

"The reason I'm asking is that RHF many times is brought on by strep throat. It gets its name because it often attacks the heart."

Edgar cleared his throat. "But you said his heart's all right."

"Yes, for now. We just have to wait and see. I've given him a heavy dose of antibiotics, and the cortisone will go a long way to help ease the pain in his hip."

"You don't think . . ." The lines in Edgar's face deepened, darkened. "I've . . . I mean, Francis dealing all summer with cleaning the bell tower and scraping the—"

"No, Edgar. This has nothing to do with pigeons or psittacosis."

"You sure?"

"Positive."

"What do we do now?"

"The most important thing is to keep this boy quiet with a lot of rest. And I can't stress strongly enough that he needs to be quarantined. Strep is contagious and the last thing you folks need is for Zach to catch it . . . say at least a couple weeks. No visitors, and he'll need to stay off his bike, avoid doing anything strenuous. As for school, we'll have to wait and see how our boy's getting along."

Doc Webber made a final notation in Francis's file and set it aside. "And Francis will need penicillin indefinitely."

"What?" Sara sagged against Edgar.

"Yes, antibiotics. They're expensive, but we have to avoid

another strep infection at all costs. If he should come down with this again, there's no telling how terrible it could be."

———

THE LAUNDRY ROOM WAS A tight fit. The washing machine tapped rhythmically against the wall. The dryer, pulled out from its space beside the washer in hope of repairs that never came, sat cattywampus with its black power cord pulled over the top. The room smelled of soap. Francis lay on a cot alongside the near wall. If he propped his head high, he could see out the small, curtainless window.

Francis had always thought that his mom spent hour upon hour washing clothes, that of all her chores, doing the laundry dominated most of her time. In his first days after the onset of rheumatic heart fever, he was surprised at how few were the times that his mom bopped in to fill the washer, how it took only minutes to switch things out. She hung the laundry outside, but still, he thought his mom would've been in the room more than she was.

Whole afternoons, he'd gaze out the tiny window and daydream about the Fourth of July and riding his bike to The End with his cane pole; he'd wonder about Zach and Rupert playing basketball, and he tried not to think about Janet, knowing it was stupid to imagine that she even noticed him as anything other than Zach's little brother.

She'd been in his homeroom last year, and they'd been partners for a little while in geometry class. She was pretty, and she had this little thing that solidified his fantasy. Every time she'd smile, it came with a little wink. That she gave it to everyone didn't matter; it made him feel warm, made him feel like he wasn't the janitor's son. The thing that really got to him, the thing that he recalled over and over while lying on the cot, was one particular time she got up from her desk after class. The room had been stifling, and when she stood up, her thin cotton dress conformed to the shape of her butt.

In the days that followed, Francis gleaned that he had a disease that wouldn't kill him but that it could be spread, and that it was necessary for him to be quarantined in the laundry room. Yet after his sentence was up, after he was no longer a danger to others, he remained unclear about what would come next. Eventually back to school certainly, but to sleep again upstairs next to his brother was murky.

For hours he'd ruminate that his predicament wasn't all that bad. After all, no one asked him to do anything. The awful sweating and chills were gone. Yet most of the time, he still had to lie on his stomach to relieve pressure on his hip, and in that position he drifted between hazy wakefulness and deep sleep.

IT WAS A LITTLE AFTER noon, the breezes hot and gentle. A laundry basket sat at Sara's feet. Her lips clamped two clothespins as she bent the legs of thick trousers over the line. She'd pinned them and pulled another pair from the basket when she saw the Mercedes pull to a stop out front. She quickly patted wisps of hair back into place, wiped the sweat from her face, and tried tugging her apron straight.

As the Monsignor approached, she smiled and said, "What a nice surprise, Monsignor!"

"It sure is a beautiful day, wouldn't you say?"

"That it is. Laundry's almost dry before I get it pinned."

She crossed the small yard to meet the Monsignor at the steps. "Shall we get out of this heat? I have iced tea."

"I don't need a thing . . . thank you." He settled down on the stoop.

"I could bring out kitchen chairs—it'll just take a minute," she said, a little flustered.

"This is fine." He adjusted his cassock, momentarily exposing his pale shins. "I don't recall if I ever sat on your back porch just to chat with you, Sara, or even with Edgar, for that matter."

Sara wiped her hands nervously on her apron.

"It's been a few days. How's Francis getting along?"

"You know Francis, he doesn't say much. I'm sure he's not fond of being cooped up."

"He must've given you an awful fright."

"Gave us both a terrible scare." She turned away.

"Sara, sit with me." He patted the stoop beside him. "There's no need to worry." The Monsignor's voice was low, soothing. "I just swung by to check on Francis and see how you're holding up. You have a lot weighing on your shoulders now."

Sara sank to the bottom step. "Doc Webber said we were lucky."

"He's been making house calls?"

"He should be here any time . . . another shot . . ." She shrugged, bit her lip, and dared not look at the Monsignor.

"I . . . I simply don't know how we'll be able to afford the penicillin—Doc Webber said he'll need it until he gets out of high school." She took a huge breath, then let it out slowly. "With Edgar's salary . . . it doesn't leave much room for medicines."

"I certainly understand that. Dr. Webber was telling me that there's a government program designed for folks like you . . ."

Sara bristled. "Folks like us?"

"That probably didn't come out right. The program's for folks who find themselves in a bad way because of unexpected medical bills. Now don't you worry, Sara. I'll see to it that Francis gets his medicine."

"Any little bit helps." Sara sat hunched, staring at her laundry drying on the line in the bright sun.

"After all his hard work this summer, it's the least I can do, Sara. Now, I thought I'd peek in on Francis, if that's all right with you."

"It's small, you'll have to squeeze."

The Monsignor stood quietly alongside the cot, gazing at the sleeping Francis. Aside from his quiet, rhythmic breathing, the only sound was that of Sara rattling dishes in the kitchen.

The Monsignor's breath quickened as he reached out, his hand trembling as it hovered inches above Francis. He was muttering, "I will miss our . . ." when a sharp rap startled him. He spun around, thrusting his hands deep into the sleeves of his cassock, as Doc Webber wedged himself through the narrow door.

"Well, well, Monsignor. Both on house calls today, eh?"

The Monsignor swiped his forehead with a hankie and cleared his throat. "Great news that it's only his hip."

"I should say so." Doc Webber set his bag on the cot while the Monsignor sidled around him to stand in the doorway.

"How ya feelin', son?"

Groggy, Francis opened his eyes. "I'm all right."

"Well, Monsignor," Doc Webber said, prodding Francis's lymph nodes. "Looks like you won't have to worry about psittacosis soon."

Taken off guard, the Monsignor stammered, "Excuse me?"

"Construction on the steeple. Psittacosis. Mrs. Cunningham's lung disease?"

"Oh yes, our pigeon problem. Construction's still going to take several more weeks."

"S'pose it'll be your legacy. Francis, time to turn on your side for your shots. More penicillin, and cortisone for your hip."

"How long do I have to stay cooped up?"

"Hmm . . . I'd say another week or so."

"I'll be able to start school Monday?"

"Hold on, son. You're going to need to take it easy. I think school probably the week after next. You won't be able to horse around or play basketball, and stay off your bike till I give you the go ahead."

"You mean I gotta walk?"

"You'll be surprised how small this town is. Enough stalling . . . here we go."

Doc Webber quickly had the pajamas down exposing the hip.

The Monsignor flushed. "Before you start . . . here's where I'll step out."

The Monsignor pushed his way through the laundry room's little door, desperate for air, desperate to clear his mind of the obsession that wouldn't go away.

CHAPTER TWELVE

Father Brennon
1945

A FRESH AND MUCH YOUNGER FATHER BRENNON PACED in front of his wide mahogany desk that dominated most of the office space. Miscellaneous files were stacked along the edge of the desk, and reminder notes were spread out randomly across the shiny surface. A statue of St. Joseph graced a small antique table tucked in the corner. Several half-unpacked boxes waited along the far wall. The office was spartan, hinting of an occupant who had more pressing issues on his mind than decorating.

There came a soft knock on his door.

Margaret Youngpeter, spinster and long-time house-keeper for the rectory, smiled apologetically as Brennon opened the door.

"Sorry for another interruption, Father, but there's a young man who'd like to have a word with you."

"Is he a member?"

"I've never seen him before. I think he might be looking for a job."

"He said that?"

"Just got the feeling, is all."

"You're usually right, Margaret. Well, we better see him, then."

"I simply don't know where you get all your energy, Father."

"We're here to lend a hand. It's what we do."

"I'll send him right in."

A man in his mid-twenties walked stiffly into the office, clutching his hat in his enormous hand.

"Welcome, I'm Father Brennon." The Father eagerly extended his hand.

"Edgar Sadler. Thank you for your time."

"Please," Brennon said, indicating the folding chair beside the desk.

Edgar sat straight, his back not touching the metal chair. Strangely cloudy, his wide-open eyes appeared eager, his worried face energized by some hidden desperation. His curly black hair had been slicked back. Even though his clothes were clean, his overalls were worn through at the knees, and his plaid shirt was faded, a missing pocket making it obvious what color it had been many years before. He held his head down as his huge fingers pinched away the tiny bits of debris that had collected on his hat.

"Coffee, Mr. Sadler?"

"Just Edgar. No thank you."

"New to St. Joseph?"

"I suppose a month still makes me new."

The Father leaned against his desk, attentive yet casual.

"So how can we help you?"

Edgar fumbled with the hat in his lap.

"I've spent the last four weeks looking for a job . . . was hoping you might have something."

"Have you tried the Bending works? They make fine furniture, and it seems they're always looking for help."

"I did when I first got to town. They couldn't help me."

Puzzled, Father Brennon skirted the desk and began sifting through his miscellaneous notes, most scrawled on scraps of paper.

"That's surprising. Let's see . . . Mr. Bonifase is on our church council. I know he does the hiring at the can factory. It's here somewhere, oh, yes, they've moved, they're over on Fifth Street now."

"I met the man." Edgar bowed his head. "It didn't work out."

"Really? What kind of work are you looking for?"

"I'm willing to do anything."

"Well," said the Father frowning, concentrating. "What have you done?"

"Mostly odd jobs this past year. Before that I was a foreman at Ajax, a big coal company back in Pennsylvania."

"I don't think I could ever work in a mine. Too claustrophobic for me. A foreman comes with a lot of responsibility."

"That it did."

"So what brings you to Indiana?"

"Back east, jobs are pretty hard to come by. Was told that I might fare better in this part of the country."

"You have family, Edgar?"

"A boy, Zach, about to turn one, and my wife Sara's due any time."

The Father raised his eyebrows.

"With all that, I surely understand your need."

"Father." Edgar took a big breath, steadying himself. "I'm willing to do anything. I can fix motors, pumps. I'm not bad at plumbing either."

The Father pulled over a chair, unfolded it and sat next to Edgar.

"I'm surprised Mr. Bonifase couldn't use you at the can factory."

Edgar bit his lip.

Father Brennon leaned in closer.

"Did Mr. Bonifase give any reason?"

Edgar said quickly and quietly, "I turned blind in one eye, and my sight in the other isn't all that good. It happened at Ajax, and they had to let me go."

"Oh . . . I'm sorry."

"But since then, I think I've done pretty well working around my little problem." Edgar tried keeping his voice upbeat. "Heck, tearing down a motor, I can memorize even the tiniest parts with my fingers."

"That so, Edgar?"

"I can do that with most anything."

"Doesn't sound all that easy."

"To be honest, Father, Mr. Bonifase was afraid with my eyesight, it'd be dangerous working around heavy machinery."

"Certainly, Edgar, you can understand his point."

Suddenly pensive, Father Brennon rose from his chair and began a deliberate slow pace in front of Edgar.

"Would you by chance have experience with steam boilers?"

Edgar managed a hopeful smile.

"I could learn."

"I'm sure you could." Father Brennon shook his head. I know you're in a predicament, but I really don't have anything. The only thing the church needs is a replacement for our boiler man, and that requires experience, not to mention a license."

"But Father, I picked up a lot working in the mine over the years." Edgar began scrunching the hat in his lap. "Just put a manual in front of me, and I can tear down anything and make it work. I could learn boilers and steam right quick, if you gave me the chance."

"I'm afraid it's not quite that simple. Maybe I shouldn't have said anything. It's a state law that we hire a licensed man to operate our three boilers. The heat for our church and the whole complex is in the basement of the grade school. I'm sure you can appreciate the need for safety when hundreds of children are involved?"

After a long silence, Edgar said softly, "It's just that with Sara due any time . . ."

He cut his thought short with a bewildered shake of his head. "I can understand that. Safety. Yes. Of course."

"Anybody can see that you must be a hard working man, Edgar."

Edgar shrugged and stood to leave.

"I much appreciate your time, Father."

Father Brennon quickly held out his arm to stall Edgar.

"Can you really learn anything with the manuals?"

"Yes, sir . . . Father."

"This makes me awfully nervous, but—what if I gave you the boiler's specification manuals, let's see . . . loaned them to you for a couple weeks. Bernard'll still be around until the end of the year to help. You learn as much as you can. Come back in a few weeks, and we'll see what we can do. Of course, I'd never be able to pay you what I'd need to pay a licensed man."

Edgar's face came suddenly alive as he jutted out his hand and shook the Father's with more than a little enthusiasm.

"There's no guarantee, Edgar. Boilers are complicated, so I wouldn't get my hopes too high."

"I know. But you'll see—I can do this, Father. I really can."

MONSIGNOR BRENNON
1959

MONSIGNOR BRENNON RELAXED BEHIND HIS oversized mahogany desk. His gold embossed nameplate sat next to an expensive set of pens engraved with his name in German. The desktop—always free of notes and clutter now—was polished to a glass-like sheen that shimmered in the sunlight.

There were still two matching chairs in front of the massive desk, but now they were elegant armchairs upholstered in fine fabrics, not scavenged metal folding chairs. The rug beneath them was woven in a delicate pattern of deep blues, maroons, and black. Photographs of dignitaries and award ceremonies adorned the walls. Antiques and religious artifacts gathered from his travels perched like trophies on elegant end tables and étagères. On a small carved table in the corner, an ornate brass lamp crowded against the old statue of Saint Joseph.

A framed quote from Roseland hung on the wall beyond the desk:

. . . ONLY A FEW GOOD MINDS ARE ENDOWED WITH

THE TREMENDOUS POWER TO ASSIST HUMANITY . . .

THERE ARE BUT A FEW GREAT HEARTS WORTHY

OF USING IT . . .

He sipped a Scotch, musing on the path his life had taken. *Even with war, Janicki, you were a tiny man. Without it, you must've vanished*, he thought, his remembered pain as potent as if no time at all had passed.

"Look at me, Janicki." He swirled the drink gently in its crystal tumbler, then raised it in mock salute. "Seminary, my own parish, power and respect," he said, savoring the last bit of Scotch. "See me now, Captain."

A knock at the door interrupted his reverie.

"Yes?"

"Your two o'clock appointment is here, Monsignor."

He banged his glass next to its matching decanter on the sideboard, then retrieved a folder from the desk drawer and tossed it on his spotless desk.

Father Yossarian marched into the office, his eyes locked straight ahead, his lips sealed together as if facing a firing squad. He stood stiffly between the two chairs, his hands clasped behind his back.

The Monsignor stared coldly at him across the broad mahogany, his anger barely in check.

"It was you who rang those bells!"

Yossarian kept his expression neutral, his gaze fixed on the wall beyond the desk. "I've already explained I'd have no reason."

"Who else but you?"

"I would never—"

"What do you take me for? I'm not an idiot!"

"Of course not, but . . ."

"You and Edgar are the only ones who even know where that panel is."

The Monsignor flipped open the folder. "I have your resignation papers to sign."

"What?" Yossarian looked from the folder to the Monsignor and back again, confused. "A forced resignation . . ." He made quick motions to protest, but sank into the chair. ". . . for something I didn't do?"

"Did you think I didn't notice?"

"I . . . I do not understand," Father Yossarian stammered. "Notice what?"

"All summer you've been spying on me, snooping for something."

"Snooping?"

"Creeping around the church at all hours . . . the way you've been looking at me suspiciously for months. And to top it off, you had the audacity to set off those bells!"

"But Monsignor, I didn't—"

"This Sunday, I will inform the congregation of your intention to return to Hungary."

"That's—"

"You're dismissed."

As the door swung shut behind the retreating father, the Monsignor said softly to himself, "That's the end of that." He smiled in satisfaction. "Good riddance." He then poured another modest Scotch.

CHAPTER THIRTEEN

Shock at the High Mass

DESPITE THE HUSTLE WITH THE NEW SCHOOL YEAR, THE congregation was still able to piece together that Sunday's Mass would be centered on some important announcement from their Monsignor. In the check-out line at Rinks, across the counter waiting for new parts for a tractor, in the store aisles stocked with fresh school supplies, the news spread that something monumental would be announced at High Mass. The mystery shrouded in white against the wall by the altar had been commented on by most, and the peculiar effervescence of the Monsignor as of late had not gone unnoticed. The fact that this was all coming together at the beginning of the new school year pointed not only to an unusual Sunday but, more importantly, to a glorious message from their monsignor. Every seat in every pew was taken, toddlers balanced on laps to make more room, and the overflow of devoted jammed into the vestibule.

Nothing about the Mass itself was out of the ordinary; there were no special hymns, no decorations of celebration, and only briefly at the end of his sermon did the Monsignor allude to the news he wished to convey to his increasingly antsy parishioners.

In closing his sermon, the Monsignor said only, "To those of you who care to stay for a few minutes after Mass, I have some announcements to make. They are dear to my heart, and I pray that you kind folks will indulge me so that I can share with you many joyous things that have been developing over these past many weeks."

With the exception of a mother with bawling twins, a few teenagers, and a drunkard who stumbled in late and fumbled out early, the people stayed locked in place. The three aisles leading up from the vestibule had become even more packed, the crowd spilling beyond the confessionals. The hum of voices ceased immediately when the Monsignor returned from the sacristy. His holy surplice and blessed bits of clothing necessary to celebrate sacrament were gone. His black cassock with its regal piping swayed gently as he climbed the few steps to the podium. The gold sash around his waist sparkled in the light streaming through the stained glass.

"I'm wonderfully pleased that so many of you chose to stay and share with me this glorious event. This is not a Mass or even a sacrament, and I'm quite sure that our Lord would allow polite vocal response to what I'm about to announce. I'll begin with only this bit of unfortunate news."

"Yesterday, Father Yossarian tendered his resignation, which I sadly accepted. He's been with us for nearly two years and more than exceeded his religious duties here at St. Joseph. As many of you know, he's been a blessing to our freshman wrestling team and has pitched in to substitute teach in our math department. I, too, have come to depend on his devotion and loyalty here at St. Joseph. But it's his wish to return to his homeland in Hungary. He will be greatly missed."

A murmur rippled through the congregation, but before this sudden and unexpected news had time to fully register, the Monsignor continued on a different, more familiar, topic.

"This past June, we all felt the sorrow of the sudden loss of Mrs. Cunningham. Her wonderful, warm smile has been missed, and her generous devotion to our charities still has found no replacement.

"With her death came the very real concern about the dangers of pigeons nesting in our steeple. Your council and I have struggled long on how to rid our church of the menace. None of us wanted poison in the house of the Lord, nor did we wish to see our steeple netted to keep out the birds, or boarded up to look like we had abandoned our faith. Thanks to Mrs. Cunningham's generosity, I believe we've at last settled on a solution we all can live with.

"I'm sure all of you have been wondering about the scaffolding already in place around the bell tower. This past month, I've contracted the Odenweller Brothers, an outfit out of Fort Wayne. They have an artist on board able to sketch out what we've come up with. I'll have it posted in the vestibule, and I'm sure you'll be impressed. Simple boarding or plywood would never work, so we came up with a shuttered barrier to our turrets. They're oak louvres and can be closed or opened from a chain system in the choir loft. With sufficient fundraising, the mechanism could even be controlled from ground level in the vestibule. Rest assured that the panels closing off the turrets, and the rest of the associated construction, should be completed well before Thanksgiving."

The Monsignor paused as murmurs rose like bees in the trees. "Are there questions? I know this has been a concern to us all."

An older man stood quickly, hand raised, waiting for the congregation to settle back down before speaking. The Monsignor arced his arms as if calming the waters, then gestured to the man. "Mr. Say?"

Say cleared his voice, then spoke deliberately, without rushing.

"Thank you Monsignor. All my life I've been fascinated by churches. I still get excited by the architecture of great cathedrals." He calmly looked around, assessing the vast volume of the church. "If your concern is about pigeons and their messes that carry diseases, I think your worry, to be blunt, is a bit foolish."

Voices floated through the congregation wondering why he hadn't spoken up before, a few whispering that the Monsignor should tell Say to sit down and shut up. Say paid no attention and continued.

"If you've ever seen the Canterbury in England, maybe you've seen pictures of it, ever been to Paris and viewed the real Notre Dame, or traveled just north of here to South Bend, every great church has pigeons, and nobody gives one hoot about them.

"Cologne, the Vatican in Rome, they all have pigeons and nobody, not even the Pope, gives any thought to them. Pigeons come with the territory. They're every much a fixture in cathedrals as marble statues. Where there are steeples and turrets, there'll be pigeons. The point I'm making is that we are about to waste a whole lot of money and energy on something foolish. Shouldn't our effort and concern be better spent on the sick or those who can't find work? I thought that's what we Christians were all about."

Eyeing Say, the Monsignor's face grew scarlet behind his wafer-thin smile.

"Mr. Say, I'm sure we've all appreciated your comments. Surely you are aware that the council is always open for comments from the parish. It meets this Wednesday at seven o'clock if you'd care to elaborate, but after long consideration throughout the summer, the work has already begun."

Mr. Say shook his head, then sank down to his seat.

The Monsignor dismissed the matter quickly with a little nod.

"Now: to the wonderful announcement I wish to share."

He paused a long while, standing straight, erect, his chin tilted up like Napoleon posing for a portrait.

"It was the most glorious moment three weeks ago when I received a letter from the diocese."

He spoke slowly, savoring the phrases he doled out to his hungry faithful.

"With the infinite wisdom of our Lord as counsel, the archdiocese has diligently searched for a replacement for his holiness Bishop Faulk, who has been gravely ill this past year. I stand before you, a small man, to announce that—" he took a dramatic breath—"the diocese has chosen me as Bishop Faulk's replacement."

A moment of stunned silence, and then, the congregation erupted with a hundred questions. The Monsignor raised his arms and quiet again filled the church.

"My nomination for Bishop has already been approved by the Council of Cardinals in Rome." Above his broadening smile, his smug face and powerful, dark eyes appeared as if he could've been speaking to millions.

"Had it not been for all of you, had you not let me into your hearts and homes to do the Lord's bidding, this humble man would never have been noticed. This is as much a celebration for all of you blessed people as it is for me."

Whispers became voices: What'll we do . . . After fourteen years, and now leaving . . . My Lord, Bishop Brennon.

"To mark this glorious day I give to you, my devoted, a small gift."

He nodded to the two altar boys.

"I present this as a lasting symbol of my gratitude and my wonderful tenure here at St. Joseph."

The boys pulled a cord releasing the white shroud covering the mystery against the wall. The shroud settled silently to the floor like sifting flour.

There were gasps, then the church fell silent. An infant whimpered in the stillness.

A twelve-foot crucifix holding the emaciated figure of Jesus Christ was mounted to the wall. The lacquered face was pale-white, with eyes painted in exaggerated agony. Black eight-inch nails punctured the wrists and feet, and garish red spewed from each wound. Dark gray paint applied around the eyes, along the ribs, and around the joints accentuated the horrific agony and imminent death. Blood streaked gaudily down the sunken cheeks of Christ's bowed head, and dagger-like spikes of thorns radiated from a scalp of plastic hair. This was his present, the crucifix would tell his flock daily of his wonderful tenure, and would remind them often that it was their sins that nailed Christ to the cross.

The Monsignor's gentle voice floated lyrically among the stunned congregation. "I stand before you a grateful man." He nodded toward another boy in the sacristy, at the control panel. The great German Bells began tolling, thundering. There were gasps. ONE. Enthralled, the faithful stood in awe with ears cocked, and nearly all absorbed the booming sound announcing that everything was again all right. TWO. "I stand before you this one last time a privileged and blessed man as I begin my journey toward a higher service of our Lord."

He turned quickly, descended the steps, and vanished into the sacristy. Yet before he'd completely disappeared, Francis began shaking uncontrollably. He'd been sitting in his usual spot next to his mom in the pew.

Gotta get outta here! his mind raced.

Within seconds, he began pumping his legs wildly and craning all around for escape. *Around Mom and straight down the center aisle would be faster,* he thought, panicked. *Past Dad and Zach, down the side aisle, might be better, less notice.*

THREE.

No time to debate, he bulled past his dad and Zach, then through the side door in a flash.

His chest heaved as he gulped air, yet his panic grew stronger. Outside, the sound of the bells boomed even louder. FOUR. It was as if his legs worked on their own, as if his legs alone would carry him to safety. Tearing straight down Second, then a right on Franklin, SEVEN, EIGHT, he'd made it all the way to town when the bells finally fell silent. The street was vacant, no one strolling along, the stores and shops closed for Sunday. Francis's breathing slowed.

Outside Lion Clothing, the owners had anchored a small bench. Sitting down in the yellow, glaring sun, Francis's tan face paled, and although his anxious body no longer shook, confusion tore at his smooth young features. For the longest time, he could do nothing more than simply sit, and in the bright sun, he suddenly felt abandoned, felt sick sitting as if naked on the Main Street of St. Joseph.

CHAPTER FOURTEEN

Basketball with Rupe and the Brothers

SCHOOL HAD BEEN OUT FOR OVER AN HOUR, MOST OF THE kids had wandered home, and there were no students left messing around on the basketball courts outside the Fatima wing. The unrelenting sun beat down, it was scorching, and what little wind there was skittered a few leaves, some fine debris, and a discarded Bun Candy wrapper in a corner next to the building. For Francis, school was still at least a week away, and he didn't give a hoot about "taking it easy." Secluded, shunned for nearly two weeks, he needed to prove something to himself, if not to Zach. Still, he was nervous about the basketball game with his brother that Rupert had arranged.

The thick iron post supporting the backboard had been painted orange. Some years ago, a Driver's Ed kid had banged off a wide swath of paint and knocked the post a few degrees off plumb. A third of the net's chain links had rusted off over the years. There were no painted lines; only a gouge in the blacktop marked the foul line. Escaping the sun before the game, Rupert, Zach, and Francis stood in the narrow strip of shade alongside the building while Rupert explained the rules.

Zach, sneering, stood apart and bounced the ball off the wall while Rupert shifted his body from offense to defense, trying to demonstrate the game to Francis.

Concentration grooved Francis's face.

"But don't we need another player to make two sides?"

Rupert raised an eyebrow and grinned. "Nope. That's why it's called Two on One."

Zach glared. "I call it 'Cutthroat.'"

Rupert shot an impatient look toward Zach.

"Yeah, Zach. Cutthroat." Rupert turned back to Francis. "It's like this. If I got the ball, you and Zach are on defense and against me; if you've got the ball then me and Zach are against you. It'll be pretty damn obvious once we start."

With a quick nod of his head, Rupert announced, "We ready to get this show on the road?"

Rupert snatched the ball from Zach and handed the ball to Francis. "You start, then me, and Zach'll go last."

What he knew about basketball, Francis learned on his own. For years he'd watched others play on the outdoor courts, and up to that summer, when he wasn't off fishing the canal, he'd spend hours alone dribbling up and down the stone alley just out back of his house. Pounding Zach's old ball against the uneven surface for countless hours, he'd honed the skill of dribbling. Odd though, he'd never felt the need to shoot baskets at school. To him, the best part of the game was dribbling. So when Rupert handed him the ball, all he really cared about and understood was that he'd have to dribble around their defense.

Avoiding Rupert, who was grinning and only going through the motions, was easy. Dribbling around his brother, who charged across the court with inexplicable anger, was easier still. Francis simply enjoyed his dribbling, and the game that had arrived so unexpectedly brought a genuine smile to his face. Back and forth, circling both, he jitter-bugged as if playing tag rather than basketball, his quarantine in the laundry room pushed out of sight, his summer of cleaning pigeon crap pushed far away. With neither player even close by, Francis shot the ball for an easy hoop, but it careened off the bottom of the backboard and ricocheted off the top of his head.

"Nice shot." Zach mocked. "Rupe's ball."

Bouncing the ball through his legs twice, Rupert drove hard to the basket around Zach and casually, "how-hard-could-it-be," made the lay-up. Zach made his short jump shot easily, then rocketed the ball to Francis, who stood beyond the free throw line simply watching.

Rupert's defense gave Francis a wide berth, while Zach waited under the basket. Francis did a few circles at the top of the court, a couple dribbles behind his back, all with a tremendously relaxed smile coating his face.

"Don't get points for dribbling," chimed Rupert. "Ya gotta shoot the pill."

Francis's uncontested shot hit nothing and went bounding far out across the playground. He tore out retrieving the ball, but just before he made it back to the court, Rupert motioned Zach aside.

"Damn Zach, would it kill ya to have fun?"

"Think you're so hot?"

Zach turned his back and strutted a short distance away.

After Rupert swished a long shot from beyond where

Francis stood watching with his hands in his pockets, Zach backed against Rupert, faked left then right, and made a crazy hook-shot.

As the game heated up, it became apparent that it was really a contest between Zach and Rupert. Since they were kids, it'd been Zach's strength against Rupert's outside shot. All the while, their remarks careened like errant passes through Francis's brain.

"You playin' or not, Francis?"

"That's suppose ta be a shot, Francis?"

"Christ, just aim the bastard."

"Zach! Ease off!"

The two friends were groaning, shoving each other under the basket, so Francis was able to dribble uncontested just inside the foul line.

"Now what, little brother?"

"Shoot the rock, Frank!"

His shot hit the backboard, grazed the rim, and dropped to the blacktop. Francis was relieved that at least he didn't have to run out and retrieve the ball again.

Beneath the glaring afternoon sun, sweat dripped from the tips of their hair and soaked their T-shirts. Zach tried being indifferent, but fumed; Rupert refereed to keep the game moving, while every so often Francis shot aimlessly without dribbling at all. The rule—that you must win by two baskets—see-sawed the game between Zach and Rupert.

Desperate for the go-ahead hoop, Zach was cutting sharply to the basket when Rupert yelled.

"Frank! Cut off the baseline!"

Lowering his shoulder, deliberately aiming, Zach

slammed full force into his brother and made an easy lay-up. While Francis bounced back to his feet and brushed gravel from an elbow, Rupert snarled into Zach's face.

"What the F, Zach!"

Rupert shoved Zach.

"Ahead by one," Zach taunted.

"I don't give a shit!"

"The hell ya don't! Your turn."

Zach winged the ball at Rupert, who quickly leaned sideways, letting the ball ricochet off the building.

"Screw this! Ya had no call ta run over your brother!"

Zach scooped up the ball.

"He can take care of himself."

"Right."

"This was your idea, Rupert!"

"Go to hell, Clinker!"

Francis leaned against the brick wall in the sliver of shade and watched.

"It's just a damn game, Zach!" Rupert glared at Zach.

"An' I F'n won!"

"Why ya have ta win so F'n bad?"

"None of your goddamn business!"

Zach wiped his face on his shoulder, exaggerated a cough then spit on the black top.

"Dumb ass idea, Rupert."

"We were supposed ta have fun!"

"Maybe I just did."

Rupert snorted and began hoofing across the playground. Francis shouted out, "See ya, Rupe!" but Rupert didn't reply or turn around.

Though he didn't dare to look at Zach, Francis could sense his brother seething.

Zach stood still, looking to where Rupert had gone. He said nothing to his brother, never let their eyes meet. Then, after a few minutes, he strode around the building with only an occasional dribble of the ball.

Francis held his face down as Zach left. It wasn't until his brother was out of sight that Francis squared his shoulders, a contented smile on his face, and announced out loud, "Hell, yeah, I called him Rupe. He called me Frank, twice!"

CHAPTER FIFTEEN

The Cat

THE TINY CREEK RAN RIGHT ALONGSIDE THE STEINLEY house. The embankment down to the slow, trickling water was steep, and just above the water, orange and rusting sewer lines spanned the creek. Not last summer, but the summer before, Zach and Francis came up with a contest, a challenge between the two of them.

The sewer lines crossing the creek varied in diameter, some as small as four inches, others close to sixteen or eighteen. They'd agreed to challenge each other, back then they called it a dare, to see who was brave enough to walk the pipe to the other side. It was a test of balance and nerve. Francis relished this fun with his brother, and from the start, he was always the winner. On the other side, he'd beam and laugh, but when Zach started over he fell silent and rooted for his brother to make it. Francis was disappointed when his brother suddenly stopped playing, when Zach discovered that Rupert loved basketball as much as he did.

This afternoon, it didn't matter to Francis that the Steinleys weren't home because the cat didn't belong to them. It had a weird black spot in the center of its forehead, so he would've recognized the cat if it'd belonged to anybody, but it was a stray. Francis didn't feel the scorching late afternoon heat beating against his neck, didn't feel the sweat trickling beneath his T-shirt as he readied himself. The sky was crystal blue, and a little breeze danced among the leaves of the trees along the creek. Except for the water flowing quietly and the gentle fluttering of leaves, there was no movement in the quiet.

In the smothering afternoon heat, out in the open beneath a white glaring sun, Francis crouched low with his arms and legs spread wide to block its escape. He moved cautiously forward. He had it cornered. It wasn't a kitten; it wasn't arching its back, and its hair wasn't raised on end. The cat was watching with curiosity as Francis closed in.

The Steinley's enormous white house anchored the corner just across Second from the high school. The bridge to the right of their porch was old and far too massive for such a small creek. Immense sandstone blocks formed the bridge's uprights. Decades ago, the stone had turned mossy in the Indiana humidity. Atop the green stone sat a red gas can.

Unaware it was trapped, oblivious to danger, the cat sat casually with its back against the stone and was slowly blinking its saucer eyes when Francis finally lunged.

In an instant, the cat sprang up, desperate for escape.

As Francis grabbed it by the scruff, the cat turned teeth and claws, its effort futile. With his arm fully extended, Francis's grip on its neck held firm.

Stretching for the gas can with his free hand, Francis's face was empty of expression, his actions mechanical, and there was no hint of thrill, no sorrow, no fun.

Cat and gas can in hand, he ducked into the bushes that lined the overgrown creek.

He pinned the bawling cat down with a knee.

Eyes wide with fright, the cat hissed as Francis soaked it with gas.

He used a wooden match.

It was late, almost 4:30, and school had been out for nearly two hours. Across the street, almost finished for the day, Alphonse had been sweeping a classroom when he saw the black smoke through the open window. The stub of his stogie slipped from his mouth as his eyes locked onto the tiny meteor screaming across Second. Hearing the high-pitched squeal of agony, he stood stunned by the window and watched the smoking cat crumble down before reaching the other side.

Alphonse's mop handle banged loudly against the floor as rage propelled him out the school's rear door and across Second Street. He didn't pause at the cat nor did he flinch at the smell of burnt fur. He charged and pushed aside the brush, finding Francis hunkered low, his back bowed, his head resting loosely in his hand.

"Christ almighty!" roared Alphonse.

Francis slowly lifted his head, blinking rapidly as if waking.

"Alphonse?"

"What the hell were ya thinkin'!"

"What?"

"You tortured that poor critter!"

Alphonse kicked at the ground viciously. Tiny stones pinged against the trees as they shot out from his boot.

"Critter?" Francis frowned in confusion.

"Ya set that cat afire!"

"Cat?"

"The dead son-a-bitch in the road!"

Francis needed to look away, but couldn't, and in that instant, shame screamed through his every fiber for something he must've done wrong. Alphonse jabbed his knobby finger, pointing to the charred lump in the street.

"The gas can! The dead cat!" Spittle flew from Alphonse's mouth. "The matches I can see in yer goddamn pocket!"

Suddenly spent, weary, Alphonse stopped abruptly and took it all in—Francis's face, the slouch in his shoulders, the looseness in his body, and the cat lying dead in the street. Bewildered, he shook his head slowly, then sank to sit alongside Francis in the cooling shade of the bushes.

After minutes, Alphonse quietly asked, "Do ya know what just happened?"

Francis stared at the ground. "I know you're madder'n a wet hen."

"Was . . ." Alphonse shrugged. "Boys yer age should be wonderin' how that cat died, not causin' it."

"What?"

"Ya knew ya were doin' somethin' wrong, cause ya were hidin'."

Then out of the blue, Alphonse shuddered, gulped air and tried belching repeatedly, with no success. He winced and rubbed his chest.

"You all right, Alphonse?"

"Belly ache."

"Maybe you shouldn't eat those cafeteria scraps."

Francis took note of the shaky knees, the knotting fists, the colorless lips as Alphonse struggled to his feet and teetered.

Francis sprang up to force him to sit back down.

"Should you go to the doc's?"

"Nope. No doc's fixin' what's ailin' me."

"But you're shakin' . . ."

"Between my ears is what's shakin' me."

"I don't get it."

"Hope ya never do. You'll be all right cause she's finally over, Francis."

"What's over?"

"Yer summer. Yer time in that damn bell tower . . . ya hearin' me? All a that shit's over!"

"Shucks, Alphonse. I know that."

"Then why . . ." Alphonse caught himself. "Ya need ta start thinkin' about school."

"S'pose so."

"S'pect I should get back 'n finish up." Alphonse stood slowly, Francis at the ready, just in case.

"Want help?" Francis asked, recovering slowly.

"Sure you wanna?"

"Yep."

"Let's do her, then," Alphonse said as they crossed Second. "You move the desks. I'll run the mop."

CHAPTER SIXTEEN

The Cemetery

RANCID GREASE DRIPPED FROM ALPHONSE'S OVERALLS, coating his boot. "Son of a goddamn bitch," he muttered, glaring at the trash barrel of kitchen grease by the ramp. Using a rag, he tried wiping the rest of the grease from his pants. Disgusted, he threw the messy rag in a barrel labeled, "Save: good trash."

After returning the empty grease bucket and popping out the ramp, his work day now over, Alphonse was taken off guard by the building thunder. He craned west, the sky growing dark, threatening, and said out loud to no one, "A thunderstorm?" His face sour, his shoulders hunched with fatigue, his eyes clouded by worry. "Not at this time a year." He'd turned, heading toward his shack, when he spied Francis in the distance meandering along the cemetery lane. After whistling for Butch, he waited, his eyes searching the nooks where his dog had always snoozed away the day. He whistled and called again, but Butch was nowhere in sight.

Sudden lightning against the blackening sky.

"Hell, Butch." He stared toward the cemetery where Francis had disappeared. "A little thunder scared ya off?"

Alphonse found Francis squatting near the base of huge tombstone.

"Howdy, Francis."

Francis spun around for a second, eyes like full moons with surprise, then turned away and crouched down even farther.

"Francis! Whatcha doin' in the damn cemetery?"

"Nothin'." Francis whittled furiously on a stick with his pocket knife.

"Whatever ya doin' best hurry. She's gonna plumb storm like a son-a-bitch."

He peeked over Francis's shoulder. "Whatcha makin'?"

"Nothin'."

"Hmm. Lotta nothin' goin' on today." Alphonse rubbed his boot against the back of his other leg. "Ya know, if those damn ladies don't stop fillin' that grease to the top, there'll be hell ta pay."

Francis didn't reply, and kept whittling.

"Ya look like ya got somethin' brewin', but I wanted ta make sure ya got that cat buried proper."

"Did like you said."

Alphonse leaned in for a closer look. "Hell's fire! Yer fixin' ta make a slingshot."

"Yeah, guess so."

"Made one when I was a kid. Whatcha plannin' on shootin'?"

"Just making it."

"Mighty fun fer target practice."

Alphonse was going to tell about hunting squirrels as a kid but stopped abruptly. There came jagged lightning, then the thunder's almost instant reply when he spied the blood on the pocket knife. Fresh blood.

"Christ almighty Francis! Did ya stick a pig?"

Francis stopped whittling, finally turning to face Alphonse, but his eyes and face were blank as if no one had asked anything at all.

Directly overhead, the sky had grown nearly black and ominous; every few seconds a gigantic rain drop smacked loudly against the leaves.

"The blood, Francis. There's shit-ton a blood on yer knife."

Francis blinked and held the knife out to examine it. "Oh . . . probably cut myself a while back."

"She looks plumb fresh ta me."

Blood on the knife was one thing, but blood oozing through Francis's shirt sleeve was something completely different. Eyes narrowed, his face lined with worry, Alphonse touched Francis gently on the arm.

Yanking his arm back in reflex, Francis resumed his rapid whittling, his face in full concentration like a little boy trying to climb a tall, slippery slide.

Before Francis could react, Alphonse grabbed Francis's arm and shoved the shirt sleeve up, revealing two neat slices in his upper arm, just below the shoulder. The blood still trickled, making lazy red tracks down his bicep. Releasing Francis, Alphonse's hands were shaking uncontrollably. His weathered face grew sickly white as he mumbled to himself, "Accident, my ass."

Slumping down, Alphonse slowly curled into a ball, knees pulled in tight, one arm wrapped around his waist, the other cradling his head.

Confused, Francis asked, "You all right?"

The reply was instant. "Need a minute."

Francis quickly used his thumb to rub the blood from his knife. His face pasty, his eyes vacant, it wasn't until Francis held his red thumb high, that he took notice of the blackening sky, that he heard the occasional gigantic rain drop crash among the ancient trees.

CHAPTER SEVENTEEN

The Letter

WITH HIS MIND CRAMMED FULL OF CONFUSION, DOUBT, and nearing panic the following morning, Alphonse tromped toward his mindless job, occasionally looking up and squinting at the sun just then peeking above the horizon. Every so often he muttered to Butch, who hobbled along behind.

"First he burned the cat, Butch."

His boots pounded down Second.

"Now he's hurtin' himself . . . cuttin' himself, Butch."

They rounded the corner and passed the church.

"A goddamn queer for a bishop? At least the bastard's leavin'."

He picked up his pace as they neared the ramp by the Fatima wing.

"The prick'll skedaddle 'n nobody'll know . . . ain't right, Butch."

The Monsignor had been standing at his office window relishing his coffee when he noticed Alphonse hustling toward the school. He glanced at the clock and scowled. It was early; unless there was an emergency, Edgar wouldn't unlock the school for another hour. Smacking the empty cup on his desk, he bulled from his office.

Alphonse gave Butch a quick scratch and let himself into the building. He was in a rush, he didn't know exactly why, but in no time he'd retrieved the mop bucket and filled it, and zoomed toward the classroom at the end of the main hall. Inside, Royal typewriters covered in gray dust covers rested on each desk. Slowly, Alphonse rolled the mop bucket down the aisle of desks nearest the windows. He paused, working the nubbin of his stogie from side to side with his mouth, and gazed long and pensively at the row of typewriters.

He slipped the dust cover off the closest machine and hesitantly tapped a key. Suddenly engrossed by a germinating idea, he didn't notice the Monsignor silently watching him from the hallway just outside the door.

The Monsignor's slight smile was odd. He studied Alphonse's face, took special note of the manner in which Alphonse worked the brown stub of cigar with his mouth. Suddenly, it'd all fallen into place, the missing puzzle piece had been found as the Monsignor strutted into the classroom, smug with a smile of recognition creeping across his face. He had suspected before, but now he was certain.

Alphonse was startled by the door slamming shut.

"Who let you in?" The Monsignor's voice reeked arrogance, clawing raw into Alphonse's brain.

Alphonse backed defensively toward his bucket and reached for the mop handle.

"Edgar's master key."

The Monsignor raised an eyebrow. "Stolen, no doubt."

"Seems Edgar thinks I'm responsible."

A crooked smile played across the Monsignor's face. His tone had quickly become oddly light-hearted as he said, "I'll have Edgar fire you today."

"Why bother if yer flyin' the coop?"

"I'll enjoy seeing your face when you're left with absolutely nothing."

"Make yerself feel good, is that it? Ya always do."

The warm, yellow morning sun streamed through the windows, casting the Monsignor's shadow against the wall, gigantic and black.

"Til the day you die, you'll be a pathetic, lonely bum."

"I ain't ever been lonely or a bum."

"But we both know you're much worse than that, don't we?" The Monsignor's grin widened to a leer, and he stepped past the first row of desks toward Alphonse.

Alphonse gripped the handle harder, confused by the Monsignor's strange new tack.

"There can't be two people having that same disgusting habit with their cigars, Alphonse. Or, should I say, *Jimmie*." The Monsignor moved another step closer. "I must admit, your silly play-acting all this time has been inventive. It's actually been entertaining, but never hurt me."

"And you can't hurt me now, murderer!" he hissed.

"It weren't no murder!" Alphonse throttled the mop handle.

"It's been fourteen years, but I remember plain as the nose on your face. Cleveland freight yard, and Clint—I even remember his name—defenseless Clint, just sitting in the outhouse." The Monsignor's eyes were sparkling and eager. "You clubbed that poor man to death."

"Clint . . . he . . . I saw . . . that little China girl . . ." Alphonse stopped to calm his shaky voice. "Clint raped and . . . and . . . butchered her. God damn it! That sweet little girl weren't no more 'n a child!"

The Monsignor gloated. "And after Clint's murder— you were a marked man. Your free and frivolous life of riding the rails was over. With your hobo law, they would've tracked you down, and you'd be dead." His eyes narrowed, finally putting the last of the puzzle together. "You must've been scared out of your mind to have followed Edgar here. Stumbled drunk into town, been hiding here ever since. I'll bet Edgar doesn't know you killed a defenseless man, does he?"

Alphonse sagged against a desk.

"And you're still stumbling through your ridiculous life pretending to be some kind of hero, a *protector*." The Monsignor practically spat the word.

Alphonse straightened up, his voice tight with fury. "Protector! Yes! God damn it, yes!"

"A failure at that, too," scoffed the Monsignor.

"Maybe. But I tried. Tried to do right." He glared at the Monsignor. "Not like you. I saw you in the jungle that night. That boy all alone and scared. Mighta been dark, but I saw ya 'n it scared the shit outta ya. Weren't close enough to hear what ya were sayin', but ya had that boy's shirt off."

"Your drunken imaginations back then, nothing more."

"History like that, I shouldn't a been surprised by what ya been doin' in yer filthy bell tower all summer."

"It's a pity I'm leaving soon. I'd enjoy seeing how far your fantasies sink you."

"Then stay. Turn down the job offer, Padre."

The Monsignor strolled to the front of the room, leaned against the teacher's desk, arms folded across his chest. "You see, old man, I'm dearly beloved here. No one would ever believe you."

Alphonse's face flushed deep red. He choked out, "Vile, evil place . . . that bell tower . . . Francis didn't stand a chance!"

The Monsignor leaned across the desk. "You'll have to work a whole lot harder," he said smugly, "to come up with something better than that hogwash."

"I know what I know!"

"I've not seen anything wrong with Francis." The Monsignor paused briefly, waiting for Alphonse's reaction. "In fact, he's performed whatever I've asked of him to the letter."

Alphonse tried speaking, but couldn't.

"You must understand that if there were something seriously wrong with Francis, his parents and others would look to you first as the cause."

"No—"

"Oh, yes, little man. You've spent the most time with that boy. Lunching in front of the church, walking the streets together, spending time at your hovel set off by itself near the train tracks, sometimes late at night, doing who knows what. It all adds up—the old hobo who lives alone, has no family. And your antics—every man, woman, and child in this town could tell stories about your crazy behavior that they've personally witnessed. So if you think something's wrong with that boy, I'd keep my voice down."

Alphonse trembled with rage, but was at last able to let

it out. "I set off those damn bells," he bellowed. "It was me!"

"Just another foolish act of a desperate old man. It's of no consequence. I'll be bishop." The Monsignor nodded slowly, pursing his lips so tightly that his mouth looked like an asshole. "And you'll be run out of town for what you did to Francis. They might even string you up for murder. Just think of all the pent-up anger when they discover a murderer all these years has been working unhindered among their children."

"Yer a damn queer! Destroyed that boy's innocence!" spewed Alphonse. "Ya won't get away with it this time!"

"Slow down, *Jimmie*. Imagine your life when this town finds out what you really are."

Alphonse slumped against the wall.

"Where will Edgar be? Zach, and even Francis, where'll they be? Who'll let you in? Who'll even stop to say 'hello'?"

"You bastard," gasped Alphonse. "All summer with Francis, ya evil bastard!"

"But you see," the Monsignor smirked confidently. "You have no proof."

"I'll find it!"

The Monsignor gave a dismissive wave. "Of course, you could stop all this foolishness and leave town on your own accord." He strolled to the door. "And, I changed my mind. I won't have Edgar get rid of you. I'll enjoy seeing how your foolishness plays out."

With that, he swept through the door and vanished down the hallway.

For a long while, Alphonse could only stare out the classroom window, fists clenched in futility. It wasn't until he spied Edgar and his sons heading for the high school that his mind began to clear. He fished a stogie from his pocket and jammed it in his mouth, then rummaged through the shelves until he found the paper. He settled at the typewriter, chewing his stogie, his eyes becoming fierce and focused, and twirled the paper in the carriage and began punching the keys carefully and deliberately.

George,
Sorry for the late notice, but I think we still have time
to work it out. As you know, Monsignor Brennon will
be leaving soon. We are hoping the paper can run a
story about his time here. You could take photos of the
church and the work that is finished in the bell tower.
Alphonse can unlock the doors for your photographer.
Thank you.
Tom Grewe

DOWNTOWN ST. JOSEPH COULD'VE BEEN any small midwestern town in the late fifties. Perhaps three blocks long, at best four, Main Street had in its stores nearly everything the good folks needed in their day-to-day. Clothing stores, hardware and drug stores, Montgomery Ward, a bar at the far end, and the First National Bank anchoring the main corner of town all lined the wide street, and from that intersection could be seen the smoke of the can factory over on Fifth, the water tower announcing, 'St. Joseph' at the municipal park, and the tall grain elevator housing that year's soy beans. Yet dominating the view was St. Joseph church, its green-coppered steeple stabbing high in the sky, and it didn't matter where anyone stood, the church steeple was impossible to ignore.

It was drizzling by the time Alphonse hoofed it downtown. Close to the bar near the end of Main Street, Alphonse located the tiny office on the second floor above Goodwill. On the door window was lettered: ST. JOSEPH HERALD; beneath, "Give us thirty minutes and we'll give you the world."

Alphonse marched straight in as if he'd been there a thousand times. The young man at the front desk looked him up and down, frowning.

"Alphonse?"

"Howdy do, young man. I have a letter fer the editor."

"A what?"

"A letter. Mr. Grewe asked if I'd swing it by after work."

"The chairman of the church council?"

"That's him. Looks to be awful dang important, too."

"Let's have a look."

Alphonse smiled and shook his head. "Mr. Grewe insisted that I deliver it straight to the editor."

"I'll see to it that he gets it."

"No, no; Mr. Grewe was very specific. 'Don't let anyone else so much as touch this letter, Alphonse,' he sez ta me. So I reckon I need ta put it directly into Mr. Bockman's hands myself, if he's here. If he ain't, then I'll just sit myself down and wait."

The young man wheeled his chair back and leaned into an adjacent office. Alphonse crammed his fists in his pockets and lowered his head. He bit his lip when he heard, "Alphonse has a letter for you."

George Bockman, proud editor of the *St. Joseph Herald*, tugged at the suspenders that stretched over his huge stomach as he eyed Alphonse.

"What's this about a letter, Alphonse?"

Alphonse carefully brought out the letter from his bib pocket.

"Mr. Grewe said it was awful important 'n you'd know what to do."

George sliced open the envelope and pulled out the single sheet. After adjusting his thick glasses, he skimmed the letter.

He glanced at Alphonse and nodded. "Yes . . . yes . . . I'll have Noonan come looking for you in the next day or two."

Alphonse descended the office steps to Main Street, where he looked around and called for Butch, but Butch had already limped home. He hunched his shoulders against the chilling wind, the dismal weather darkening his already dour mood. He could hear the faint sound of a freight train across town. With his brain still twisting from his confrontation with the Monsignor and his thoughts of Francis, innocent and helpless, still tearing at his every fiber, Alphonse pulled his collar high on his neck.

Sprinkles began dotting his weary face. He sighed loudly. Slowly, he began trudging home alone in the rain.

CHAPTER EIGHTEEN

Jimmie from the South

BACK THEN, HE WAS CALLED JIMMIE, TO SOME, JIMMIE from the South, and it was a night that Jimmie knew would happen sooner or later. Yet, he never imagined it would turn out the way it did.

Railroad jungles were tucked away not far from the bustle of almost every freight yard in America. The jungles were places for the lone traveler and the bewildered, secretive places where they would wait for another freight to haul them toward the rumor of a job or away from wherever they could no longer stay. The jungles concentrated the lazy, the disillusioned and angry, and the hobo, whose only desire was to travel the country, requiring little more than the clickety-clack of a jostling boxcar for company.

Hidden beyond the reach of the freight yard's glaring lights, perhaps down in a hollow, maybe secluded in the trees far from the staging rails, the jungles had sprung from desperate human necessity, thriving despite efforts to close them down and chase out the rough—and not so rough— souls who passed through.

Jungles had their own pulse, their own set of laws, each as unique as the characters passing through. Jimmie had ridden the rails for years and had learned early on to be wary, to listen, to wait and watch. He did his best to comfort the innocent and defenseless, to look out for the unfortunate the best he could.

This night, he was still in Cleveland, where he'd been for the better part of a week. The water tower and a freight spewing black smoke at the far end of the yard were backlit by the setting sun. Dozens of curving train tracks reflected light from the fading day. Railroaders pushed handcars of produce and dry goods while mice scurried and birds pecked for grain beneath boxcars.

Near the jungle's center, smoke still rose lazily from the coals beneath a huge black kettle. The fog crawling in from Lake Erie mingled with the smoke, while faraway snores and wheezes floated with the stench.

Jimmie from the South leaned his back against a stump deep in the shadows of Cleveland's jungle. His hand throttled a bottle of 'shine.

His overalls were mottled, sticky and stiff with grease and bits of debris collected from his travels. Fish scales, bark from a Florida Cyprus, and indefinable hints of other stops created a sort of catalogue of where he'd wandered.

His angular face was softened by a beard two months in the making, and beneath the dented brim of a bowler hat, his blue eyes were not cloudy from 'shine but searching, wary. Even so, he didn't notice the men skulking in the nearby shadows.

"Looky there, Stubs," Sheeter whispered. "Jimmie got hisself all liquored up."

"Let's cut 'im up now!"

"Quiet, ya dumb bastard." Sheeter elbowed Stubs. "'member what he did ta Clint."

"Yeah, so we should cut 'im, right, Sheeter?"

"We ain't a killin' 'im. Leavin' that ta others, fair trade fer killin' Clint. Me and you, though, we gonna hurt that asshole bad . . . I mean real bad."

Sheeter pinched a louse against his neck and grinned, revealing a row of rotting teeth with a black gap center front. His scarred and blotchy face framed tiny eyes and a crooked nose bent oddly to the side. His hat was nappy at best, stained and flecked with twigs and bits of grass, though still marginally cleaner than his pants and shirt.

Stubs was even filthier than Sheeter. His shoulders slumped perpetually down and one arm ended in a stump just shy of his wrist. He was a big man; despite his stoop, he was still inches taller than Sheeter. His face was expressionless, and his mouth hung continually open as if he were some unfortunate who'd been clocked in the head once too often. He couldn't form a smile; when he laughed, his mouth never moved.

Sheeter scanned either side, checking that they were alone.

He exaggerated a cough, then called out, "Ya there, Jimmie?"

Jimmie heard, and understood instantly that it'd finally come down to this.

"Me 'n Stubs here come ta have us a little talk."

Jimmie tipped his bowler slowly to the back of his head and calmly watched Sheeter and Stubs inch their way through the grainy light.

"Don't have much time fer tramps," Jimmie drawled.

Sheeter shot a bullet of chew in Jimmie's direction.

"I come in here wantin' a little pow wow, 'n yer gittin' all snooty."

Stubs bellowed, "Me, too, Jimmie," then began to cackle. The cackle became choking, and after a huge hack, he quieted down and waited for Sheeter's next move.

Jimmie pulled his knees tight to his chest and tightened his grip on the bottle, ready to spring up, but waiting.

"Yer friend Clint got what he deserved! Rapin' that little girl and throwin' her guts under the wheels." Jimmie's voice softened. "She was like a China doll . . . painted lips, little painted nose." He jabbed the cork in his bottle and stood up. "Ya assholes think ya gotta score to settle? It was hobo law!"

Sheeter flipped open his knife and held it close to his gray face, admiring the glint of the polished blade.

Stubs's wide eyes tracked the shine of the knife. "Ya wanna cut 'im Sheeter . . . ya wanna cut 'im up real bad don't ya?"

"Shut it, Stubs. This is what I'm a thinkin'." He pointed the knife toward Jimmie. "Ya always say yer lookin' out fer the fella that can't defen' hisself. Way I see it, hell, we all see it this a way, is ya clubbed my partner Clint ta death. He was takin' a shit he was, 'n ya popped his head open like a melon."

Jimmie said through clenched teeth, "His filthy hands crawling over her smooth, innocent body. She weren't no more 'n thirteen!"

"Just a takin' a shit . . . and no knife or nothin' ta defen' hisself."

"I'd do 'im again fer what he done. So you boys bring it on!" Jimmie brandished his bottle as Sheeter pressed closer.

"You'll be ridin' in a boxcar all alone thinkin' yer safe, but you'll know we're a comin'," said Sheeter with a demented smile on his scabby face. His knife blade, silvery sharp, glinted in the dismal light. "Be scared ta even take a wink. Yer ugly head'll git sawed off with yer eyes plumb open."

"C'mon, Sheeter, c'mon!" Stubs's voice rose with excitement. "Cut the bastard good! Wanna see ya use yer knife!"

"Said we ain't cuttin'!" Sheeter swung around and clocked Stubs on the jaw. Stubs stumbled back, more confused than hurt. "Leavin' that fer the other boys. Wanna make this son-of-a-bitch suffer, by God—"

Sheeter lunged at Jimmie. Jimmie swung the bottle and missed. Tripped by Sheeter, he lost his balance, and Sheeter thundered his boot against Jimmie's skull. Stubs landed a wicked kick to Jimmie's gut.

"Ain't nobody ta help ya now," chortled Sheeter, grinding his boot into Jimmie's back, pressing him face-down into the rocky ground.

He shoved a length of rope at Stubs.

"Tie 'im up!"

Stubs looped the rope around Jimmie's ankles, yanking it tight. "Got 'im now Sheeter!"

Sheeter stuffed a rag in Jimmie's mouth to muffle his moans, then ripped down Jimmie's overalls. "Quit dancin' and hold his damn feet, Stubs."

Stubs held tightly while Sheeter pulled Jimmie's arms behind, coiling more rope around the wrists.

Deep in the shadows, unnoticed, a dark, solitary figure watched and waited.

Jimmie struggled, but it was hopeless.

Like a hyena, Stubs circled and barked his odd laugh.

"Stubs, yer a worser horn dog 'n Clint. Git yer damn pants off!"

Stubs made an excited giggle then tugged open the buttons on his fly.

"Git ta work Stubs, rut 'im good. Wanna watch his eyes."

Stubs dropped to his knees over Jimmie.

"I said hard, Stubs!" Sheeter leaned down, grinning into Jimmie's face. "How ya feelin' now, ya high 'n mighty son-of-a-bitch?"

Jimmie managed to twist his head away.

"Whooo-wee, Sheeter! This is better 'n a good time!"

"Lay the wood to 'im! Don't ya worry none, Jimmie. Just relax 'n enjoy the company."

At each shove, Jimmie's face raked raw against the stones and dirt.

Sheeter loomed above Jimmie's head, his shiny knife still out and ready.

While the rag in Jimmie's mouth bloodied, he remained aware and focused.

The solitary figure slinked forward from the shadows, his full attention locked on the thrusting.

Though humiliated, in pain, angry, and lying useless like a discarded pair of old boots, Jimmie's eyes still connected with the watcher, to that face with the wickedly scarred jaw, to that savoring smile devoid of compassion. And in that instant, when Jimmie saw Brennon's crooked grin, Sheeter had suddenly vanished, and Stubs's heavy breathing was no longer there.

CHAPTER NINETEEN

Trouble in the Woodshed

THE SMALL METAL SHED SQUATTED ALONGSIDE THE GAR-age. Inside, it was stifling hot.

The shed was Edgar's escape from duty and worry. He clamped a chunk of oak in the lathe and hit the switch, using a chisel to carve the spinning wood. Those troubles the scream of the machine didn't scrub away were covered over and shoved out of sight by the intense noise. He turned the lathe off, unclamped the finished piece, and held it close to the original dowel, gauging the match he'd made.

Pausing just outside, Alphonse swallowed hard, took a giant breath, and began squeezing inside the shed, saying, "Ain't room, Butch. Sit."

"What ya workin' on today, Edgar?"

Edgar squinted at the new piece. "Still trying to fix this dang thing."

Alphonse craned over Edgar's shoulder and whistled. "Damn shot better 'n I could do."

"Been trying to repair this damn cabinet for weeks." He set the dowel on the bench, then looked up and eyed Alphonse. "What're you doing here on your day off?"

"Hopin' ta have us a visit, if ya ain't too busy."

"Kick that door open . . . damn it's hot."

"Francis 'round?"

"Not sure where he went off to."

Alphonse glanced around the tight space. There was no place to lean, no place to sit.

"Zach?"

"Christ, Alphonse."

"Didn't want yer boys 'round is all."

Edgar rummaged on his work bench. "Just us. What's so damn private?"

Edgar flipped the switch and the lathe's squeal filled the shed.

Alphonse rolled his eyes. For what he was about to do, he needed quiet.

"Kinda important, Edgar," he shouted.

When his chisel caught a knot, splitting the wood, Edgar shut the lathe off. In the abrupt quiet, he tossed the chisel clanging to the bench.

"That was a damn waste of time!" Edgar winged the stump of wood at the scrap pile and scoured the heap for a new piece.

"Edgar—"

"Jesus, Alphonse. What's so important?"

"It's 'bout Francis."

"What now?" Head down, Edgar continued scrounging.

"Ya probably hain't noticed."

Rejecting a new piece, Edgar tossed it back on the pile.

"Francis's been spendin' the last couple days at the marsh down by my shack." Alphonse, coiled with anxiety, could no longer contain his frustration. "God damn it, Edgar! Would it kill ya to at least look at me?"

"All right! Spit it out!"

"I said, Francis's been at my marsh the last few days."

"So? He hasn't been able to work, won't be in school for another week."

"He's been killin' frogs with a slingshot he made."

Edgar straightened up, a hint of a smile on his face. "I started with squirrels, rabbits, anything that moved . . . we all did it."

"This ain't the same." Alphonse doled his words out carefully. "Edgar, he'll spend a whole day smashin' frogs. When I ask him why, he don't say a thin'. It's like he's in some kinda trance."

Edgar pulled a fresh piece of wood from the pile. "Reckon maple'll have to do . . ."

"Edgar! That boy a yers is hurtin'. Been hurtin' all summer!"

Edgar smacked the dust from the wood and began clamping it in place.

"I watch out 'n see thin's . . ." Alphonse took a deep breath to steady himself. "Ya ain't gonna believe me 'n it'll probably sound like bullshit to ya." He wiped the brown juice from his lip. "Yer gonna hate what I'm tellin' ya, but that bastard Monsignor's been diddlin' yer son all goddamn summer!"

Edgar slowly pulled his hands from the lathe. In the stillness, as soft as sawdust, he eyed Alphonse's deeply creased and serious face.

Alphonse continued quickly, "You're probably thinkin'

it's just crazy ole Alphonse, but it ain't. It started gettin' bad back in June after he 'n Yossarian cleaned out the bell tower. Christ, Edgar, Francis doesn't know where he is half the time . . . it's like his brain's blocked everything out."

Edgar's face turned sour, his eyes dark. "Are you done?"

"I'm tellin' ya Edgar, Francis doesn't know why he's unhappy, has no clue what he's even hidin' from."

"Hiding from?"

"What's been happening to 'im in the bell tower with that bastard."

Edgar reached for the switch, then stopped.

"You know what you're suggesting?"

"Ain't suggestin' nothin'! I'm a tellin' ya!"

"Christ almighty, just say ya hate the Monsignor 'n be done with it."

"I hate the son-a-bitch! But forget that. I'm worried ta death about Francis."

"C'mon . . . the Monsignor hurting Francis?"

"All goddamn summer!"

"Bullshit."

"I've been keepin' track. On Fridays that son-a-bitch made yer boy stay late ta sweep the bell tower. It doesn't take but two shakes ta git 'er done. Most a the time he never made it home 'til after nine."

"He likes his time alone."

"He wasn't alone! He was with that bastard!" Alphonse, pushing close to Edgar, face to face, spoke in slow low tones. "That Monsignor's been diddlin' yer son."

"Diddlin'?" Edgar scowled.

Alphonse closed his eyes.

"He's been rapin' Francis."

"What?"

"Ya don't need to hear the words again."

But when the words finally registered, Edgar suddenly raised his fist and his voice boomed, "How dare you! March your skinny ass to the rectory 'n be done with him!"

"It's a fact, Edgar!" Alphonse shook his head slowly from side to side. "Wish it weren't so, but all god damn summer!"

"Garbage! Nothin' but horseshit!"

"Why would I make up something this horrible . . . I love that boy!"

"Get out." Edgar's growl sounded as from a cave.

"Francis doesn't know 'cause he's got 'er blocked outta his mind. I go crazy thinkin' what'll happen if he ever finds out."

"I said get out . . . get the hell out!"

Edgar turned his back to Alphonse, flipped the switch, and in the squealing racket, needed one hand to steady the other guiding the chisel.

CHAPTER TWENTY

The Sadler Boys

ON SATURDAY FRANCIS HOBBLED BACK INTO HIS THIR-
teenth year. He'd been held in suspension, disconnected
from school and work, separate from Zach and his parents
since he first fell ill with rheumatic heart fever. After strip-
ping his cot of the dirty sheets and replacing them, he
changed from sweat pants and bare feet to jeans and tennis
shoes. When his mother whipped in to change over the
laundry, wisps of hair curled down along her drawn face,
she didn't bother looking up as she pulled the wet clothes
from the washing machine.

"You've free time now. Your father wants you to visit his
mother."

"Just me?" His last visit was awkward and horribly bor-
ing, and that was with his brother.

"Your father and brother have had to work extra without you. Take your grandmother the food I've made—it's in
the ice box."

It was an edict leaving no crumb for discussion.

His grandmother existed in a one-bedroom apartment
above Tri-County Hardware. Right off, Francis knew he
was in for it. The miniscule apartment reeked. Everything

in the place smelled old, as if even the nooks were coated with staleness, as if the weight of neglect anchored every inch of the place motionless—a dead place in a still-life.

He put the food away, trying to be polite and staving off boredom as long as he could. "Zach couldn't come. He's going to be a big shot in high school. Your hair looks nice, Grandma. I put your food in the ice box. Zach's going to make varsity this year. Dad wanted me to tell you 'Hi.' How are you feeling? Does Mrs. Nesch still drop by to check on you? Don't know if anyone told you, but I got real sick. Want your radio on, Grandma?"

Francis had it all covered in less than ten minutes. He scanned the tiny place for the third time, then plunked down on the floor by the radiator. Sitting so, he got the full effect as she squatted down to the foam seat of her rocker. A whoosh of putrid urine hit him full force. Turning his face quickly away, he began working loose a hair pin caught in the grill of the radiator.

He missed Zach; these visits were always easier with his brother. Desperate for escape, he allowed his mind to stray and remembered that snowy day with his brother years ago at Alphonse's shack. Francis figured he must've been around eight then, because he'd been in Sister Roberta's fourth grade class.

———

THE YOUNG BROTHER'S SNOW DAY

THE BROTHERS TRIED THEIR HARDEST to concentrate on a checkers game atop the rickety kitchen table. Wearing a great smile, Alphonse hovered at Zach's back; all the while, heavy snow kept piling up outside his shack.

Zach had a finger on a piece in his back row, but his focus was clearly on the snow outside when Alphonse instructed, "Never move from your back row. It's the key, Zach."

Alphonse tapped Zach's shoulder for emphasis. "Without a king, your enemy'll have a shit time winnin'."

"Sometimes ya just gotta, Alphonse."

"Sacrifice everything, but don't ever leave your back row open."

"Hurry up, Zach!" Francis skittered from the table to the window and back. "Just make your stupid move."

Zach sacrificed a piece, which Francis jumped with relish.

Zach couldn't take his gaze from the window as the snow continued falling fast. Already several inches deep on the sill, he couldn't contain himself and popped from his seat, asking, "Do ya think it'll snow all day, Alphonse?"

"Now Zach, I ain't in charge a snow."

"She looks good for packin', Francis!"

Francis suddenly charged the window again and pronounced with certainty, "I think snow days are better 'n regular vacation days. It's like they're free, Alphonse."

Zach rolled his eyes. "Geeze, Francis. They're just a surprise is all. Think we'll get another snow day tomorrow, Alphonse?"

Alphonse, his expression dead-pan, cocked his head toward Zach. "I'd say if she doesn't stop snowin', we could be in fer a shit ton a snow."

Zach thought for a minute, then turned toward Alphonse with a silly grin. "Goll, Alphonse, that's a stupid thing to say."

"Seein' if ya were payin' attention is all."

While Francis whipped from the table to the window and back again, Zach couldn't take his attention from the outside. He finally announced, "It's too nice outside to be playin' checkers, Alphonse. Hey Francis, wanna build a fort?"

Francis grabbed his coat, yelling, "We'll make two!"

"You comin', Alphonse?" shouted Zach, shoving his hands in his gloves. "Snow's gettin' deep! We can all make a fort!"

"Every job needs a foreman." The warm smile that Alphonse beamed declared that this day was all he ever needed. "I'll supervise."

———

HIS ONEROUS GRANDMA DUTY FINALLY discharged, Francis headed down his grandma's staircase as fast as his aching hip would allow, the smell of urine wafting behind him, already forgotten. Outside, at last comfortable to breathe, it was still Saturday. It was a rare day when he had absolutely nothing to do, and the luxury to do whatever he wanted felt odd, made him feel almost guilty.

Three blocks from Tri-County Hardware and his grandmother's apartment, along a railroad spur, St. Joseph's grain elevator pointed its gray, corrugated siding high into the muggy sky. Francis sat on a curb across the tracks, watching the dump trucks tilt and release tons of soy beans through the iron grills to the storage bins below. It was harvest time, and truck after truck lined up while a freight rolled in slowly, groaning and vibrating the ground. It wasn't until an errant pigeon shit a near miss by his shoe that he shook his head clear, jumped to his feet, and ambled toward the canal that ran lazily behind Main Street. He wandered aimlessly along the alley behind the row of businesses, the memory of that long ago snow day at Alphonse's looping over and over through his mind.

He wasn't sure how he eventually arrived there, but Francis found himself gawking at the giant posters of last year's varsity team taped inside the windows at the First National Bank building. *Reckon Zach's picture'll be up there in no time*, he thought. A casual glance at the steeple clock suddenly stunned him. He stood shocked for a long minute, wondering where the time had gone, where he'd been. *Dang—almost four o'clock*, he thought in panic.

Francis picked up his pace as if he had somewhere important to be. He was heading down Second just past the Choo-Choo, the soda shop where the high school kids hung out, when he spied his brother quickly hoofing his way.

Still faraway, he yelled, "Hey, Zach! Watcha doin'?"

Zach closed the distance in a hurry.

"Meetin' Rupe, if he ain't with his girlfriend." Zach shot a fast look around. "Finally feelin' better, little brother?"

"Yeah . . . don't I look all right?"

"Hell if I know."

Zach suddenly grabbed his brother's arm, forcing him to keep moving farther away from the Choo-Choo. He spit his words from the side of his mouth.

"The Choo-Choo's not for grade schoolers."

Francis yanked his arm free, his face heating red with anger. "Wasn't goin' in that shithole anyway."

"Well, look at you . . . fakin' sick's changed your attitude."

"Maybe it did, maybe it didn't." Francis rubbed his arm. "Why ya shovin'? Afraid somebody might see ya talking to me?"

"Bingo!"

"You can go to hell if you think I was faking it!"

"Keep it down, asshole," said Zach, glaring. "You're acting crazier 'n Alphonse."

"Alphonse ain't crazy."

Zach jeered. "That old man's tiltin' almost a hundred 'n he's got bats in the belfry."

"He's practically family, Zach!" Francis shouted, desperate to defend his friend. "Remember the Fireman's picnic?"

"Who cares?"

"And building snow forts at his shack?"

"I ain't a kid. And I don't give a shit about Alphonse." Zach glanced back at the Choo-Choo and snarled, "He likes hanging around with you. You can have 'im."

"You're jealous."

"Jealous of what, idiot? Mom told me what time you left this morning. You've been pallin' around with him the whole F'n day."

"I ain't seen Alphonse, and Mom doesn't give a hoot where I've been."

"Nobody does. And don't think you're sleepin' upstairs again."

Francis stiffened, clenching his fists. "It's my room as much as yours."

"No way am I sleepin' next to you."

"I ain't sick anymore. Ask Dad, hot shot!"

"The room's mine."

Tears welled up in Francis's eyes.

Zach closed in tighter. He poked his brother's chest, saying, "Look at you. Snivelin' like a baby." He turned and pointed. "If my friends weren't back there . . ."

"At yer dumb hangout!" Francis stammered. "You're, you're not good enough to make varsity!"

They ignited. Suddenly, nearness to the Choo-Choo didn't matter, that Zach was bigger and stronger didn't matter. There were no more words, no swearing; the only things left were grunting and vicious swings. The brothers clawed and grappled, and the blow to Zach's stomach was retaliated by a clamping headlock and a wicked throw to the sidewalk. Neither understood nor cared how it had come to this, and neither was aware that across the empty street, Alphonse stood hidden as silent witness.

CHAPTER TWENTY-ONE

The Marsh

EAST OF TOWN, BEYOND WHERE THE PAVEMENT STOPPED
on Second Street, cattails grew tall in the marsh. Given that
it was already the first of September, the place still held water enough, where mallards tipped to succulents and sparrows pecked for seeds among the willows, and where, every
so often, a heron poised like a carving on orange skinny
legs. A tiny stream curved through the tangled grasses and
in places ran out in the open. The occasional tree drooped
over the pools, where gusts of wind often toppled beetles
from its limbs, and they would splash atop the still water.
Grasshoppers grew meaty in the weeds as angling sunlight
reflected in their bulging eyes. This was the place where the
tadpoles of early summer had become the frogs of early
autumn, and as they poised on rocks hungry for bugs flit-
ting by, they became easy targets for Francis.

Scrunched down low on the bank, Francis squinted an
eye and locked his arm, taking careful aim with his slingshot. He steadied briefly before quickly relaxing the rubber
bands and letting the slingshot slip from his hand. In the
quiet of the marsh, he rested his back against the solid
trunk of a tree.

In summers past, he'd spend hours fishing along the banks of the canal, hoping for a sign from his bobber, and even if he weren't rewarded at all, he'd relish being out of doors and didn't mind being alone. Yet in this space between summer and autumn, in the space between his illness and school, his time on the edge of the marsh reflected no joy or sadness, no memories of summers past, no excitement about what might lie ahead.

Instead, something he could not explain compelled Francis to smash little green frogs against granite. Though he kept track of his killings at first, lately he no longer cared.

Uniform pebbles at his side were organized like bullets on the dirt. With his face expressionless and flat, and with his jar of drinking water still cool in the shade beside him, he paid little attention to the adolescent frogs squeaking out over the marsh. His hands lay limp in his lap, and his tennis shoes remained planted firmly against the clay with no hint of when his feet moved last. Birds flitted among the willows that bowed silently with the breeze, while Francis held motionless, hunkered against the tree.

It had been just after four thirty when Alphonse again spied Francis from across the marsh. He studied him for a moment, rubbing the whiskers on his cheek. Worry creased his face. After surveying the scene, his exhaled breath loud with exhaustion and doom, he tucked his hands in his overalls and trudged toward Francis. Kicking stones, intentionally stepping on twigs and cracking them with his boots, he talked gibberish to himself as if he hadn't a care in the world. Even so, Alphonse was nearly upon Francis before

the boy turned, his blank stare slowly giving way to aware-
ness.

Alphonse nodded toward the slingshot. "Yer gettin'
damn good with that thin'."

"Think so?"

"Maybe too good. Wouldn't want ya killin' all the frogs
'round here."

Alphonse slowly squatted next to Francis and picked up
the slingshot, turning it over thoughtfully.

"Don't mind me sharin' yer spot."

"Ain't my spot."

"Well . . . when a fella hangs 'round one place long
enough, it sorta belongs ta 'im. Ya know, squatters' rights?"

Alphonse settled cross-legged on the ground. "Ya sure
had a bout." In setting the slingshot down next to Francis,
he gave him a little nudge and a silent wink. "How ya feelin'
these days?"

Francis said just above a whisper, "Ain't sick anymore."

"Damn glad, but I gotta say, ya scared the shit outta
me."

Minutes passed before Francis said, "Back to school
Monday."

"How's that sittin'?"

"Heck if I know." He finally faced Alphonse. "Doc gave
me the go-ahead."

"Reckon a new schedule'll feel mighty good."

Alphonse mindlessly began snapping twigs he'd found
nearby. He held the bits of twigs in his sweaty palm. Francis
didn't seem to hear the snap or the mallards landing in the
marsh, or see the yellow sunlight filtering through the reeds.

"Maybe . . . ya know, Alphonse, how I plumb like fishing?"

"Hell, I never knew that." Alphonse smiled, letting the twigs trickle from his hand, then gave Francis a playful shove on the shoulder.

"I'm serious."

Alphonse leaned to pick up a stick and let a giant black ant crawl on board. Rotating the stick slowly, he watched the bug trying hopelessly to keep up with the revolutions.

"Except for a little blue gill 'n my cats at the fishing derby," continued Francis, "I didn't get much fishing in. Where'd all my time go this summer? Dang, Alphonse, feels like I spent it all just sweeping up pigeon crap."

"Ya did."

Alphonse shook the ant free. "Best ferget about that pigeon crap and that damn bell tower. Ya got a new school year ta think 'bout now."

"S'pose so . . . not lookin' forward to Sister Loyola's homeroom though."

"What's wrong with her?"

Francis snatched up a few pebble bullets, shaking and clicking them in his hand.

"Ever hear of a calling, Alphonse?"

"Who's calling?"

"No, I mean the calling. That ol' nun said I had a calling to become a priest. Guess she 'n the Monsignor got together 'n they think the Lord himself is calling me to become one of them." He snorted sharply. "Me, a priest . . . imagine that, Alphonse. They think I'm gifted."

"Jesus Christ, Francis . . . she said that?"

"Yep. Right before I got sick."

"What'd yer parents think?"

"Didn't tell them."

"Think ya should?"

"Heck no! Can't imagine having to wear one of them stupid cassocks every day."

Alphonse grinned, playfully nudging Francis with his boot. "Not fond a wearin' a dress, eh?"

Francis scowled.

"Meant ta be funny. Ain't seen ya laugh in a long-ass time."

Francis quickly sat up straight, his mouth working to find the words.

"This'll probably sound stupid, Alphonse." He paused briefly, heavy concentration wrinkling his forehead. "But I can't stand to look at those black cassocks."

"Christ, its part of their friggin' uniform."

"It's the bottom of it that gets to me; sometimes, it even makes me wanna puke. I can't stand the way it swooshes against the floor without a sound."

For a moment, Alphonse studied Francis, his face, the droopy eyes, the stoop in his young shoulders. Finally he said with a far away, distracted tone, "That pissant Monsignor can't skedaddle soon enough ta suit me."

"You always had it in for him."

Alphonse pitched his stick to the weeds.

"And you should, too."

"He was just my stupid boss."

"Wish that's all he was."

"What's that suppose to mean?"

"Nothin', but what ya said 'bout cassocks ain't stupid, Francis . . . try as hard as you can, it's mighty hard ta get some pictures outta yer mind." The dark furrows circling the old eyes grew deep. "Just be glad you'll never have ta look at a cassock again."

A quiet splash followed by a duck's quack broke the stillness. All of a sudden, Alphonse cleared his throat loudly. "What's with ya smashin' all my frogs the last couple days?"

"Ain't yer frogs."

Raising his voice, "Ta hell they ain't!"

"Why are you gettin' all . . ."

Without warning, Alphonse suddenly leapt to his feet, his fury ignited.

"Because we had the same goddamn talk when ya burned up that cat!"

Drowning in confusion, Francis could only reply meekly, "Whatsa cat got to do with frogs?"

Alphonse grabbed a handful of dirt and winged it to the weeds.

"Goddamn it, boy! That cat did nothin' to ya 'n ya burned it!" Alphonse snapped. "Tortured it! These frogs did nothin' to ya 'n what do ya do? Ya smash every goddamn one of 'em ta hell 'n gone!"

Francis looked away.

"Ya wanna kill everythin'? Wanna start on those ducks next?"

Viciously, Alphonse kicked his boot against the ground. His face scalding, his eyes narrow and fierce, he kicked repeatedly.

"Kill every son-a-bitchin' thin' . . . just 'cause a yer shit summer?" Dirt exploded from his boot. "Just 'cause ya had ta spend every goddamn Friday night with that bastard in the bell tower!"

Falling silent abruptly, panting, Alphonse turned slowly and took in the scene, Francis, the marsh, himself towering above Francis and shaking.

At last, he slowly sank down alongside Francis, and said softly as if nothing more would ever matter, "What's the point?"

After a long while, Francis said sheepishly, "Alphonse, explain about the frogs."

"You've been killin' these frogs here with yer slingshot."

"Today?"

"Last few days."

"Reckon I was just goofin' around. I wasn't shootin' at anything. Not really."

Alphonse shook his head. "That's not what's important. Not important at all."

Francis flung his pebble bullets into the brush, then picked up his slingshot and smirked at it with a tiny snort.

"Alphonse . . . it's just . . ." Abruptly, he sent the slingshot sailing out of sight toward the marsh.

"I'm not killin' any more frogs! I'm not gonna kill anything anymore!"

"Look, Francis . . ." Alphonse began, tracing lines in the soft dirt with a finger. "Ya got every reason in the world ta be mad. To be pissed as hell 'n confused. I'm sorry I got so mad, but sometimes . . . well . . . I see things 'n can't help myself. I just go crazy seein' innocent stuff ruined."

"S'pose yer right. That cat was innocent."

Alphonse dismissed the comment with a tiny shake of his head.

"And ya need ta start treatin' yourself good. Ya hear me? Good."

"Alphonse . . . I'm not as bad a killer as you think."

"Hell, Francis, I know that. Yer a good young man," Alphonse persisted. "Ya know yer good, don't ya?"

His face pinched in thought, Francis said, "But if I can't remember stuff, I could be turning into an awful bad person and not know."

"Ya won't. Ya ain't."

"The thing is, Alphonse, I'd be sitting here and get to listening to the water trickle . . . seeing the boatman skitter . . . ducks paddling through the cattails . . . and before I knew it, the day was shot, and I don't know where the time went or what I did."

They sat for a time gazing out over the marsh.

Suddenly, Alphonse yelled, "Got it, Francis!"

Startled, Francis jerked back.

"What?"

Alphonse popped to his feet. "Besides frogs and ducks, ya know what else lives in this here marsh?"

"Seen a 'possum once."

"Ain't talkin' 'bout no opossums." Alphonse animated, pointing toward the marsh with an excited boyish face. "See where all them reeds are pushed down . . . like trails criss-crossing 'n twistin' all over the place? Guess what made 'em?"

"Snakes?"

"Ain't got no snake 'round here."

"Then what?"

"Them trails were made by rats."

"Rats?"

"Not just any ole rats . . . muskrats."

"Ain't they all the same?"

"Hell no, they ain't! Muskrats are special. Got fur that's damn valuable!"

"Rats are valuable?"

"Only muskrats. What would ya say if I lent you my old traps?"

"Why?"

"Their hide's worth plenty, and ya might as well do somethin' worthwhile before ya head ta school. Hell, Francis, ya could trap them muskrats 'n take 'em to the junkyard! Know fer a fact that Watney would pay at least fifty cents a rat."

With his face and eyes anxious to smile, Francis searched the old face.

"Like become a mountain man?"

"Sure, like a mountain man. Be a damn trapper and make some money fer yourself."

"Wow . . ." Francis's face filled with wonder, and he finally allowed his smile to broaden. "Never made any money before."

Alphonse spread his arms wide.

"Look at all them trails! Wouldn't take nothin' at all."

"Watney really gives money for rats?"

"Muskrats are a damn commodity!"

"I don't know anything 'bout trapping."

"Ain't much to it . . . let's go dig out them traps!"

They'd gone a few quick steps before Alphonse held out an arm and stopped abruptly.

"I'm loanin' ya these traps, 'n I don't mind. I'll teach ya ta set 'em. But there's one thin' ya gotta promise me, Francis."

Alphonse paused, his expression dead serious. "This is mighty damn important."

"Okay."

"Ya gotta check yer traps every morning, early. Early, ya hear? 'n ya can't let a morning slip by without checkin', no exceptions. Ya got it?"

"I got it, Alphonse."

"It's damn important!"

"Geeze . . . I promise."

Enjoying the excitement in the young face, Alphonse stuck a stogie in his mouth. With Francis, he ambled toward his shack, a relieved smile coating his face.

"How many traps ya got Alphonse?"

"We got five."

CHAPTER TWENTY-TWO

The '54 Ford

THE WHITE-OVER-BLUE FORD SEDAN SPARKLED IN THE SUN. It had wide white-wall tires and rested on the playground beside the grade school. Edgar was circling the car slowly when Alphonse sauntered over, shaking his head, the joy of chewing his stogie obvious.

"Well, well, well, Edgar . . . what have we here?"

"She's a '54 Ford."

Edgar continued his slow walk, admiring but never coming closer than an arm's length to the car.

"Whatcha think, Alphonse? Looks damn near brand new."

"Shinier 'n a new dime. What the hell's it doin' here?"

"Old man Raabe brought it for me to look over."

"That car dealer? What possessed him to do that?"

"Said it was deal at seven hundred."

"Ya crazy, Edgar? Yer damn near blind. You ain't drivin' it."

"Zach'll be drivin' next year."

"Buyin' a car's one helluva big deal, Edgar."

"Sara could learn, too. Be a nice surprise for her. She's

been awful down." Edgar tightened his circle. "I know a ton about motors, but a car and seven hundred bucks?"

"How 'bout a TV or a new dryer? Christ, a car's a ton a jack."

Alphonse leaned through the open driver's side window. The ignition key dangled enticingly from the lock.

"Well, now that it's here, whatcha gonna do?"

"Guess check 'er over, inside 'n out. Take a long look at the engine." Edgar jammed his fists in his pockets. "Damn big decision."

"Christ, Edgar, ya can't do nothin' 'til ya drive the son-a-bitch."

"If I got caught, they'd throw me in the clink. Ever drive a car, Alphonse?"

"Seen it done." Alphonse shot Edgar a long wink. "I'd say we just need ta tool around the playground. Maybe through the cemetery fer good measure, couldn't be that hard. No way 'round it Edgar, we gotta drive this beast."

"Hell, I'm nervous to even sit in the thing."

Alphonse sat behind the steering wheel like a veteran, feeling the space, while his eyes and hands explored the components on the dash. Edgar eased tentatively into the passenger side, then sat with his shoulders hunched and his hands clamped to his knees, all the while staring through the windshield at the school's brick wall.

Alphonse was like a kid with a new train set.

"She looks good, Edgar, mighty good. She's an automatic. This is the shifter ta go drivin' ahead, 'n move it down ta back. This here—" he tapped the speedometer—"tells ya how fast yer goin'."

Edgar moved only his eyes to look.

"And you'll be happy ta know she's got brakes."

He pointed down and pumped the pedal.

"We turn the key 'n pop this baby into drive 'n we're off. Ya followin' me, Edgar?"

Edgar's eyes were opened wide, but he didn't respond.

"Know fun ain't yer long suit, Edgar, but ya ready?"

Edgar gave a jerky nod.

Alphonse started the engine, shifted into reverse, and let the car slowly idle backwards.

"Christ almighty, she's fine!" Alphonse slapped Edgar on the knee. "Hell, ain't even touched the gas yet."

Through locked teeth, Edgar said, "Maybe we should try forward."

"Relax, Edgar, ain't even nothin' ta hit 'cept the grade school." Alphonse shifted into drive.

Edgar cringed as the car drifted forward.

Alphonse grinned. "Time fer a little gas."

Moving no faster than a brisk lope, Alphonse aimed the Ford straight down the playground and past the basketball courts. At the high school, he made an excruciatingly slow, wide turn.

"Jesus, Edgar! This is the smoothest car I ever drove!"

"It's the only car you ever drove."

"Hah! But she's still smooth as shit, though I'd never be caught ownin' this contraption." Alphonse glanced at Edgar's pale face. "Ain't like we're gonna die. Lighten up, Edgar."

"You're not the one thinkin' of buying it."

"Cars ain't my style. Not that she ain't a beauty. I'm a walker, ya know."

"Just the same, a little encouragement."

"We got the playground ironed out. How 'bout we head over to the cemetery? We'll pick up some speed, see how she handles."

"Don't be knockin' over any tombstones."

Alphonse gently pressed the accelerator.

Edgar pointed. "We gotta car heading this way. Slow down!"

"Any slower 'n I'd be stopped." Alphonse accelerated a tad. "Will ya looky there, Edgar. Here comes our supreme leader, him 'n his fancy Mercedes."

"Slow down, Alphonse!"

"Don't git yer gonads in a twist. If it were up to me, I'd run the son-a-bitch over."

"He's waving for us to stop."

"Jesus." Alphonse scowled down at the dash. "Damn near caught myself havin' a good time. Yeah, we'll just have us a little chat with our shepherd."

Gravel crunched loudly under the Ford as they slowed and stopped. The Mercedes pulled close alongside.

Smirking at Alphonse, the Monsignor cranked his window down.

"Somebody actually gave you a license to drive?"

Alphonse looked him in the eye. "That'd be one stupid son-a-bitch, now wouldn't it?"

For what seemed an eternity, no one said a thing. The Monsignor, ignoring Alphonse in the middle, watched Edgar stare straight ahead through the windshield at nothing.

"Well, it's about time, Edgar." The Monsignor finally spoke around Alphonse. "I saw Tom driving it over this morning."

Edgar smiled weakly, asking, "Whatcha think, Monsignor?"

"For a Ford, it's not a bad car."

"I don't know . . . he wants seven hundred."

"I'd love to see Sara's face when she lays eyes on it," the Monsignor said. "Tom Raabe's a good man. I'll talk to him again. I bet he'll go down to six hundred . . . maybe five-seventy-five."

"You'll do that?"

"Of course." The Monsignor began rolling up his widow, then paused. "Oh, and I wanted to tell you that before I leave town, I need to go over that raise with you. Been a long time coming, eh, Edgar?"

Edgar nodded mutely, too shocked to speak.

"Off to my last meeting with Mr. Grewe and the council. We'll talk later this week, Edgar."

The Monsignor drove slowly away.

Suddenly in a hurry, tires spitting a few stones, Alphonse wheeled the Ford from the cemetery and parked beside the grade school. Neither he nor Edgar made a move to open the doors.

Alphonse finally broke the silence. "Well, Edgar, that's yer little test drive."

"Got so much floatin' in my brain, don't rightly know what to do."

"Seein' that prick probably didn't help."

"Everything at once. It's damn hard to take it all in."

"Edgar, I know yer head's spinnin' with the car, and if you can believe that ass, maybe a raise." He steadied himself with several long breaths. "About Francis. With him startin' school Monday, he needs ta get off on a good foot."

"Good God, Alphonse!" His serious eyes locked onto Alphonse. "I don't want to talk about Francis. Especially, not now!"

Alphonse wiped his chin and cleared his throat. "We've been close since my hoboin' days . . ."

Edgar shook his head. "Jesus, Alphonse, just get on with it!"

"Ya know I've been worried 'bout Francis all summer."

"We've been through that. Forget about it!"

Alphonse's fingers whitened on the steering wheel; his voice rose just below a shout. "That's one thin' I won't do! Yer gonna sit there 'n hear me out."

"Last thing I need today is more worry and bullshit!"

"Ain't bullshit!"

"You heard what the Monsignor just said."

"Yer raise? The bastard probably feels guilty!"

"Of what?"

"Of cripplin' yer boy!"

"Your hate's screwin' with your brain!" Edgar unleashed a fist against the dash. "You have any idea the gamble that man took for me, hiring a blind man? I won't betray that."

"If I was a father, I'd never wanna hear this shit again. But yer gonna listen Edgar, 'cause ya have ta."

"I said drop it!" Edgar reached for the door handle.

"Ain't lettin' ya hide!" Alphonse grabbed Edgar's arm. "All those Fridays when he got home late . . . a moron could sweep that place in twenty minutes! Ya can't be that blind ta not know what's been goin' on."

"God damn it! Your hate's playin' tricks on you."

Ignoring the comment, Alphonse thought that if he could only forge ahead, he might at last get through to Edgar.

"I watched them head up to the bell tower 'n disappear for hours."

"How'd you ever get in?"

Alphonse sighed. "Yer master key, years ago."

"You've been sneaking 'round inside the church?"

"Not sneakin', Edgar."

"But you never really saw anything, did you?"

"No, but I stood in that church 'n heard it all."

"What the hell does that mean?"

"That queer's been rapin' Francis," blurted Alphonse suddenly. "Sorry Edgar, but it's been happenin' all summer . . . Fridays when he worked late."

Edgar sat still, no longer searching for escape, finally allowing the words to tumble through his mind.

In that instant, Edgar's entire world folded in on itself. He sank deep, then deeper still as everything he knew—his home, his wife, the fancy car, the promised raise, his sons, the hobo who'd been his friend for so many years, all collapsed into nothingness.

Agonizing rage suddenly powered Edgar from the car, as the word "rape" clawed and stomped through his brain.

"Goddamn you, Alphonse!" Edgar stormed away from the car.

Alphonse sped to catch up and latched onto Edgar's arm.

At the touch, Edgar whipped around, grabbed Alphonse by the coat and pinned him against the school wall high enough that his feet dangled above the ground. Alphonse didn't struggle.

Edgar's violent anger gradually dissolved, and he loosened his grip, allowing Alphonse to slide slowly down the brick wall. Each stood alone in the long silence until they could finally look at one another.

"Alphonse . . . I'm . . . I'm . . ."

"I know." Alphonse clutched Edgar's shoulder and said softly, "Terrible shit."

"Hard to get my brain around it."

"Remember last week when the church bells went off for the first time in forever? Whole goddamn town wanted ta know what the hell was goin' on."

"Reckon that was you."

"You knew?"

"Not 'til now." Edgar nodded. "You had a key."

"It was me who set those damn things off. I couldn't stand it. Was hearin' what was happenin' in the bell tower 'n had ta turn 'em on . . . but they weren't near loud enough."

Edgar took a shaky breath. "Don't know what to do."

"It's probably a stupid idea, but I've been hatchin' a plan."

A new thought suddenly wormed in Edgar's brain. He shook his head, thought more, and scrutinized his friend.

"If what you say is true, how does anything help my son now?"

"He can't get away with it. Not this time! Won't let 'im!"

"Alphonse—is this about Francis? Or is whatever you're scheming only for you?"

"He's gotta be found out for what he did." Alphonse

tried curling his fingers into a tight fist, yet his hands shook.

"Alphonse, look at you. You're quiverin' like a leaf."

Alphonse looked away.

"You're not all torn up just because of Francis—or me, either. Alphonse, revenge is a . . . a . . ."

"I know what yer sayin'," began Alphonse. "For years I've done everything I could to screw with that bastard's world, the only kind of revenge I could muster."

"Maybe all this stuff about Francis . . . maybe your history with the man, your mind's playing tricks on you."

"It's not!" Alphonse pounded the wall, then wilted, suddenly weary. "It's not, Edgar."

The two began slowly making their way around the back of the school.

"From here, Edgar, I don't know where I'm goin'."

"You're not thinking of leaving?"

"Gotta see it through, ya know that. After all this, who knows?"

"Where would you go, Alphonse?"

Alphonse gazed down at his spotted hands and muttered as if already far away, "Does it really matter which direction a lost man steers?"

CHAPTER TWENTY-THREE

Two White Rat Feet

THE COMMUNITY POOL HAD CLOSED WEEKS AGO; THE ditty from Mister Softee had faded from the neighborhoods, and the kids of St. Joseph had long since stopped goofing around by the curbs, anxious for school to start.

For Francis though, there was little space between working for the church and his walking toward the marsh, from when he watched Alphonse plummet to the mud after sawing through the limb he sat on to when he scolded him for killing the frogs. That he was supposed to finally return to school this coming Monday never entered his mind, and he bopped down Second with the bell for first period not ringing in his ears. He knew his classmates sat across the way, knew their names; he knew that Janet, the girl he had a crush on last year, swayed through the halls, but none of it mattered. He'd been gone so long, he was sure no one remembered what he even looked like.

On that early morning, muskrats scampered through his brain, and Alphonse had insisted that Watney would pay fifty cents a pop. Zooming down Second past the church, he wondered how many rats it would take to buy Zach a new basketball. That would get his brother's attention, he thought, for sure it would.

In the marsh, diamonds of dew poised on the bowing reeds, and haze drooped low like silk over the water. Grackles pecked for bugs in the gravel, frogs scooted atop rocks to warm themselves, and a flotilla of green-headed ducks spun in circles out in the open, where they quacked before tipping over in the chilly water.

He'd never been at the marsh that early before. He stood still on a small rise, his alert eyes canvassing the scene. There was no wind, and except for the occasional quack, there was no sound. In due time, he focused on where he'd staked his traps last evening, baited with peanut butter: two in the reeds, two strategically placed along the bank, and one near an old culvert that glowed rusty orange in the early morning sun.

Francis wanted to charge ahead, but mystery held him back; he needed to linger in the 'just maybe' he'd not felt since The End. His mind galloped: Will the rats be dead? Could be bigger 'n coons. Would they bite? Why was Alphonse all worked up about checking the traps early? *Heck, it couldn't be even close to eight*, he thought, he was sure of it.

The sound of a pounding freight suddenly jarred him aware, jerked him suddenly back to the marsh. The cool shade and shadows of morning had gone, and he was surprised that now he was sitting in the glaring, baking sun of late afternoon. A rivulet of sweat trickled down his neck; a green late-summer fly buzzed near his ear. Intense thirst finally drove his hand to latch onto the jar of now hot water. He squinted at the slanting light, the sun already in the west. *How did it get so late*, he worried.

Scrambling to his feet, he grabbed the broken limb he'd found to use as a club. He thought he was ready, but his first steps upstream were tentative. Gradually he inched close to the spot. The trap was empty. He released the breath he didn't know he'd been holding as he lowered his club slowly and pulled the trap from its stake.

On to the next: the dangling trap ticking against the stones; he readied his club. Then there it was. His round eyes soaked in the wonder of his first trapped—and very dead—rat.

The jaws of the trap clamped the rat's neck. The blood that had oozed from its mouth was dried; the tip of its exposed tongue had already dried stiff in the sun. The smell of peanut butter remained strong as he reached down to touch the fur. Before unclamping his prize, he paused, gauging the animal's size, its glistening fur, the flies that explored the tiny, cloudy eyes.

Soaring with excitement, he charged full speed toward his third trap, near the rusting culvert. Success, again! Carrying his two muskrats as if he were a seasoned trapper, he puffed out his chest and wondered why he hadn't been trapping before, and he wished that someone had been watching all along.

Francis carefully placed the two muskrats next to his water jar beside the tree. Despite the thrill screaming through his veins, he cautiously crept though the reeds to his last two traps.

It all became magical. It was the 1800s, and he heard

the mallards in the distance, heard the wings of sparrows splitting the air overhead. He paused to watch a black cricket spring from his arm, then bent low to see the hair on a woolly caterpillar as it chewed through a leaf. His face was peaceful with the harmony he'd found amid the tangled reeds and, at that moment, his world was in perfect order in the heartbeat of the marsh.

But then, all of a sudden, his tiny world crumpled down. His fourth trap had been sprung. He shuddered and stared. Sickly pale and wide-eyed, he pressed his quivering hand against his clammy face as the avalanche of evidence came crashing through.

The jaws of his trap gripped a tiny white foot. Sinking to his knees, Francis carefully released it, brought it close to his face, then ceremoniously put it in his pocket.

He splashed recklessly the dozen or so long strides to the last trap, only glancing down before grabbing it and charging back to the knoll. Not until he knelt, did he look. Again, the foot in the jaws was white and bloody. Francis pressed his lips tightly shut as he sank to the ground.

Much later, he remained folded down low in the deep shade. Before him, two dead muskrats lay next to the five cold traps, and in his pink palm rested two rat feet. His body no longer shook. His cheeks had long since dried, and after a while, his hand closed protectively around the tiny feet.

FRANCIS KNEW HE NEEDED TO hurry if he were going to sell his rats. He could smell them on the work bench in the shed where he'd left them the night before. He quickly slid his prizes into a burlap bag, then hustled down Franklin Street and across town.

While he'd been at the junkyard many times, it'd always been with his dad, never alone and never trying to sell anything. He remembered only that Watney was a huge burly man with brown, rotting teeth. Francis stood at the gate, a little nervous, then, his face and posture all business, he stepped through.

At first, he thought there might be some organization to the junk, but he couldn't be sure. Dead iceboxes were on the left out front, and behind them the screen doors looked to be stacked by size. All the way back were jalopies, cars without doors, missing windows, hoods propped open, tail pipes to one side, rusting bumpers to the other. The three aisles down the junkyard were crooked. Above the first hung a sign announcing aluminum, the next iron, and the last sign, "misc." Two large bins were labeled "new clothes, like off the rack." A vat of black oil, a bin of coiled copper. A crate of blue insulators, a heap of bent bicycles. Dead motors and more clustered way to the far back. Francis stood motionless. The sun beat down.

Watney's voice tackled him. "Whatcha want!"

Francis jumped and turned around, sheepishly holding out the bag. "I'd like to sell my two rats."

"Ya wanna do what?"

"Alphonse said you buy muskrats."

"That ass. Ain't you Edgar's boy?"

"He's my dad."

"Tell yer old man I'm tired a sittin' on his damn parts."

"Yes sir. You bet I'll let him know."

Watney leaned his wide butt against a workbench. "Let's see what ya got. Hand 'er over."

Watney upended the bag and dumped the rats on the ground. A tiny laugh peeped from the gruff hulk of the man. Then, after choking and spitting, came the full-throttled belly laugh.

"Jesus H. Christ!"

Francis scowled. "What's wrong?"

"Alphonse put ya up to this?"

"Alphonse said . . ."

"That crazy bastard!"

Francis bristled.

"He said muskrats are valuable, that you'd pay good money for 'em."

"And . . ." Watney tried stifling his laugh. "Ya want cash?"

Francis straightened his back and glared.

"Take it easy, boy. Muskrats are worth plenty, but watcha got here is two scrawny sewer rats." Watney shook his head, still chuckling. "Boy . . . these ain't worth a pot to piss in."

Clamping his mouth shut, Francis spun around to leave.

"Now, hold up a minute," Watney called.

"You got no right to make fun of somebody," Francis shot back quickly.

"Alphonse shouldn't a . . . wait, boy."

"My name's Francis."

"Okay, Francis, here's what I'll do fer ya, since ya brung 'em clear across town. My ol' shoat could use a snack. How 'bout I give ya a quarter fer the both?"

His face scarlet, Francis stomped away.

"Hold on! Don't ya want yer money?"

Francis yelled back over his shoulder, "Don't need yer stinkin' quarter!"

"WHAT THE HELL YA DOIN'!" barked Alphonse.

He staggered out the front door waving a whiskey bottle. Shirtless, the straps of his bibs had slipped from his shoulders. A drip of green chaw poised on his chin.

"Since when did ya start sneakin'?"

Startled, Francis could only muster, "Nothin'."

After his heartbreak with Watney at the junkyard, Francis had sped home and grabbed the traps. He'd placed the tangle of traps by Alphonse's front door, on the uneven planks. Being extra quiet, he was tiptoeing from the creaky porch when Alphonse caught him. Butch had wandered over giving Francis a quick sniff, then waited with a whimper for attention and a scratch.

But Francis couldn't take his eyes from Alphonse, the sloppy way he was standing, his quivering eyes, the shaky hand as he tilted the bottle. Finally, Francis had to avert his stare.

"Watcha gotta say for yerself, boy?"

"Just bein' respectful."

Alphonse thumped down the steps then plopped at his picnic table, motioning with the bottle. Warily, Francis sat across from him.

Francis was at last brave enough to ask, "You drink whiskey, Alphonse?"

"Havin' a belt is all," he said, rubbing the spots on the back of his hands. "What I do when times are rough . . . not like some fools, who drink 'er like sody pop."

"If you got rough times, I reckon it's all right."

"Damn straight it is!" Alphonse aimed his spit at a bush, saying, "Why ya sneakin' like a fool cat?"

"Just bringing back yer traps is all."

"Do whatever ya want." Alphonse took a snort. "But don't be a damn sneak 'bout it."

Near where Butch now snored, Francis watched the leaves skittering with the breeze.

"S'pose it's nice havin' a dog around."

"Changin' the subject, eh?"

Francis looked up sheepishly and said softly, "Sorry you're having a rough day, Alphonse."

"Not that it matters a hill a shit ta anybody, but I've been better." Alphonse set the bottle firmly in the center of the table.

"Ya wanna tell me why ya brung back my traps?"

Francis couldn't look at Alphonse. "With school finally starting 'n all . . ."

"So?"

"Nobody traps these days, you know that."

Alphonse leaned closer, his eyes drilling.

"And . . . ?"

"Well . . . I just dropped by to return 'em."

"Them was my traps. So what happened?"

"Nothin'. Nothin', really, Alphonse."

Francis suddenly shot to his feet and was nearly out of sight when he yelled back, "Gotta go!"

LATER, IN THE EARLY EVENING, Francis meandered past the grain elevator, then along the canal behind the stores on Main Street. He'd wandered for nearly half an hour before stopping abruptly. After turning and looking back around, he started forward, but stalled again. He swiped a hand at his wet eyes. Finally, his hands knotting, his face rigid, he hoofed it as fast as he could back toward Alphonse's shack.

Butch snoozed on the porch, but Alphonse had gone. For long minutes, Francis sat on the picnic table, his eyes searching, canvasing. Struck with a sudden thought, he popped from the table, and hustled up the rise toward the rail bed.

The sun was low on the horizon, and the tracks silvered in the light as they narrowed in the distance. Shielding his eyes, Francis spotted the tiny far-way silhouette and knew it had to be Alphonse. He sprinted.

Despite being out of breath, he kept running and yelled, "Alphonse!"

In the stillness of the evening, Alphonse had heard. He turned, waving "hurry" with his spindly arm. As if nothing had gone before, as if Francis had never stormed away, they walked together and talked.

"How far ya goin', Alphonse?"

"A fair piece."

Francis halted to catch his breath. Then, from his shirt pocket, he withdrew the two white rat feet and offered them in his open palm to Alphonse. Alphonse only glanced at them before grabbing and tossing them to the cinders.

"Was a time, Francis, I could run down these rails."

Francis raised his eyebrows. "What?"

"In my day I was fast. I mean real fast."

"Look awful skinny and slick." Francis tried balancing on the rail for several steps, but reverted to walking the ties.

"Somethin' as simple as walkin' a straight line, a lot a times turns out to be a son-a-bitch." Alphonse shrugged. "But at this rate, we ain't gettin' very far."

"How far we need to go?"

"Now there ya make a good point."

Francis slowed to almost a stop, but said nothing.

Alphonse smiled, asking, "Ya wanna turn back?"

"Not yet."

Neither picked up the pace.

Francis bit his lip and finally ventured, "Ain't you goin' to ask me about the rat feet?"

"That's just the way animals do 'er sometimes."

"But I was there early, Alphonse."

"Bet you were."

"But . . ." Francis halted completely to look up at Alphonse. "Before I knew it, it was already late afternoon."

With a gentle nudge on the shoulder, Alphonse urged Francis to walk.

"Guess you can tell what happened after that."

"Maybe ya should tell me."

"I was there plenty early. But this is what makes my brain go crazy. I was sitting and wondering if rats bite, 'cause I didn't know if they'd be dead or not. And the next thing I know, it's late in the afternoon." Shamefaced, Francis said, "Sorry Alphonse . . . I broke my promise."

"Ya didn't." Alphonse bent down to pick up a stick. "Ya got there early, that was the deal."

As they walked, Alphonse tapped his stick against the rail. "I'm worried 'bout ya losin' track a time. Did ya start thinkin' again 'bout that baby pigeon ya found in the bell tower?"

Francis considered this for a moment. "I guess I always think about it. Heck, Alphonse, it was dead over a hundred years and still not rotten, and those wings just tiny nubbins."

The next several minutes were silent except for the click of Alphonse's stick.

"Alphonse, is there something wrong with me?"

"Somethin's always wrong when yer thirteen."

Francis puzzled over that for a moment, then suddenly perked up.

"It wasn't all bad, though—I didn't tell you—" He bounced higher on the ties. "I did get two whole rats though!"

"Really?"

"Yep! Only—"

"Only, what?"

"Well . . . I took 'em to the junkyard this morning."

"What'd that ol' coot Watney say?"

"Told me they were sewer rats . . . not worth a pot to p . . . spit in."

"So what happened?"

"He laughed at me and said his hog could use the snack. Offered me a lousy quarter for the both."

"What'd ya do?"

"Told him he could keep his stinkin' quarter."

Alphonse grinned. "Ya did?"

"Yep."

"Ya stuck up fer yerself 'n ya did good." Alphonse ticked his stick against the rail for emphasis. "Real good!"

"Felt weird."

"Doin' somethin' fer the first time always does."

"The thing that still gets me, Alphonse, is those little rat feet. Dang, they chewed clean through their leg."

"That they did."

"Musta hurt awful bad."

"Nothin' likes bein' trapped."

"But chewin' right through the bone?"

"Was their only way out."

"Feel awful about crippling those rats for life."

Alphonse slowed a tad to consider this for a moment, then continued on waving his stick like a conductor.

"Well, Francis, do ya think them rats can count?"

"That's stupid. They're rats."

"Of course they can't count! Rats don't even know how many feet they's supposed ta have. Come next spring, I reckon I'll be lookin' at three-legged rats."

It was nearly dark when they finally turned, slowly making their way toward the shack with its tin roof reflecting the last of the evening light. Soon, the shack came into full view, silhouetted against the fading sky. Butch, limping in close, sniffed Francis, then hobbled alongside Alphonse as they eased off the rail bed.

Alphonse winged his stick into the night. "Was a time when Butch woulda had that stick before she dropped."

"Reckon he's pretty old, all right."

"Had 'im as a pup when I gave up hoboin' . . . well . . . that was a lot a years ago." Alphonse sighed. "Looks ta me like ya better scoot . . . school tomorrow, and it's yer turn ta get smart."

Francis quickly skirted the porch, heading for home. Nearly out of sight, he yelled back, "I liked our walk, Alphonse!"

Alphonse smiled in the dark, saying to himself, "Damn glad ya came back, Francis."

CHAPTER TWENTY-FOUR

A Lousy Note in a File

THE SWELTERING, MUGGY SUMMER WASN'T GOING AWAY, no matter what the calendar said. Those crisp days of autumn with cool, clean air, when the red and yellowing leaves of the maples and hickories shouted that summer was over, those days had yet to come.

Even so, during the first weeks of September, the boiler room remained the center of everyone's attention, the hub where urgent requests for repairs and remedies were made. It was also the time when the huge boilers had to be inspected and clawed free of clinkers, the sixty flues atop each wire-brushed clear of soot, made ready for the coming winter months.

Zach wielded a long-handled wire brush, running it back and forth through a flue, the brush flicking gray ash against his face. His eyes were ringed in dark grime. Soot coated his neck and clung to his sweaty shirt, and the granular air blackened the fine hairs of his nostrils.

Finally finished, he clanged the boiler door closed while his dad, at the sink in the back, scrubbed his face and hands. After propping the brush and ladder in the corner,

Zach carefully ventured in low tones, "Flues are done, Dad. S'pose I can still make the Sunday scrimmage."

Edgar didn't bother looking over. "Somebody's gotta wheel out those clinkers . . . and this place needs a good sweep before tomorrow."

"Where's Francis? I've had to do—"

"Enough!" snapped Edgar.

"But Doc gave him the go-ahead days ago."

"I said drop it!"

Edgar had just toweled his face dry when he looked up to see the Monsignor striding quickly into the room, a small briefcase in his hand. In an instant, his brain revolted with dread, impatience, and disgust.

"We need to talk," said the Monsignor in a grim, stony voice.

"You're the boss." Edgar spoke flatly.

Edgar wadded the towel and tossed it to the sink. The Monsignor gave Zach a small nod of recognition.

"My office, Edgar. Won't take long."

———

EDGAR SAT UP STRAIGHT IN the velvet chair, appearing lost and out of place, like an abandoned refugee waiting for a bus. The Monsignor strutted near his mahogany desk.

"I have a lot on my mind, Edgar," began the Monsignor. "I want to tidy up a few things. First off, it must be a relief having Francis finally back in school tomorrow."

"It is," said Edgar cautiously. He was miffed about the interruption, but even more than that, and his burgeoning fear and disgust with the man, he was at a loss as to why the meeting needed the secrecy of the rectory. He felt trapped, knowing that whatever was on the Monsignor's mind must be important and sensitive to require his office.

"As I promised your wife, I've enrolled you in a government program that will supply your son's penicillin. It's free. When we're through here, I'll have you sign the papers."

"We're appreciative."

"I also talked to Tom Raabe. He's not able to give you a break. I think seven hundred dollars for a Ford in that shape is a fair price." The Monsignor paused in front of Edgar. "Perhaps down the road, when Zach gets his license."

"Maybe." Edgar nodded warily.

"You seem a bit out of sorts, Edgar."

"Just a lot to do." His voice was matter of fact. "It's that time of year."

"With South Bend just around the corner, I haven't much time either." The Monsignor paused in front of Edgar, looked down, and said in a cold, stony voice. "I did though, find time to write a rather extensive note to my replacement about your overdue raise."

Edgar paled. "A note?" He didn't slump in his chair. "You . . . you wrote a note?" He sat stiff, gripping hard his knees.

"I'm sure it'll be taken care of quickly." The Monsignor resumed pacing. "Now, to the reason I wanted us to speak privately. It's about Alphonse, and . . ."

"He's almost family," interrupted Edgar. He shifted slightly, his arms now out straight, his hands gripping the chair's arm as if bracing.

"Yes . . . and you're the only reason I haven't fired him. Your . . . friend is convinced that my work with Francis this summer has harmed your son. This is, of course, preposterous. Has he mentioned this to you?"

Edgar exhaled loudly, his body suddenly releasing its tension. He could do nothing but wait for the inevitable. "He might've mentioned something."

"Don't be glib with me!"

The Monsignor halted and jutted a finger at Edgar, his scar flaming scarlet against his chalky face. "He's accused me of some very hideous things."

Edgar stared blandly at the Monsignor's threatening finger.

"Let's be clear on this. You have a wonderful son, and if there was ever a problem with his summer, you need to look long and hard at Alphonse." The Monsignor spoke quickly, as if reading off a list. "He lives in a hovel by that rat-infested marsh. He's a worn-out hobo, never married, living alone. Think about it, Edgar. There's no telling how badly living like that could warp the brain."

Edgar struggled to contain his building-by-the-second anger and suspicion. He said mockingly, "What do you expect me to do?"

The Monsignor stopped, turned and eyed him. His mouth was slightly ajar for a second or two, while his mind tried unwinding Edgar's odd behavior.

"What I expect is for you to remember this." His voice rose, his words spoken like lecture. "The hobo that rescued you and Sara years ago is not the same man that now sneaks around inside the church! He's stalked your son this entire summer. I've tried everything I could to protect Francis, but in my position, there's only so much I could do."

"Alphonse would never harm either of my sons."

The Monsignor leaned in close. "You're a fool if you believe that. He's a liar—a predator—and a murderer!"

Edgar bowed his head, biding his time until the storm passed.

"And he's been with Francis this entire summer!"

Finally hearing enough, Edgar jerked his head up and stared directly at the Monsignor. "And I said he'd never harm Francis!"

"Open your eyes!"

"They're open!" Edgar bolted up defiantly. "I know exactly what Alphonse is accusing you of."

"Then you know he's crazy to come up with those lies."

"He's never been crazy!"

"What!" roared the Monsignor. He took a fast step forward, jutting out a shaky finger at Edgar. "If you think there's a fiber of truth in that fool then you're treading on thin ice!"

"You—" Edgar caught himself and stopped.

"If you want to continue your thought . . ." The Monsignor narrowed his eyes, calculating. "You're welcome to look for another job in this town. With the recommendation I could leave behind, no one would ever think of hiring you, even if you had perfect eyesight."

Edgar couldn't move.

"Are we clear on this?"

Edgar couldn't think.

The Monsignor yanked open his briefcase, pulled out

the papers and smacked them against the table. He pointed
a pen at Edgar.

"Sign if you want that medication."

CHAPTER TWENTY-FIVE

The Burnt Flashbulbs

AT LAST, AUTUMN HAD ARRIVED. IT WASN'T COOL, BUT THE summer's baking heat had gone, and with the gentle breezes, the changing leaves of the maples winked in shades of reds and yellows. Alphonse squatted like a gargoyle in the shade on the church steps. His hands were clamped firmly to his knees, and only his eyes moved as they tracked the cars buzzing down Second. *He said he'd be here,* he thought. *I'll wait 'til the son-a-bitchin' cows come home if I have ta.* Finally, Noonan, the *Herald*'s photographer, pulled to a stop in front and loped up the walk, a large Speed Graphics camera hanging from his shoulder by a strap.

Alphonse jumped to his feet and whistled in appreciation. "That's one helluva camera. Looks damn expensive."

"Cheap. Army surplus." Noonan cracked his gum. "Someone actually gave you a key?"

"Yep. With the Monsignor busy leavin' town, and Edgar up ta his ass gettin' stuff done, just leaves me ta see ya 'round."

"Boss wants shots inside the steeple." Noonan tipped his head back and stared up at the tower. "Gotta tell you, I'm not a fan of heights."

Once inside, Noonan was quick. He pointed, clicked the shutter, and popped out flashbulbs as he moved from the vestibule, to the choir loft, and finally to the bell tower, chewing gum nonstop. A tiny smile of satisfaction crept across Alphonse's face as he followed behind, snatching up the burnt flashbulbs like a squirrel gathering nuts for winter.

The photo session quickly over, they emerged through the brass front door, where Noonan paused briefly on the walk.

"What's with the damn flashbulbs? I appreciate your picking them up, but they're trash. You were like a kid hoarding Easter eggs."

Alphonse gave a lopsided smile, but said nothing.

Noonan shook his head. "You do beat all, Alphonse."

As Noonan hoisted his camera strap higher on his shoulder and headed to the car, Alphonse grinned like a kid with a secret and patted the bulbs stuffing the pockets of his bibs.

CHAPTER TWENTY-SIX

Fruit Canning Time

WEEKS AFTER THE FRANTIC HUSTLE OF THE NEW SCHOOL year had subsided, when the boiler room was no longer the center of attention, had always been a special time for the Sadlers. It was fruit canning time.

In the kitchen, steam clouded the lone window, and water beaded against the yellow enameled walls. The linoleum floor grew tacky around the table where Edgar sat cranking the apple peeler. Sara's face glistened in the haze of steam above the stove as she bent over the kettle, stirring the simmering apples. She wiped sweat from her forehead, tucking stray curls back into her coiled hair, and smiled contentedly at her husband.

"Last year, they were all wormy." Edgar plucked an apple from the peeler. "Only a few so far, in two and a half bushels."

He plopped the peeled fruit in a bowl of cold water with a dozen others, then grabbed another from the bushel basket that sat near his feet. The peeler was ancient, cast iron with black springs, and as he cranked, its rhythmic squeak measured out their methodical work.

Francis wandered in, nonchalantly eyeing the process and his parents.

"You're late." Edgar barely glanced at Francis. "Thought you wanted to help."

"Sure, okay."

Slowly, with care, Sara lifted the steaming pints from the pressure cooker. Not taking the chance to look at her son, she said pleasantly, "If you're going to help, grab a knife."

Francis settled at the table and began quartering the peeled apples on the scarred cutting board. He'd made it through a half-dozen when Zach waltzed into the kitchen.

"Well, well," said Edgar. "Will you look who we have here, Sara."

She ignored them both, busy searching for another pot in the lower cabinet.

Edgar nodded toward Francis. "You might give Francis a hand."

"He's got it under control," said Zach flippantly. He was antsy and kept shuffling his feet.

"Would it kill you to at least say 'Hi' to your brother?"

Zach rolled his eyes but gave Francis a quick, "Hi."

Francis beamed. "Hey, Zach! How's it goin'?"

"I'm really busy, Dad. I'd like to help, but I gotta get ready for the dance."

Edgar stopped his crank. "You better not be getting uppity."

"Everyone's gonna be there."

"Just the same, don't be ignoring your family."

"I'm not—gotta go." And with that, he backed quickly out of the kitchen.

In short order, Francis had caught up with his dad and had to wait until he'd peeled more apples.

As Edgar stabbed another apple onto the peeler, Francis grabbed a bright red one from the bushel. After buffing it against his jeans, he snapped off a huge bite, closed his eyes, and never noticed the drip of juice hanging on his chin. His manner and face said he relished the sound of his crunching as much as the apple's sweet taste.

Edgar stopped, mid-crank. "How's the apple?"

"These apples are good, Dad." His words jumbled around the fruit.

"Settling into school?"

"S'pose so."

"Looks like . . ." Edgar cranked. "You're starting to make yourself scarce, like your brother."

"Not really, but sometimes I just like goin' for walks and thinkin' about stuff."

"Figure anything out?"

"Alphonse said walks are always good. Dad—" He reached for the newly peeled apple then looked over, directly at Edgar. "At the assembly this afternoon, you sure were mad."

"Had every right ta be!" Edgar pitched an apple to the bowl of water. "The school needs a damn new P.A. system. I've got better things to do than traipse in just to reset the damn thing."

"You almost took the principal's head off."

"All that nun had to do was flip the switch after she jiggled the damn wire."

Francis carefully sliced the apple in half. "It's just that

the gym was packed . . . and . . . everybody was watching."

"So that's it!" snorted Edgar. "I embarrassed you."

"Well . . ." Francis kept his eyes down and cut quickly. "Sometimes, they all start making cracks. It's not like when they call me 'Clinker.' I'm used to that."

"Hear that, Sara?"

Edgar speared another apple but fumbled it. It splattered to the floor and skidded across the linoleum. Francis retrieved it, but Edgar never noticed.

"I am an embarrassment to our son. Next thing ya know, the whole damn place'll be confusing me with Alphonse."

"Oh, Edgar. Relax."

She wiped her hands across her apron. "And Francis, you know better than to pay any mind to those comments. Your father's simply doing his job. Now help me lift this tray. I need to start another batch."

———

LONG AFTER FRANCIS HAD WANDERED off to bed, Sara wiped down the cooling stove while Edgar mopped the kitchen floor. Pushing against a particularly sticky spot beneath the table, he said bluntly, "The Monsignor put a note in my file." He dug the mop hard against the spot. "It says that somebody needed to give me a raise."

"What? He wrote a note?" Sara stopped in mid-wipe. Stunned, her mouth open, she stared at her husband. "That's it? You now have a note in a file?" She tried wiping down the stove again, but couldn't.

Edgar leaned the mop against the counter and reached for a chair. "Every time I think that man's on our side he pulls this crap! Fourteen years, and I get a lousy chicken-shit note. Hell, Sara, these last couple days, I can't stand to even look at the man." Sliding the chair across the floor, his grip looked more like a chokehold.

Sara pulled her chair out and sat, then quietly patted the seat of Edgar's chair.

"Last couple days? What's new?"

Edgar sighed and scratched his stubbled chin before sitting down. "Maybe it's his leaving, but he's skittish, nervous. Had to have our little chat in his office. It had to be private, everything hush-hush like."

Her face was pensive, haggard, and she sat with her fingers curled tightly in her lap against her dirty apron. "We should've known we'd be stuck like this."

"It's like he can't get out of town fast enough. All his damn sermons—concern and worry for everyone . . . but not us." Edgar kicked the mop bucket toward the corner.

Sara rested her hand on Edgar's arm. "What did you say?"

"He didn't leave much room for me to say anything."

"He'll leave, and leave us high and dry, then."

Edgar was about to speak, but held back, something more serious clearly reflecting on his face. He couldn't control the slight quiver in his hands.

"Edgar?"

He didn't respond.

"What else happened, Edgar?"

"It's more than just his lame note." Edgar combed his

hair back with his fingers. "Today with the Monsignor . . ." He took a huge breath and let it out loudly. "Alphonse and I had a long talk yesterday. He said some pretty ugly things, and they've been stewing in my head."

"What? You and Alphonse had a fight?"

"No, no. Alphonse—" He thought for a moment. "Alphonse is worried. And it's strange, but I think the Monsignor's scared of Alphonse."

"What? If I weren't so tired, I'd laugh."

"The more I think about it, the more I'm convinced of it."

"Alphonse may act the fool, but we both know he's sweet and harmless. What could the Monsignor possibly be afraid of?"

"Not sure." Edgar stalled, exhaling exhaustion. "You weren't there today to see his face. I'm telling you that priest has changed! He's not the same man that hired me."

At that moment, Edgar knew he needed to let it all out, to confide in his wife about Alphonse's accusations against the Monsignor. He could barely voice to himself the possibility that Alphonse had been telling the truth all along, let alone try to find the words to explain to her what happened to her son in the bell tower all summer. With that lying in front of him, the threat of losing his job became insignificant.

"The Monsignor believes Alphonse is making up some horrible lies about him."

"Good Lord, Edgar, what—"

"Hell, I don't know," he lied. "But . . . It was Alphonse who set off the bells."

"What could've possessed him?"

Deflated, feeling feeble and weak, he was unable to voice out loud what he was more and more convinced was the truth. He sputtered, "Alphonse has been doing crazy crap like that for years. You know that."

"Those bells with all that noise . . . and so late—it was after nine."

"Didn't think it was that late." Edgar shoved his chair back and began pacing. "You know how he hates the Monsignor. Reckon he just wanted to piss him off, I suppose."

Sara frowned. "I don't know why he never liked the Monsignor, I've only gotten pieces of his story. Still, if Alphonse's hatred has gotten worse . . . well, I'd be leery of any man who centers his life on hatred."

Edgar said quietly, "He's not all hatred, Sara. He's looked after our boys since we got here."

He rubbed a weary hand across his eyes. "Sara, I don't know how Francis could've gotten by without Alphonse this summer."

"Edgar, don't blame this on your . . ."

"It started with pigeon shit!" he said cutting her off. "Francis scraping the walks, dealing with the church, and his shitty schedule . . . Alphonse was there for him all summer. Probably did more for Francis than we're even aware of."

Sara searched Edgar's face, certain there was more to her husband's anger than he was willing to tell her. After a long silence, she said, "Edgar, what're we going to do about the money?"

Weary and lost, Edgar sagged in his chair, propping his

head on his fist. He could find no answer for anything right then, and he shuddered at her question that hung in the air like a bad smell in the kitchen.

CHAPTER TWENTY-SEVEN

At Howard's Left
1945

BLACK COAL SMOKE WEAVED WITH THE FOG THAT DROOP-
ed low over the tracks as evening dissolved into night.
Cleveland's freight yard moved with clanging machinery
and switching boxcars. Yard lights stood like cold sentinels
high overhead, scrutinizing railroaders working at a frenetic
pace, scrawling on clipboards and pumping handcars along
the cindered beds. Sixty-pound blocks of ice slid down
chutes to men who stacked them on the dock. At the yard's
far end, engines lined up to take on water from a tower
higher than the ice house.

Beyond the reach of the yard's probing lights, in the
quiet of an alcove among the trees, Sara sat on her pillow,
her pregnant belly straining the pleats of her blouse. Edgar
squatted close, his hands clamped hard against his thighs.
Wood snapped in tiny fires on the hillside, and muffled con-
versations too distant to be understood drifted on the air.
Sara rested her hands protectively on her belly and whispered, "I don't like this. Not one bit. That lady warned us."

"I know," said Edgar. "But this is the fastest way to Indiana. We're plumb out of time."

Edgar was thirty. His face was drawn. His eyes, though, were fierce, and they had the nervous jitter of a man who found himself desperate in a strange place, a young husband desperate to make things right for his pregnant wife.

"How will we know which train to take?" she said, peering into the darkness.

"There's gotta be somebody to help. You ready?"

"Still queasy, but I know we need to go."

She held Edgar's arm for balance and struggled to her feet.

The stench of rot wafted with the smoke pressing down against the jungle. Edgar squinted in the direction of a dozen shadows circling a huge kettle, but he got his bearings from their voices—snippets of stories, the fragments of crude jokes. Curled up in the weeds, a man snored beneath giant shards of cardboard. His shoes were off, and he'd tied them hobo-fashion with the laces to his ankles.

Sara's grip tightened as they eased through the gloom.

"Those men . . . good Lord, Edgar, they're all liquored up."

"I can smell them. We need to stay back."

"What we need is a friendly face."

They huddled together beyond the cookfire's light, hearing the crash of breaking glass as an empty bottle was tossed to the darkness, seeing the glint of another bottle of 'shine as it circled the kettle.

A tattered, skinny man bent over the fire, shoving wood into the flames, just as someone appeared from the shadows and grabbed him on his shoulder. The skinny man spun around, ready to take a swing at the newcomer, but quickly checked himself and flashed a tremendous grin.

"Jesus goddamn! It's Jimmie! It's Jimmie from the South, boys!"

"Been a long spell, Mitts." Jimmie clapped his friend on the back, his thin whiskered face beaming. He glanced around the circle.

"Don't s'pose any a ya folks are hungry?"

From somewhere in the darkness came a shout, "I'd eat the asshole out of a chicken!" followed by a quick, single hoot of laughter.

Jimmie upended a seed sack and flopped a giant carp onto the stones.

"This here carp's better 'n a fifteen pounder."

Excitement rippled through the small group.

Edgar leaned closer to Sara. "Hear that? That fella brought fish for the group. Sounds like he knows his way around. Maybe he'll lend us a hand, Sara."

"God only hope so." She cradled her belly. "I have the feeling it better be fast."

"What! Now?"

"Not that, Edgar. It's just that we need to get to Indiana . . . somewhere clean. Maybe where there's a woman around."

Jimmie moved casually through the jungle, every so often pausing by a campfire before moving on, now and then sitting to chat, but in good time, he made it back to the kettle now steaming with fish.

For those new to traveling by freight, like the young Sadlers, little about Jimmie set him apart from the other hoboes. His clothes were filthy, tin covered the holes in the soles of his boots, his hair was scraggly, and he was in sore need of a bath. His restless eyes reflected his soul's need to wander, yet the manner in which he moved through the jungles made him unusual; the ease and honesty he had for the down-and-out made him unique. And though he drank 'shine, the same rotgut as the other hoboes, his blue eyes were not clouded with liquor. Within Jimmie, there thrived an uncontrollable drive to make certain that everyone he met was treated justly, no matter how unfortunate, or naïve, or young.

Rounding the kettle, Jimmie announced, "I'm puttin' in fer all ya. Fish stew is what we got cookin' 'n we got plenty."

Shadows scrambled; men rummaged for spoons, rooted among trash heaps for cans to use as bowls.

Edgar pulled Sara to her feet.

"That Jimmie fella is going to feed the lot of us. Can't remember when you last had a hot meal. God knows you need it."

Mitts and Blinky, Sheeter and Clint, and nearly another twenty travelers settled in near the kettle. Jimmie was sitting with Blinky on a log near the fire when he spied the Sadler's cautious approach. He elbowed Blinky, then jumped to his feet.

"You may have just one eye, Blinky, but even you gotta see that young lady's gonna need a seat."

Blinky's face reddened. "Reckon I was already eatin' stew."

"Might be just hoboes, but we still gotta have manners."

The Sadlers smiled sheepishly and sat down. Jimmie offered them a can of stew, then settled beside Blinky on the ground next to them.

"We surely appreciate it, sir," Edgar said, as he dug his spoon—one of their few possessions—from his pocket and handed it to Sara.

"Sir?" Jimmie guffawed, slapping his knee. "Ain't no 'sir.' Name's Jimmie. Some call me Jimmie from the South, on account a that's where I'm from."

"I'm Edgar. This is my wife, Sara." Edgar gave a hesitant smile.

"Well . . . I'll be go ta grass . . . yer Sara looks like she could pop on the spot."

"We're scared the baby could come any time."

"Damn . . . what're ya folks doin' here, then?"

"When we left, we weren't sure how far along she was. The last couple months, I got caught up in looking for work."

Jimmie nodded. "These days that ain't no different 'n most."

"Back East things are bad. People are scared, no money and no jobs. I talked to a lot of folks that think this part of the country might be better."

"From what I seen, she's bad all over."

"We heard there's a lot of factory work in Indiana."

"Travelin' by freight, I don't rightly know, Edgar." He rubbed his whiskers thoughtfully. "No offense, Sara, it'll be tough but we might be able to get ya loaded up in a boxcar."

———

AS THE FIRST LIGHT PEEKED over the horizon, Jimmie stationed lookouts, and had four others besides Edgar ready to hoist Sara into a boxcar. After checking up and down the rails, he signaled "Now!" He had no sooner slid under the coal car than an explosion of white steam whooshed from beneath the car, the screaming sound pissing off the engineer.

"What the shit!" he yelled through the tiny window. "Smitty, check the goddamn brakes on the coal car!"

It'd been dicey, but the delay was just enough to allow Jimmie and the Sadlers to settle into the car. As they eased from Cleveland's freight yard, they could see through the open door the Cuyahoga River's placid and forlorn waters fade away in the distance.

Yet after making it to Dayton, their journey got no easier. Jimmie was determined to locate another freight that would head to Fort Wayne with the fewest stops, one close by where he and Edgar could more easily move Sara without being discovered. Slipping among the staging rails and eyeing the symbols on the engines, Jimmie had finally located the right freight when a railroader and the yard bull spotted him.

"That him!" The yard bull's voice sounded like gravel. He pointed to where Jimmie was scrunched low, trying to hide behind a caboose.

"That's the son-of-a-bitch who ran from the two-oh-eight!"

The railroader was more curious than angry. "Don't find many like him anymore."

"These bastards are all the same," growled the bull. "I'll show ya how to handle 'em."

In an instant, the yard bull thundered his way to where

Jimmie huddled and slammed him flat against the caboose, pinning him in place with a beefy forearm. Blood trickled from Jimmie's scalp and mouth.

"Yer a god damn thief! Stealin' rides from the railroad!"

"I ain't no thief—I'm just helpin' a pregnant lady is all."

The bull shoved his arm against Jimmie's throat.

"Lyin' bastard! No thievin' hobo'd help anybody but his-self!"

"She's in a bad way," Jimmie gasped. "Baby's probably poppin' now. Beat me all ya want, but it's a goddamn fact."

The railroader tugged the bull's arm. "Take it easy, Smetts."

The bull lightened his grip but didn't release Jimmie. "You stole your last ride," he grumbled. "Tell your lies to the coppers!"

"If ya don't let me help her . . . ya gotta do it yer own-self."

"Let him go, Smetts."

"What? You believe this bullshit!" Smetts glared at the railroader. "Hire me ta do a job, 'n ya get all soft."

"A pregnant woman, Smetts."

Smetts snorted. "Not in a freight yard, there ain't."

"And if there is, I don't want anything to do with it. Let him go."

Smetts swore but released Jimmie with a shove. Jimmie lost no time. He scurried across the rails and out of sight.

EIGHT CARS BEHIND THE FREIGHT'S coal car, the Sadlers and Jimmie were packed tightly like cargo. Edgar had helped Jimmie rearrange crates labeled 'Palmolive' in order to form a bench for Sara and had secured it all by restringing the straps. After rolling on her side with her back to the men, Sara was weary but comforted to be on her way to Indiana at last. For mile after mile, she buried her head in the crook of her elbow, pretending to sleep, the men's voices and the train's rhythmic clickety-clack a soothing comfort.

"Didn't like Pennsylvanie, eh?" Jimmie asked.

Edgar reached back and patted his wife protectively. "Starting our family in a smaller town sounds better to us."

"Been ta Pennsylvanie," Jimmie laughed. "They gots plenty a small towns."

Edgar closed his eyes against the countryside whizzing past, and didn't reply.

"Sorry, didn't mean ta snoop." Jimmie shrugged. "Was just passin' the time, Edgar."

"It's all right," Edgar dismissed the matter with a little wave. "The truth is, I had a good job at the coal mine, but I got fired."

"Never had a job. But I bet it's a damn dirty shame."

"S'pose they had no choice . . . I went blind in one eye. They said working around the mine was too dangerous."

"Ya still gots another eye."

"For now, it's holding its own."

"Sure be the shits if yer other went bad."

"I can't worry about that."

"S'pose yer right."

"We thought maybe coming out here where it's a little slower . . . I don't know, maybe people would relax the rules a bit."

"Know there's lotsa friendly folk in Indiana."

"We know Indiana's a gamble. It was even a wild idea before we knew about the baby. But now . . . I need to find something fast."

A little later . . . heading toward Fort Wayne.

"Why 'Zachariah'?" For a bit they fell silent, both lost in their separate worlds as the freight rolled west.

Edgar finally said, "Sara likes the sound of 'Zach.' She thinks it's biblical."

Suddenly, the thundering freight screeched its brakes and slowed rapidly. Edgar catapulted to his feet and leaned far out the door. He pivoted and yelled back inside.

"Fort Wayne! Sara, we made it to Fort Wayne!"

Jimmie stood alongside and shook his head.

"Not yet, Edgar. This is just a shit-ass turn. All the freights have ta slow down and grind to a halt here. We hoboes call it, "Howard's Left."

Edgar lingered at the door, staring at the slowly passing farms.

Sara stirred, her eyes opened wide in alarm. Her lungs begged for air, but she couldn't breathe; she wanted to call out to Edgar, but she couldn't find voice. She felt the moisture in her lap and knew her water had broken.

They were out of time.

"EDGAR! UNHOOK THAT STRAP!"

The men scrambled while Sara sat frightened and confused on the ledge, her feet dangling above the deck.

"Git the other one!"

Edgar tossed the strap aside, for a second stroked her hair, and asked anxiously, "You okay?"

She could only nod.

Edgar's voice shook, "How much time do we have, Jimmie?"

"Two . . . maybe three minutes."

Despite his own jitters, Jimmie relished this moment— the excitement, the challenge of helping others, the feel that he was worthwhile, and it all was reflected unmistakably in Jimmie's eyes, the thrill on his grizzled face.

Choking smoke swept past the door, the freight's releasing brakes shot out clouds of steam, and one by one, the boxcars banged loudly as they tightened.

"Here we go, Sara!" Jimmie popped from the car, waiting with his arms up, while Sara sat on the lip of the car.

Edgar stared at the drop. "We'll never get her down, Jimmie!"

"Toss me some crates and that pallet!"

In no time, Jimmie had stacked it all firmly against the rail bed.

The engineer leaned on the freight's horn.

Jimmie reached up again. "Ease 'er down ta me!"

"We're movin', Jimmie!"

"Now!"

Edgar helping to lower her from above, Jimmie steadying her from the rail bed below, they maneuvered Sara out of the car and onto the stacked crates. She teetered briefly before Edgar hopped down, and from there, he and Jimmie helped her off the cindered rail bed. As the train moved steadily around the turn, the ground vibrated and the rumbling of wheels against rails faded away.

Sara, supported by Edgar on one side and Jimmie on the other, stepped carefully across the rails to a narrow dirt lane. She looked across the fields, shading her eyes against the late afternoon sun. "What is this place, Jimmie?"

"This be Howard's Left. Ain't much, but it's a damn shot better'n a freight yard or a boxcar."

She said softly, "I'm . . . we're mighty beholden, Jimmie."

"Ain't nothin'."

"Almost there, Sara," said Edgar.

"Howard's a damn nice man, and Mrs. Swetnam is one helluva friendly woman. She's got three kids a her own so she knows a thing or two."

Sara closed her eyes, saying softly, "A woman . . . my prayers've been answered."

———

HOWARD'S BEDROOM WAS TINY. IT had a single window, nightstand, a lone picture of a freight train barreling over some wooden bridge, a rickety floor lamp in the corner, but for Sara, lying in the narrow bed, it was a luxury she'd not felt in nearly a year. As Edgar perched anxiously on the edge of the bed holding Sara's hand, Mrs. Swetnam, a portly woman, mid-forties with a square red face, bustled in with towels and a basin of water. Though her words were kind, she called out orders like a sergeant.

"Now Edgar, me and Sara got this under control. You

visit with the men folk on the porch. I'm here to give your wife a bath."

"Oh my," sighed Sara. "Hear that, Edgar? A bath."

"Now you go on, Edgar." Mrs. Swetnam shooed him off the bed. "We're goin' to have us a long night."

———

EDGAR SAT ALONGSIDE JIMMIE ON the stoop. In the distance, a pudgy man meandered up the lane toward the freight tracks. Jimmie nodded toward the figure.

"Ya know, Edgar, Howard's a real nice fella."

"I'd say so, since he opened up his house for us."

"Every ride through here I see his big-ass smile—him wavin' ta all get out at the freights needin' ta stop at that turn. He's one helluva character."

"Doesn't look like he works his farm."

"He doesn't."

"What's he do?"

"He waves at the freights passin' through. Hell, the damn railroad couldn't function if that man wasn't down there every day sittin' on his stump and wavin' like shit."

"That's it?"

"Reckon that's all he needs." Jimmie's face darkened. "Whole buncha years ago, Christ, had ta be at least fifteen, was passing through here and got me one helluva shock. I saw Howard's barn afire. Found Howard, head all bashed in bad, bleedin', everythin' around him burnin'. The Swetnams got 'im to a doc, but they say he ain't ever been the same since. Coppers figured it was robbery, that whoever done it got mean and beat him near ta death." Jimmie's voice rose, high pitched, and gave the stoop a quick thwack with his clenched fist. "The sons-a-bitches busted in his brain then burned his damn barn ta the ground!"

"They ever catch them?"

"Hell, no!" Jimmie sprang from the stoop. "Might as well a shot him dead! He can't think, can barely talk—" He stomped back and forth in front of the stoop, shaking his head violently in disgust. Stopping suddenly, momentarily confused by his tirade, he looked back at Edgar sheepishly, "Christ, Edgar . . . sorry. It's just that when I see innocent people bein' hurt sometimes . . . well sometimes I go crazy 'n can't help myself."

He settled back on the stoop. "Didn't mean ta get all preachy. Ya got more important things on your mind than listening ta this ol' hobo."

Edgar slapped Jimmie on the knee saying, "All I know is me and Sara would've been in a helluva pickle if you hadn't helped us."

Jimmie didn't respond, his mind clearly elsewhere, and they sat motionless for some time. Overhead, a naked lightbulb cast long dark shadows across the porch, and somewhere in the pitch blackness crickets chirped for mates. There was no wind; it was a stifling, muggy Indiana night. Knifing suddenly from the house, Sara's piercing scream propelled them to their feet. For a second they shared wideeyed stares then tore inside the farm house.

"What—" Edgar, panicked, barged into the tiny room.

"She's fine." Mrs. Swetnam turned calmly to face him. She smiled and held out a small bundle. "And so is your new son."

Edgar stumbled to the bedside and grabbed Sara's hand tightly. Mrs. Swetnam gently tucked the swaddled infant between them.

"Zachariah," Sara crooned softly. "Baby Zachariah."

Speechless, his mouth ajar, Jimmie's eyes locked open with surprise and wonder. He wedged himself in the corner by the floor lamp trying to steady the shaking in his legs.

———

LAVENDER THISTLE BLOSSOMS, ALMOST AN acre near the farm house, shivered with dew in the early-morning quiet. Edgar slumped on the stoop, his face drawn. Jimmie sat nearby, on the edge of the step.

"One helluva night, Edgar."

"One helluva trip." Edgar found a brief smile. "Never thought we'd make it."

"Just goes ta show ya. Ya gotta keep puttin' 'em down."

"Thank God. My wife can finally rest easy."

"Damn right! Ya done good, Edgar!"

Edgar rubbed his bloodshot eyes. "Don't know if the hard part's over or just starting."

"Yer in new territory, that's fer sure."

"Don't get me wrong, Jimmie. I couldn't be happier about Sara and baby Zach. But bein' out of work this long . . ." He shook his head. "I can't lie. I'm scared to death."

Jimmie stood up to wring the kinks out of his back.

"Hell Edgar, look at yer hands. Anybody with half a brain can tell you'd make a damn good worker."

Edgar held his unusually large hands up and stared at

them. "Foreman. I was foreman at the mine for four years."

"I knew it! Ya don't need eyes ta know how ta get shit done."

"I just need to find someone around here who believes that."

"You will! I'm not the only intelligent son-a-bitch in these parts. But then, I never had much use fer a job.

"You're a lucky man." Jimmie's eyes clouded as he plunked down next to Edgar. "Got yerself a pretty wife, a brand spankin' new baby boy."

Edgar turned, trying to read Jimmie's sudden shift in mood.

Jimmie stared off across the expanse of thistle. "'spect ya need ta take a long breath 'n see what ya really got."

"You have family, Jimmie?"

"Nope."

"Traveling the rails like you do, don't you ever get lonely?"

"Nope, at least not your kinda lonely."

"My kind of lonely?"

"I like the shit outta visitin' 'n helpin' out, but I reckon she all boils down ta the fact that I need to be alone. Sittin' on some crates in a rockin' boxcar, 'n listenin' to the clickety-clack of the freight, that sound washes away all the ugly things I see, erases the worried and scared faces from my brain. Funny, I enjoy people 'n like hearin' about their lives and lendin' a hand where I can, but she don't take long before I gotta run away 'n be by myself. Lonely? Christ, Edgar, ridin' 'round this ole country, I get ta know a whole passel a folks."

"Like in Cleveland. You had a regular band of hoboes helping out. I suppose they're your family."

Filtering through the door came the sounds of a whimpering baby and the soothing tones of a mother. The men smiled at one another, and their smiles lingered as they sat silently on the porch with the light of dawn coloring their faces pink and warm, and softening the deep lines around their worried eyes.

THAT EVENING, AFTER A DAY of helping the Swetnams with chores and sharing a simple supper with Howard, Edgar and Jimmie settled on the stoop in the fading light. Sara and the baby were tucked away in the little bedroom. Howard stood on the porch steps waving toward the train that he heard stopping at Howard's left.

Jimmie leaned his back against the post. "Wasn't much to it, Edgar. Ya wake up one day 'n find yerself livin' a life 'n yer not sure how ya got there. Seems slippin' inta hoboin' was easy, a natural thin' ta do, but it weren't." He reached down and plucked a long grass stem.

"Mighta been different if there weren't no war." He smoothed the green stem between his fingers. "My Pa got hisself killed in that war." He tossed the grass away and fished a stogie from his bibs. "Was around twelve when Ma got that yellow telegram."

"Course, it wasn't good without Pa, but Ma took up work in a textile factory. Macon, Georgia it was, 'n we was gettin' by." Jimmie's mouth worked the stogie. "So one day she got her sleeve caught in one of those big machines. Tore her arm clean off." Jimmy shook his head. "They all said she'd die, but she didn't. Took a shit ton a time, but she went back ta work just the same." Jimmie's face grew dark, his voice quaked. "Havin' only one arm, her damn bosses said she wasn't fast enough, wasn't good enough anymore, and they fired her."

Edgar began to reply, but Jimmie waved him off.

"We was desperate, but she weren't gonna send me to no workhouse. 'We'd make it through,' she said." Jimmie gazed at the night sky, his voice distant. "They traipsed through our shack, all hours a the night, all strangers, mostly. I slept in a corner of the porch, out of the way where they couldn't see me, but I watched 'em come 'n go. Well . . . in truth Edgar, I needed to sleep on that porch. I couldn't stand what was goin' on inside."

"Jimmie, that's—"

"I never saw it comin'. One night, one a the bastards got jealous . . . the son-a-bitch crashed out the door yellin' loud 'nough ta wake the dead, 'Got what you deserve! You one-armed cheatin' whore!' He set the house afire. Bastard probably used gas 'cause everythin' was burnin' so fast. I was helpless ta get Ma out. Firemen said she'd been stabbed before the fire got ta her."

He shook his head. "After that, I had nothin' . . . nobody. I wasn't more 'n thirteen, so I took ta the rails 'n been ridin' ever since.

"I still remember . . ." Jimmie rubbed his eyes. "Up to the end, she always liked readin' ta me. I still miss her, Edgar. I surely do."

Much later in the pitch black, Edgar's voice floated through the darkness.

"Jimmie, I don't know how we would've handled it if . . ." Edgar's throat tightened. "If you hadn't been there, if you hadn't found a way to get us here . . ." His voice shook. "How we can ever repay . . . the only thing we really have is a thank you."

"Yer welcome. But I really did nothin'. I needed . . . needed ta do 'er fer my ownself . . . to see you and Sara make it ta Indiana." Tears welled in Jimmie's eyes. "Last night when it was all over, I was just a sittin' out here all by myself, thinkin', hopin' everythin' would turn out all right." Jimmie wiped his runny nose with his sleeve. "Was just a sittin' here when I heard baby Zach cry. Hearin' that cry, Edgar . . . well . . . it was like havin' my own boy. Don't think I'll ever forget that. Never will."

CHAPTER TWENTY-EIGHT

Butch

FEEBLE LIGHT LEAKED THROUGH A CRACK IN THE CORNER of Jimmie's one-room shack, softening the meager furnishings: the scarred kitchen table, two small folding chairs, and an ancient mattress which occupied a fourth of the room's space. Despite the cramped quarters, there was tidiness to the place. The covers on the mattress had been folded neatly back, smoothed over where a pillow should've been.

A magazine picture of a locomotive spewing black smoke, pulling a long chain of boxcars, was tacked on the wall above the table. Pinned low, close to the mattress, was a glossy black and white photograph. In it, Sara held baby Zach, Edgar beaming at her side, his arm around her. A much younger Alphonse stood close, and even though most of his body and the tip of his head had been cropped off, there remained enough to see clearly the exuberance on the hobo's face. On the kitchen table lay a neatly folded blanket, a chunk of two-by-four, its ends gnawed to splinters, and a bowl.

Outside, rain pelted against the tar paper and corrugated roof, the drumming so steady it could've been mistaken for a hum.

Alphonse fingered a corner of the blanket. Faded navy blue, stained, flecked with dog hair, the blanket still held legible its origin: C & O RAILROAD, ERIE, PA.

He rose gingerly and peered out the window. Toward the west it was clearing and the rain was easing, and he knew it would soon stop. He moved methodically, gathering the things from the table, and soon made his way along the muddy path past the outhouse. Further on, much closer to the rails than to his shack, a spade stuck from the ground. Butch lay beside the open grave.

In the sprinkling rain, Alphonse spread out the blanket, placed Butch in the center, and tightly wound the blanket around his dog. He tucked the ends in just so, then paused to study the bundle. After adjusting Butch, he redid the blanket. With the C & O RAILROAD lettering now centered, he was at last satisfied and gently lowered the bundle.

He gave the dirt a final pat with the spade, his muttering barely audible, "We made it ta hell 'n gone, didn't we, Butch?" And with that, it was over.

The passing storm had lightened the sky to a hazy blue, and he was turning back toward his shack when heard the far-away freight train charging up from Vandellia. Squatting near the tracks, the wind from the pounding freight ballooned his shirt and hastened its drying. All too soon the train's racket faded to the north.

Pushing to his feet, he was shocked to see a stranger rapidly approach down the center of the rails. *What the . . .* he thought, confused, and moved out in the open to watch. "The bastard walks faster 'n me."

The man strode on long, willowy legs, quickly closing

the distance. He popped from the tracks, eased down the rail bed, and hoofed toward Alphonse, who stood staring, his tan and weathered face perplexed.

Alphonse couldn't help it, and knew it was impolite, but he couldn't take his eyes from the man's incredible grin. There was no getting around it, the man's mouth was peculiar. His grin exposed an immense row of immaculate white teeth, none of them crooked, all precisely spaced like a picture of teeth you'd see at a dentist office. To Alphonse, still many paces away, the teeth were an oddity, extra long and wide, as if the man himself were insignificant as he followed behind his gigantic, benevolent smile.

The smile bellowed, "Howdy do, stranger!"

Stunned, Alphonse couldn't keep from staring.

"Damn nice day! Hell, I'm already dry."

The man behind the grin was skinny and hairy. Thick black hair matted his hatless head and merged into a full beard. His filthy clothes were worn through at the joints. He wore thick-soled boots and lugged a carpet bag, which he dropped to the ground as he shoved out his hand.

"You can call me Goodman."

Alphonse shook the hand automatically.

"Most call me Jimmy." The stranger pumped Alphonse's hand. "Jimmy Goodman."

Alphonse stared at Goodman's mouth forming the words.

"Gotta name, old timer?"

Alphonse blinked and shook his head from the stare. "Go by Alphonse, these days."

"That yer shack?"

"Yep," Alphonse said pointing over his shoulder. "Ain't much."

"Headin' ta California, I am."

A smile slowly sprouted across Alphonse's face. "Californie, ya say?"

"That's where I'm aimin'."

"Goodman, would ya . . ."

"Jimmy."

Alphonse chuckled and stuffed his arms in his bibs. "Jimmy, would ya like ta have a visit, take a load off?"

"Damn right I would!"

They sat at the picnic table, its top still puddled with water.

"Ya want anythin', Good . . . Jimmy? Might have a chunk a cheese somewhere."

"This here water's just fine."

"Ta Californie, eh?"

"You bet I am."

"Looks ta me like yer headin' the wrong direction."

"Never been one to take the direct route," said Goodman, gulping water. "Figure Fort Wayne then west to St. Louis . . . but I could head to Chicago and then west. Last time there, I ended up in Canada for a year. Pretty country up there."

"Yep . . . damn pretty."

"Colder 'n shit though."

"Colder 'n a witch's tit," said Alphonse, closing his eyes briefly and smiling. "Been ta Californie myself."

"Yeah? Like it?"

"Spent a shit ton a time takin' in that ole Pacific Ocean.

Heard somebody say once she's called the 'ocean of forget-fulness.'"

"Why's that?"

"Hell, don't rightly know, but maybe she's so beautiful ya ferget yer past, yer sorrows."

Alphonse leaned over the table, and as he spoke, his head bobbed a little as he talked.

"The time I tripped ta Californie, she was a damn bitch."

"How so?"

"Ever hear o' 'Black Sunday'?"

"Hell, yeah! Long time ago."

"'Thirty-five, it was. I was there, trippin' a freight through Oklahomy. Never seen anythin' like it, that black blizzard, she came barrelin' down like a tornado spinnin' on its side."

Jimmy's toothy mouth gaped in surprise.

"You were there?"

"Took four days ta clear the dirt off the tracks. Drifted higher 'n a tall squaw's ass, it was. Shit, Jimmy, I seen parts of that ol' Dust Bowl south inta Texas, and way the hell west inta Colorady."

"Damn, Alphonse, you're one seasoned son-of-a-bitch."

"Seen lotsa country." Alphonse straightened himself up and shoved out his chest. "Not much lately, but I've been around."

"Still though," said Goodman. "I 'spect riding the rails back then was a hell shot easier 'n today."

"Why's that?"

"For starters, the freights are a helluva lot faster. Makes it tricky to hop in a car—hell, the bastards even got rid of the damn grab bars."

"Ya still got yer arms and legs."

"Yeah, but ya gotta be damn careful."

Alphonse scratched his whiskers. "Back in my day, I still had ta keep my wits about me."

"Another thing," continued Goodman. "There ain't but a handful riding the rails these days."

"But ya still got yer jungles, don't ya?"

"Big yards mostly. Way off the beaten path."

"And that big ass kettle?" Alphonse studied Goodman's face for clues. "Ya still got those black kettles steamin' in the jungles, don't ya?"

"Damn straight they're there! Wouldn't be right having a jungle without the kettle, now would it?"

"I 'member listenin' ta jokes, 'n stories . . ."

"And they still drink 'shine, Alphonse."

"Sharin' stories 'bout where they been . . . where they're headin'." Alphonse gazed toward the tracks, far beyond Goodman.

Goodman banged his jar against the table, then stood, giving the shack the once over, clearly ready to be on the move again.

Alphonse shot to his feet. "I could find that hunk a cheese, Jimmy."

"Appreciate it. But I get by."

"Got yerself one helluva long walk ahead a ya."

"Don't mind one bit." Goodman lifted his spindly leg and banged his foot against the table. "Got me some mighty fine boots." He lowered his leg and grabbed his carpet bag. "I plumb like ta walk, Alphonse."

Alphonse watched Goodman scramble down the path

past the outhouse and the soft soil that marked Butch's grave, then tracked him scampering along the rail bed, north toward Fort Wayne.

"Them was the days, Butch," he said softly. "Them was the days."

———————

ALPHONSE SPENT MUCH OF THE following morning circling his shack and stomping back and forth between his shack and picnic table, but the truth was, he didn't need to ruminate, for his mind was already made up. He needed to delay work and be done with it, but he didn't want to abandon Edgar and knew he should take his time before charging ahead. He was in for a slow torturous day.

Finally off work that afternoon, but well before the last Mass, he marched straight down the playground toward the church. Eyes narrowed, shoulders squared, he charged up the church steps two at a time. Shoving in the master key, he turned the lock and strode through the main door.

His boots pounded against the marble floor of the center aisle, the sound echoing off the gilded ceiling and stone walls, reverberating through the tremendous space of the empty church. Whipping past the communion rail, he cut straight in front of the altar, and had no sooner pushed through the sacristy's door than the outer door to the causeway swung shut.

Moving deftly through the sacristy, he ignored the pungent smell of old incense and scowled at the details of the room he hated. Light from the ornate window shimmered on the marble countertop and illuminated the open binder listing upcoming funerals, weddings, and special celebrations. A box of Kleenex sat near the sink at the far end of the counter. Religious periodicals rested in a neat stack beside a purple velvet chair, a dog-eared copy of *Mercedes Monthly* tossed casually on its seat cushion. Taking it all in with nothing more than a glance, Alphonse stormed quickly through the door to the causeway outside.

"Brennon! It's time!"

The Monsignor, robed in black, was paused outside the rectory door. He looked up, turning slowly toward Alphonse, then resumed his attention to the letter he held. He skimmed the short message, then carefully folded the paper and slid it back into its envelope. His smile was condescending when he again looked up.

"Time for what, old man?"

"Ya ain't gettin' away with it! Ain't lettin' ya!"

The Monsignor smirked. "The more you slither around my church like Quasimodo, the better."

"The world's gonna know!" Alphonse spit his chaw to the walk. "Bishop, my ass."

"Tell me this isn't about Francis."

"I have proof!"

"You don't have a scrap."

"In black 'n white!"

The Monsignor scoffed and reached for the door handle to enter the rectory.

Alphonse charged and jabbed a finger against the Monsignor's back.

"Yer all high 'n mighty now, but I'll git 'er done!"

The Monsignor twisted around jeering, "And what, exactly, do you think you'll get done?"

"Expose yer sick ass fer what it is! Let this goddamn town know watcha do when the damn doors are closed!"

The Monsignor crossed his arms over his chest and stared calmly down at Alphonse. "You have nothing. You're nothing."

Alphonse held his ground. "Ya were a sick son-a-bitch back in Cleveland, 'n yer still a sick bastard now."

"You—" The Monsignor's face suddenly flushed red as he began cocking an arm.

Alphonse's face lightened. He saw an opening. He wanted, needed, it to happen, to finally see the Monsignor deal with something beyond his control. Alphonse didn't let up.

"Tell me, Brennon, do ya have ta diddle boys ta be bishop?"

The Monsignor lowered his arm and hissed, "Get out of my sight!"

"Got me proof, padre!"

"Revenge! You want revenge?" The Monsignor shoved his jagged grin close to Alphonse's face. "You won't even have that when I'm bishop."

CHAPTER TWENTY-NINE

No Way Back

ALPHONSE COULDN'T WAIT. HE WAS PLAYING HOOKY from work; he'd wanted to let Edgar know about his plans, but didn't since he'd headed toward Vandellia before sunrise. When the first pulse of movement began, he'd been perched atop the broken pallets he'd stacked several feet high in the crotch of the boxcar walls, his wrinkled weathered face grinning like a giddy kid.

A few minutes north of St. Joseph, simply sitting on pallets wouldn't do. With careful, tiny steps for balance, he slowly shuffled about the boxcar. Shards of cardboard and a useless seed bag swirled with grit near the open door of the jostling car. Pausing at the door, he leaned his head far out and marveled at the speed with which the Indiana countryside whizzed past—the telephone poles, the colors of autumn, the neat white farm houses where family men lived out their entire lives trying desperately to scratch contentment from the land—all the while relishing the sound of the clickety-clack beating in time with his hobo brain. *They all can go ta hell*, he thought. He was tripping to Fort Wayne, and come hell or high water, he'd be warming himself by the jungle fire, drinking 'shine and eating hobo stew from the kettle that night.

The bowler he wore, with its dents and scars and decades of forgotten stains, was a trophy of sorts, a badge speaking clearly about his life of wandering. To him the magic of riding the rails again would be incomplete without his bindle. In it he'd arranged fishing string, a couple hooks, a box of Strike Anywhere matches, a pint of Southern Comfort, and an extra pair of socks. He'd thrown it together in a hurry and wasn't clear if he'd need any of it, but to him, a hobo without a bindle was no hobo; it was as integral to riding the freights as the clickety-clack of the iron wheels on the iron rails.

From the far end of the car all the way to the door, crates had been stacked and strapped in place. They were stamped for Sears-Chicago and labeled TE-PO-CO TOILET FIXTURES, with a tagline beneath: "Seats Conforming to Nature's Curves." Alphonse leaned his shoulder against the door jam, eyeing the cargo, a grin on his face.

Miles had built upon miles when he finally pulled open his bindle and brought out the pint. Unscrewing the top, he held it up to light and just before swigging, he clicked his tongue and gave a sharp nod, a toast, a salute, to the life he'd dearly missed.

He savored a slow gulp and tilted the bottle for second swig, but stopped and eyed the level in the bottle. As if mowed down by a runaway freight, it hit him full force, and he trembled with the power of a sudden burgeoning fear. Twisting the cap on the pint, he sank slowly down the door jam and slumped against the pallets. He let the pint fall away and splinter against the receding rails.

His intense, vivid dream of glimpsing again the pulse of the hobo jungle vanished as the clickety-clack of the rails all but faded away. St. Joseph—its church and bell tower, Edgar and his boys, the Monsignor and the sins, all of it he could not escape. Even for this one day trying to unearth a former life, attempting to savor again the joy of the jungle, feel again the warmth of the kettle fire, that other life was gone. Alphonse was hobbled, handicapped with the present he could not run from, chained to a loyalty and hatred from which he could find no relief.

The freight suddenly lurched. Couplings crashed; steam whooshed. The rhythm of the rails slowed. Alphonse braced himself against the door jam on wobbly legs and tried shaking his head clear of its spiraling descent as he hopelessly watched the sign for Fort Wayne come into view. Finally stopped, he turned and canvassed the crates of toilet seats, the grit and the walls, the pallets where he'd sat, his bindle still propped in the corner. Sealing his eyes briefly, his nose inhaling a huge breath, he held for a moment the memory of smells, the sensations of the way it had always been.

He'd made it to Fort Wayne, but now it meant nothing. He clutched his hip and eased himself down to sit on the door jam. With his fingers cramping against the door frame and his legs dangling yards above the rail bed, he swallowed hard then released his grip. Like a discarded sack of grain, he thudded in a puff of dust against the ground.

Not bothering to swipe away the dust or the gravel from his bibs, he hobbled along the rails searching the black engines for a sign. Recognizing the southbound through Vandellia, he hurried the best he could to the boxcar's open door. His shoulders level with the bottom edge of the door, he managed to swing in an arm and yank out the pallets. Just barely high enough now, he was able to clamber up and pull himself inside.

He huddled far back in the car, his forearms anchored to his knees, and it wasn't until the freight had fully stopped in Vandellia that he lifted his head up from his bracing hands. Gazing out the door at the small yard, tears grooving through the dirt of his wizened face, it took many moments for the booming voice to register.

"Hey you! Old timer!"

Alphonse jerked around. There was nowhere to hide.

"Best climb on outta there."

"Yes, sir." Alphonse took a shaky step toward the boxcar door.

Hands propped on hips, the man cocked his head. He looked confused. Taking his time to gauge the tattered old man teetering in the door, a smile gradually crept across the railroader's face.

"Where the hell did you come from?"

"Well, young fella, I was born in Macon, Georgia."

"You didn't just come from Georgia with nothin'!"

"Travelin' light." He swiped at his eyes. "Headin' back ta St. Joseph."

"I'll be damned . . ." The man extended a hand to help him down. "If you ain't one helluva fossil."

"Ya haulin' me ta the clink?"

"What?"

"You the yard bull?"

"The yard—what the hell's that? C'mon, I'll get you down."

Warily, Alphonse lowered his butt to the floor. "Now that's right friendly."

"It's damn high for a codger," the man said as he helped Alphonse half-slide, half-fall from the car.

Shifting his feet to steady his standing, Alphonse pronounced, "Coulda made 'er with the grab bars. Why ya boys got rid a 'em, I'll never know."

Unable to take his eyes from Alphonse, the man spoke slowly in gentle tones as if his voice would break something, "You know, I haven't seen the likes of you in a coon's age."

"Ain't seen many like you neither. I'm mighty appreciative of ya not callin' the coppers."

"Why would I do that?"

"Fer stealin' a ride."

The man chuckled. "Times've changed."

Alphonse tipped his bowler. "That they have, they have fer damn sure."

He clamped his hat back firmly on his head, turned and began walking.

"Hold on. St. Joseph must be at least a ten mile walk."

Alphonse stopped only for a second, then gave a salute over his shoulder, saying, "In my day I was a walker . . . I surely was."

THE SHADOWS WERE GROWING LONG when Edgar spied Francis's bike parked against the tree whose limbs drooped far out over the canal. Squinting, he could make out bobbers dangling from its limbs, and though he'd not been there in years, he was sure some had to be his son's. While Alphonse's disgusting accusations still gnawed at his brain, and he'd paid closer attention to his son's behavior as of late, Edgar still couldn't comprehend, let alone accept, the horrific details of the bell tower and Francis. Yet that afternoon there was something he couldn't explain which compelled him to trudge to The End to seek out his son.

Francis sat alert on a grassy hillock, his cane pole held in a prop he'd pushed in the ground close by his feet. Unseen, Edgar hunkered down on a log to watch.

It didn't take long before the bobber began twitching sideways, but there was no hoopla, no hopeful shouts for a prize blue cat, no joy of anticipation coating the young face. Francis barely moved. But when the bobber dipped beneath the surface, Francis quickly grabbed his pole and raised a wriggling fish into the air. He gently lowered the blue gill to the bank, a faint smile finally sprouting on his face.

Edgar could make out the outline of his son as he held the fish up to the light and then released it back to the placid canal, and he became convinced that surely everything must be all right, as he marveled at how naturally his son laced another worm to the hook.

At last, Edgar was ready and after clearing his throat loudly, he clomped toward Francis and plopped down close by.

Like some hidden secret of his had been discovered,

Francis spun around, even more alarmed when he saw who it was.

"Dad! What're you doing here?"

"Always liked watching you fish, ever since you were a squirt."

Francis frowned, saying quietly, "You walked all the way down here?"

"It's okay, ain't it?"

"S'pose so."

"Saw you catch that fish."

"It wasn't even close to the crappies we used ta get at St. Mary's."

"But you looked happy for the catch anyway."

"Like catching any fish."

Francis locked his sight on the bobber while Edgar pulled grass and made a small pile between his feet. For a long time they simple sat in the quiet.

Finally, Edgar shrugged and said awkwardly, "With you not working in the boiler room all summer, we haven't had much time together."

The bobber suddenly dipped. Francis grabbed the pole. He released the blue gill without a hint of pleasure, while his dad sported an exaggerated smile that Francis ignored.

Francis dug a juicy worm from a can, stabbed it on his hook, and after adjusting the bobber, he winged his new offering far out to the canal. As he settled down to wait, Edgar looked on silently, biding his time, all the while unable to steady his galloping mind.

He said at last, "Reckon it feels good to be back in school."

"Guess so."

"Probably didn't seem like you had much of a vacation, did it?"

Francis shrugged. "Getting sick really messed things up."

"Bet it did."

Francis stared out across the canal saying, "Feels like I let you down." He hunched his shoulders. "You 'n Zach doin' everything at the start of the year 'n all."

"Nobody plans to get sick." Edgar clawed the dirt with his heel. He waited a tad, then continued clumsily, "And I'm sorry your trapping didn't work out."

"What do you mean didn't work out!" Francis shot him a panicked look. "You talked to Alphonse, didn't you?"

"Always do, but not much about that."

With a scowl. "What'd he say?"

"Everybody messes up, Francis." Edgar kneaded his fists. "Wish you would've told me when it happened."

"Didn't think you'd wanna be bothered." Francis slumped. "Bein' busy and all."

"I should've figured something was up."

"Mom says people have enough of their own bad things to worry about." Briefly, he looked square at his Dad. "I hide bad stuff pretty good."

Edgar tensed.

Francis reeled in to check his bait and tossed it back, then leaned close toward his dad, a sudden smile lighting up his face. "But I got two other rats, Dad!"

"You did?"

"Yep!" Francis blurted quickly. "Went to sell them at the junkyard! I was gonna buy Zach a new basketball."

"Why would . . ." Edgar caught himself. "I know he would've liked it."

"I wanted to see Zach's face when I gave him a new ball that I bought myself."

"I would've liked to see yours."

"Huh?"

"You would've been damn happy to do it."

"Yeah." He thought for a moment. "But what I really wanted was to make a bunch of money 'n give it to you 'n Mom."

"What? That's why you wanted to trap rats?"

"Yep!"

"You shouldn't worry . . ." He patted Francis on the knee then fell silent.

"But it didn't go so good at the junkyard. Watney said my rats were sewer rats, said he'd give me a quarter for both, a measly quarter." Francis shook his head. "He laughed at me, Dad."

"That's a shame. Don't have much use for that ass either."

"Alphonse told ya about the rat feet, didn't he?"

"He mentioned it."

"I was at the marsh early, Dad, just like I promised."

"You didn't mean for it to happen."

"I don't know where all my time goes. At the marsh—I guess just daydreaming. That's why those rats are crippled."

"They'll survive just fine."

"Seems I can't do anything right."

"Feel that way a lot of times myself."

"At The End here, it feels okay. But everywhere else—I

just get to thinking and the next thing I know—it doesn't matter what it is, I'm always late."

"Probably has to do with you being sick like you were."

"Heck Dad, it started back around the Fourth of July."

"That long ago?" Edgar's face grew white, his face now wet with sweat. "Do you think it mighta started when you stayed late cleaning the bell tower?"

"Maybe . . . somewhere around there."

"Remember anything?" He paused, desperate to find the right words. "Remember anything . . . uh . . . weird happening when you cleaned the bell tower with the Monsignor? What I mean is . . ."

"Got a bite! Dad!"

Edgar bowed his head and stayed seated as Francis sprang to his feet and lifted the small fish from the canal.

"Another blue gill. Wish it was a cat!"

Releasing it, Francis then wound his line around the pole. After emptying his worm can in the weeds, he waited for his dad to get up before asking, "You all right, Dad?"

"Of course."

Francis bubbled. "It was fun havin' you here to watch! Just as good as Alphonse."

"I liked it too. I'm just glad you and Alphonse have been able to spend time together this summer."

"He's fun, Dad. But he sure can get mad."

"Don't I know it."

"Thing I don't get . . . I see the way he watches Zach play basketball, but with me it's different."

"You're special to him."

"Did Zach do something wrong?"

"Of course not. Alphonse loves Zach and you both the same."

"But I don't get why he treats me so different."

"You two boys are night and day. Even when he was little, Zach's always liked being around others, being out front doing things like playing basketball." They began sauntering toward the bike. "You like being alone, like the outdoors and fishing. I suppose you remind Alphonse of when he was your age . . . quiet, by yourself, always wanting to help others when you can."

"Still doesn't make a whole lot of sense."

"We don't talk about it much, but remember Alphonse is your godfather."

"I never think about that."

"But he does."

"Alphonse ain't religious."

"You might say you've been fishing in his church." Edgar gestured across the banks of the canal.

"What?"

"That man's spent his whole life outdoors, riding the rails from ocean to ocean, going to bed under the stars. He's been a lot of places, seen lotsa stuff, but for him, sitting here by the canal watching his godson fish . . . well, for Alphonse, I bet that's like going to Mass."

Edgar reached for the fishing pole.

"I got it, Dad."

"I know, but you're riding your bike."

Francis grabbed the handlebars, but didn't climb on. Down the dirt path and onto the road, he beamed a tremendous smile. His dad, though, carrying the cane pole in his meaty hand, showed no joy, and his eyes clouded with some future dread coloring his face.

"Dad! Zach's first game's Friday!"

"Don't I know it!" He rested his hand gently on Francis's shoulder as they sauntered toward home. "Thank God. It's about time." Distracted briefly, his exhale was loud and long. "I'd say we all could use a breather."

CHAPTER THIRTY

Edgar's Coal-Hardened Fist

IT WAS CLOSE TO TEN IN THE MORNING, A SCHOOL DAY. Francis had hustled home and bounded up the stairs, where he found Zach sitting on the edge of the bed, looking confused and sour. Catching his breath, Francis blurted, "What's wrong with Dad?"

Zach glared. "Christ, what're you doing home?"

"Sister Loyola wanted me to check. Said Dad didn't show up for work."

"He's downstairs in the bedroom."

"He ain't sick, is he?"

"Never heard Mom and Dad fight like that before."

"Geeze, Zach." Francis paced; the linoleum squeaked. "Something bad's happening."

"Got that right."

Francis waited, but Zach didn't elaborate. "So why are you home?"

"Season opens Friday, so no P.E." Looking straight ahead, Zach paused and stared blankly. "Damn, Francis, it was ugly."

"What was it about?"

"Dad kept yelling something about Alphonse," said Zach. "Mom just clammed up and took off."

"Where'd she go?"

"Probably the grocery."

"What ya think we should do?"

"Hell if I know."

"Should we go downstairs and check?"

"No way! Ain't gettin' close to him."

Francis rocked his feet against a squeaky spot, making it squeak over and over. "It's really getting screwy. Yesterday Alphonse didn't show up for work either. And now Dad." He kept rocking. "Dang, don'tcha think that's pretty strange."

"Will you stop that! Christ."

Francis started walking again.

"And quit pacing!"

"But—" Francis stood awkwardly, hands outstretched.

"Oh, hell, just sit on the bed." Zach moved over to make room. "You ain't sick anymore. You might as well sleep back up here, too."

"Really, Zach?"

"Christ, yes! Especially with the way it's been going downstairs."

Francis sat tentatively on the bed's edge. His quick smile said relief at last, and he kept it hidden from his brother.

It was quiet for a bit before Zach said flatly, "Just so ya know, I saw what happened yesterday."

"What?"

"On the playground." Zach glanced at Francis. "Me 'n Rupe've had our eyes on that asshole, Jettinghoff."

"Oh, that." Francis tucked his feet up to sit cross-legged. "He tries pushing his weight around with everybody."

"I didn't like what he called you. Clinker's one thing but—if Rupe hadn't held me back I would've punched his F'n lights out."

"You would?"

"Damn straight, I—"

"You two get down here!" Edgar's stony voice boomed up the staircase.

Rolling his eyes, Zach whipped down the steps, with Francis close behind.

Edgar's face was blotchy and unshaven, his black hair tangled and pressed flat in places, and his wrinkled clothes made it obvious that he'd slept in them. He certainly hadn't taken his morning bath, which only deepened the mystery. His hands were coiled tightly into fists, his huge knuckles turning white.

"What're you two doing home?"

Francis peeped a few words about Sister Loyola.

Edgar growled, "Get back to school!"

"But, Dad—" tried Zach.

"Both of you! Now!"

On their way to back to school, Francis asked, "Did ya see his fists Zach?"

EDGAR HAD EVERY INTENTION OF going to work that morning, but after his blow-up with Sara, he couldn't bring himself to head there. He couldn't deal with the sinking, helpless feeling of forever tending to the boilers, the coal, the pumps and soot, the incessant demands of the nuns.

Taking his time, minutes after his boys were out of sight, he decided to take the long way to work. His tromp down Third Street was slow. He then hooked a left on Franklin. In turmoil, head down, he listened to his work shoes crunching pigeon shit. As he marched closer, he felt the powerful need to avoid looking up at the church steeple, the place where his imagination would run horribly free.

The black Mercedes squatted in the driveway of the rectory, its trunk yawning wide. The Monsignor was bent over, half hidden in the trunk. Two bags and several boxes waited close by.

Across the street, third graders filled the playground with noisy chaos and fun. A shrill whistle signaled the end of recess, and strategically placed nuns began herding the children into lines before marching them back inside.

Spying the Monsignor from across Second, Edgar suddenly balked. *Christ, it's all plain as day right now*, he thought. *The asshole's already packin'. It's now or never.* At last, he'd made room in his brain for the unspeakable, and understood that it was finally time to face his dread, to confront its source once and for all. Charging close, he halted abruptly behind the Monsignor and spewed out instantly, "See ya can't get out of town fast enough."

Startled, the Monsignor cracked his head against the underside of the trunk lid, then turned around to find Edgar.

"Ah, Edgar. I was hoping to have a word with you before I left."

"Doubt that."

"Excuse me?"

"You were hoping to never see me again."

The Monsignor slapped the dust from his hands. "I don't much care for your tone this morning."

"You ain't leavin' till you hear me out."

The Monsignor snorted and turned to pick up the larger of his two suitcases while Edgar took note of the tire iron lying tantalizingly close near the car.

Detached as if he were not there, as if he were watching himself, he slid his hand around the cold metal, lifted the iron, and tapped it against his free hand as if gauging its weight.

The Monsignor arched an eyebrow and slid the suitcase into the trunk smirking, "What do you expect to accomplish with that?"

"Maybe find a little justice."

"That's a bit radical, but say your piece, Edgar." He lifted the second suitcase. "I'm busy."

Edgar shifted the iron from hand to hand. "Francis and I had a long heart-to-heart."

"We've been over this before—"

"Francis doesn't lie!" He pointed the iron directly at the Monsignor's face. "I know what you did!" He felt the cold, heavy iron; he felt the scalding, pounding in his ears.

"I'm a bishop!"

"You're a sick son-of-a-bitch!"

The Monsignor's dark eyes narrowed. "Your friend's the one who's sick."

"Bullshit! Yesterday I saw it all in my son's face! I saw

every damn Friday he spent with you in that filthy bell tower."

The Monsignor leaned in close. "You'll lose everything —your job, your town," he said softly as if letting Edgar in on a secret. "And God only knows how badly you'll hurt your family."

Edgar gripped the tire iron with both hands, holding it close to his chest and stammered, "You—you—"

The Monsignor gave a satisfied chuckle saying, "Or did you forget you're half blind? Besides, you're making a fool of yourself with that . . . that weapon."

Edgar's thoughts folded and refolded, and he felt himself falling away, stranded and alone. He stared down at the iron in his hand as if seeing it for the first time. A sudden shriek flew from his mouth, as he sent the tire iron winging toward the garage.

The Monsignor smirked. "Take a deep breath, Edgar, and I'll explain the reality of what's happening."

Edgar trembled; his mouth quivered.

The Monsignor, hands to his waist, leaned back casually, confidently against the trunk of his black Mercedes. His smile was soft, his voice gentle as if he were helping a boy with a puzzle. "Boys Francis's age are influenced by all sorts of things," he slowly illustrated. "Unfortunately, Alphonse is quite a different man from the one who helped you and Sara years ago." He added a slight bob of the head to his smile. "Quite frankly, I'm worried about Francis, too." He then said in lower tones, "Hopefully it isn't too late."

Edgar felt himself waver, doubt creeping in.

"Alphonse has infected you with his wild fantasies.

Imagine how much worse it must've been for Francis. Promise me you'll separate your son from his—from that—influence."

Edgar tried shaking his head clear but the Monsignor pressed on. "Think, Edgar. Francis has never said a bad word about me, has he?"

The more he listened, the more each word grew heavier as Edgar bowed his head under the weight and closed his eyes.

"I didn't think so, Edgar."

Edgar thought of yesterday, recalled again Francis's words.

"I lost that whole day . . . and now those rats are crippled . . . I feel awful, Dad."

Edgar slowly lifted his head, his eyes clearing, his voice growing strong.

"It all came clear yesterday at the canal with my son."

"And just like that, Alphonse is the hero?"

"In his wildest dream, Alphonse couldn't make this garbage up."

"He did!"

"Until yesterday, I was blind." Edgar's throat tightened yet he managed to belt out, "You took advantage of my boy!"

The Monsignor stepped closer and his self-assured smile stretched tight his jagged scar.

"But you see . . ." The Monsignor smirked, his small black raven eyes unblinking, impenetrable and confident. "I'm a servant of the Lord."

"You raped my son!"

"And you'll never be anything more than a puny janitor."

Seemingly of its own accord, Edgar's arm cocked, readied, then rocketed.

Like an avalanche, his coal-hardened fist smashed against the Monsignor's condescending face, striking so hard and suddenly, it shot the Monsignor off his feet, driving him down against the concrete onto his back. His black cassock floated in the air, then settled softly just above the knees, his anemic legs glowing white in the morning sun.

CHAPTER THIRTY-ONE

Zach's First Basketball Game

AT LONG LAST, ZACH'S FIRST BASKETBALL GAME HAD arrived. Francis figured he hadn't looked forward to a Friday since last spring when school was nearly out for the summer, when he'd finally be tearing off on his bike to The End.

By the time Francis hoofed it to Alphonse's shack, he was so nervous he could hardly contain himself. The shack door gaped open when he hopped up to the porch. But right off, he was miffed. Alphonse was just sitting at his kitchen table talking to the air as if his dog were still alive: "Been waitin' fer this a long time, Butch . . . things've been awful bad." Water dripped from his wet hair to his bare chest. A bit of blood-spotted paper stuck to his cheek.

Inside, Francis shifted on his feet impatiently. "Hurry, Alphonse. You need to finish getting ready. I wanna get close to the front."

Nonchalant, Alphonse looked up grinning.

"S'pose ya do."

"Maybe you should start puttin' on a shirt."

Alphonse's toothy smile broadened. "In due time, my man, in due time."

"Alphonse—"

"Ya know Francis, I'm feelin' awful good." His ancient eyes flickered clear and young. "After our piss poor summer and that prick finally leavin', it's about goddamn time we enjoy ourselves a little."

Francis rolled his eyes.

"So don't ya think we oughtta get going?"

"We need ta savor the moment."

"Geeze—Alphonse."

"It's like if ya haven't had a pie in a helluva long spell, the last thin' ya wanna do is gulp it down. You'd a missed the tastin'."

Francis gave a little snort.

Alphonse laughed. "Glad ya agree."

Alphonse finally rose from his chair and lifted his well-mended shirt from its wall peg when Francis finally noticed. "Holy moly, Alphonse! You shaved!"

"Don't tackle the job often," he said, running his fingertips along his jaw. "Only one nick."

"And you washed your hair?"

"That I did. Can't be too spruced up for a big night." Painfully slow for Francis to watch, Alphonse pushed his arms through the sleeves of his shirt. "Be a damn hoot just walkin' there."

Alphonse quickly sat back down then leaned back in his chair and put his hands behind his head.

Francis groaned. "We'd be ready if you'd finish getting dressed."

"We gots time, Francis."

Francis refused to return his smile. "Don'tcha wanna get a good seat?"

"Hell, ya know I do. Always like bein' close ta the action."

After several thoughtful minutes, Alphonse got up and began buttoning his shirt. Suddenly giddy again, he leaned close to the tiny mirror tacked to the wall.

"Ya know Francis . . . I used ta be a looker. Had more women than I could shake a stick at. One helluva looker I was, yesiree Bob."

"Good for you, now let's get goin'."

Francis grabbed Alphonse by the arm and began urging him toward the door.

Once outside on the porch, Francis finally noticed that his friend had done more than wash his hair and shave.

Alphonse's gray hair was slicked back, and it was obvious where he'd sheared blunt the ends. There were no grease stains on the knees of his bibs, no caked dirt on the sides of his boots. The straps of his overalls lay neatly against his clean shirt.

"You look . . . nice, Alphonse."

"That's it?" He winked. "S'pose 'nice' is nice."

Shoulders squared, he strolled down Franklin, puffing a stogie and pointing at odd things as though he were a tour guide. Francis danced along impatiently by his side.

They hadn't gone more than a block or so down Franklin before people began hustling past. High schoolers coagulated and yapped, and whole families moved around them swiftly, anxious to get there.

"Everybody's hurrying," Francis complained.

"A coon's age ago, my Ma told me, 'Ya have ta stop 'n smell the roses.'"

"The front seats are the best," protested Francis, more than a tad louder.

"Now look at that collie sittin' on that porch. They're fine dogs, mind ya. Butch was, too, in his heyday. He never gave a shit that he was old . . . could care less that his hip wasn't worth a good goddamn." Alphonse waved his stogie in a broad gesture. "People could learn a lot from their dogs."

"You doing this on purpose, Alphonse?" Francis asked through tight lips.

"Now take a gander at that cloud."

Francis groaned.

"That big fluffy one right there," Alphonse pointed. "I say she's shaped like a lion."

"Whatever you say."

"Now hold on, boy. She's a changin'. By Christ, she's startin' ta look like Butch . . . whatcha think, Francis?"

Francis, not bothering to look up, stuffed his hands in his pockets and sighed. "Sure, just like Butch."

"I plumb enjoy lookin' up at the sky."

"That's nice."

"Spent almost thirty years sleepin' under the stars."

"Doesn't everybody?"

"All right, all right. Just playin'." Alphonse chuckled and flipped his stogie at a hedge. "Reckon she's time ta scoot."

As they neared the school, the crowd thickened and the hundreds of excited voices tumbled into a loud steady buzz. From Monroe Street, even as far as Fourth, people sped along. At the overflowing parking lot, more than a block away from the high school, people jockeyed for a space. Elbows elbowed elbows; a man shoved his kid in front to wedge himself forward. It wasn't until they were almost there before Francis began noticing that folks were giving him and Alphonse a wide berth—a tiny island in a rowdy sea that gradually shifted ahead to get in the high school's main door.

Once inside, the crowd condensed further, and its collective energy carried Alphonse and Francis along as if there was no need to walk at all. They surged past the back-lit trophy case and its dozens of gold plastic trophies giving tribute to former glories, past the sparkling banner above it that proclaimed "St. Joseph Blue Jays" in blue and gold, past the principal's office on the left and at last through the double doors into the gym, where raucous noise thundered. Francis's eyes widened: *this must be the biggest crowd ever*, he thought.

In making their way through the crowd, Alphonse's demeanor had changed. No longer teasing, easy-as-it-goes, he'd become jittery, tense, and pale. Gone was his casual stroll, and as they'd passed through the doors, he tried nervously to pat his hair back in place.

A thousand shoes stomped out the rhythm against wooden bleachers. A thousand eyes scanned for a hint of their team.

When Alphonse finally spotted Edgar, his tenseness suddenly dissolved. He pointed. "There's yer dad!"

"Dad? Where?"

"Yer dad reserved us some fine seats." Alphonse clapped Francis on the shoulder. "We had 'er all planned out, Francis."

"You and Dad?"

"Damn straight we did."

Edgar sat four rows up in the center, balancing three sacks of popcorn in his lap. Francis took two steps at a time, Alphonse trailing behind. They'd just made it to their row when the PA announcer's voice boomed through the gymnasium.

WELCOME . . .

TO THE OPENING GAME OF OUR 1959 BASKETBALL SEASON . . .

MAKE SOME NOISE FOR YOUR . . . VERY OWN . . . ST. JOSEPH BLUE JAYS!

As the place erupted, Francis squeezed in next to his dad, while Alphonse leaned forward and gave Edgar a thumbs-up. He yelled across Francis, "Ya ready!"

Edgar put his hand to his ear; Alphonse bellowed again.

"Ready fer Zach?"

Edgar nodded, and after fumbling with his own thumbs-up, he passed bags of popcorn to Alphonse and Francis.

Alphonse yelled, "Thought Sara'd be here."

"She was afraid she'd get too nervous," Edgar yelled back. "I know for a fact she's got the radio blaring in the kitchen."

WOULD YOU PLEASE STAND FOR OUR NATIONAL ANTHEM?

Francis peeked at Alphonse, who stood reverently, his hand over his heart. The last note had no sooner stopped ringing before "When the Saints Go Marching In" began pulsing through the auditorium. A few bars into the song, cheerleaders bopped to center court and held up a gigantic

Blue Jay banner. One by one, the varsity show-boated through it. The crowd exploded in cheers and foot stomps as the whole team worked through its warm-ups to the beat.

All was ready at last. The teams sprinted to their benches while the gym throbbed with the building music. Francis chomped popcorn. Edgar leaned far forward straining to make out the players, searching for Zach, while Alphonse took in everything, each player, the crowd, the coach doling out last minute instructions.

Their opposition, Fort Jennings, hailed from twenty or so miles west down Highway 30 and was much smaller than St. Joseph. The several dozen visiting folks at the game took it seriously, but years ago they'd come to understand that their annual game with the Blue Jays was merely a warm up for the defending champs, and that St. Joseph used this match-up more as an introduction of its players than viewing the Jennings' Wildcats as any real competition.

A frenzied drum roll crescendoed to a cymbal clash.

As each home player was introduced, the place rocked louder. "At guard . . . Jimmie Grothouse . . . at the other guard, Jerry Carter . . . and last at center, Larry Menke . . ." In the din, the teams lined up at half court, the referee tossed the ball high, and the Blue Jay's opening foray into their new basketball season began.

Francis tried nudging Alphonse, who was standing stiff as if still at attention for the anthem, but Alphonse was so engrossed in eyeing the Blue Jays' bench, he never noticed.

Edgar turned and roared at Francis, "They should've announced all the damn players!"

"They only announce the starting line-up! He'll get his turn, Dad!"

From the opening tip-off, it was obvious why the case in the front hall was crammed with trophies. There was no doubt that this year, the Blue Jays would again go far in the state tournament.

St. Joseph swarmed on defense while their offense seemed to score at will. By halftime, the team was politely cruising over Fort Jennings by fifteen. Despite the score, the entire first half Edgar, Francis, and Alphonse remained on the edge of their seats and never took their eyes from the court. Their breath caught at every whistle, and, though they never voiced it, each knew that what they anxiously waited for was Zach's first appearance in a varsity game. But at halftime, Zach still remained on the bench.

While the band played its program at center court, people plowed back and forth, desperate for snacks and toilets.

Francis elbowed past Alphonse. "You need to move. I gotta use the bathroom."

Edgar, shouting to be heard over the din, said, "Quite the shindig! Whatcha think, Alphonse?"

"There's a shit ton a people 'n noise!" Alphonse scooted next to Edgar. "All this hoopla gots me quiverin' like a leaf. But damn if Zach don't look good in his uniform! Looks strong!"

"Coach is groomin' him for strong forward."

Alphonse suddenly soured. "Glad that prick ain't sittin' on the bench tonight."

Grimacing, Edgar said, "Has me worried."

"Ya clocked that bastard pretty damn good. Too bad the shiner ya gave him ain't permanent."

"Need to hash it out with you later."

Spotting Francis in the crowd below, Alphonse pointed and said, "Doubt that he'll follow his brother's footsteps."

"He never cared much for basketball."

Alphonse rubbed the smoothness of his cheeks. "Wasn't talkin'bout basketball. Francis'll find his own way."

"Hope you're right." Edgar glanced at Alphonse. "I appreciate you cleaning up for the occasion tonight. But you look like you got more brewin' than just Zach's basketball game."

"I surely do, Edgar. Maybe after the game, I could run a few things by ya."

As the announcer thundered over the PA, Francis pushed through the throng to his seat.

"Ya get lost?" Alphonse teased, blocking the way.

"Man, was it crowded . . . move over Alphonse."

"Yer son's gettin' bossy, Edgar."

"C'mon! It's about to start."

In the second half, the game never seesawed, and the Blue Jays easily stayed far ahead. The crowd glided through the third period and into the fourth, and that they were far less boisterous had nothing to do with boredom, nor relishing every basket the Blue Jays made; they'd simply grown accustomed to expecting no less than a sound trouncing.

In spite of the lead, both Edgar and Francis remained alert and antsy, popping to their feet at nearly every play. Alphonse, though, didn't jump up or yell; instead he stayed locked in place, scrutinizing the court and keeping track of Zach on the bench.

The game was winding down when Alphonse suddenly jumped to his feet and began smacking his thighs repeatedly. He jabbed Francis hard in the ribs.

His voice dripping with anxiety, Alphonse said softly and reverently to only himself, "Christ almighty . . . he's a goin' in."

"Holy moly! Dad!"

After a piercing whistle, Zach caught the pass. His face paling in panic, he frantically searched the bench for a clue. Calling time-out, the coach patted Rupert on the butt and shoved him toward the scorer's table.

With just over a minute left in the game, all was winding down and many began filing toward the exits. The Sadlers and Alphonse though remained standing, united in the bleachers. They wouldn't budge one iota until the final buzzer.

A nervous kid had the ball when Rupert popped out to catch his pass. Rupert dribbled tentatively to his right, did a donut, then was dribbling left when he found Zach open close to the basket. The ball arced, a long soundless curve that felt like slow motion to those watching, and at last reached Zach's panicked grab. A pause, then Zach spun and leaped, and his arm shot up, his hand released. The ball banked off the white square and fell through the hoop for the final score.

Zach looked surprised and a little confused, but as the realization hit, he began to grin and was soon jumping and whooping with Rupert and their teammates.

Alphonse muttered, "Well . . . I'll be go ta grass," then he lunged around Francis and grabbed Edgar as if his world would stop spinning.

"We gotta get down there!"

Edgar led the way, a forward wedge against the tide pouring toward the exits. Laughs, blue, pats on the back, jabs, gold, the team was packed so tight they moved toward the hall as one.

"They're headin' to the locker room," Edgar called over his shoulder. "We can't get through!"

"She'll wait, Edgar!" Alphonse tugged Edgar's arm.

"Son-a-bitch, Zach scored a basket!"

"Hell, yes, he did!"

The gym was emptying fast when Alphonse nodded toward the bleachers. "Looky there, Edgar! Seems Francis has found himself a girl."

"Well, I'll be . . . don't stare, Alphonse!"

Outside the high school, a few stragglers still gabbed, but nearly everyone had gone by the time Alphonse and Edgar eased down to sit on a school bench away from the glaring lights of the entrance.

"Had ourselves one mighty fine night, Edgar."

"That we have."

Edgar suddenly turned serious. "What about the Monsignor?"

"Hope ya ain't worried about the coppers, Edgar."

"Don't know what I'd do if the police knocked on my door."

"If I know anythin', that bastard's hidin', 'n he ain't gonna say shit ta anybody." Alphonse pulled out a stogie and studied it. "Wish I'd a been there, Edgar. I surely wish I coulda seen his face." Alphonse rolled the stogie thoughtfully between his thumb and finger. "I might have a card left ta play." He shook his head doubtfully. "It's a damn long shot."

"Card?"

"Maybe . . . Hell, I don't know." He lit the stogie and took a long draw.

Edgar waited but it was obvious that Alphonse wasn't going to elaborate. He finally stood up and stretched his back. "I'm bushed. Wanna get home and talk to Sara about Zach's first game."

———————

ALPHONSE STARED AFTER EDGAR AS he disappeared in the darkness beyond the street lamp. The basketball game, Edgar, and the boys all vanished as he turned up Second toward the colossal hulk of the church, its steeple knifing high into the black sky.

She's now or never, he thought.

He skirted the back of the church and scampered up the stairs the altar boys used, unlocked the door, and slipped inside. On the top shelf in a back closet, he located the sack he'd hidden days before.

He moved quickly from the altar boys' room to the sacristy and flipped on the light. Grabbing a pen next to the church planner on the Monsignor's desk, he was about to scrawl a note on the bag, but thought for a moment, then tossed the pen aside, saying out loud, "The prick'll know."

He set the bag squarely on top of the planner, scanning the room he despised. His grimace changed to a smirk as he glanced at the control panel for the bells.

He left the light on and retreated back the way he'd come, out into the coffin-black night.

CHAPTER THIRTY-TWO

Jimmy Goodman

IT WAS LATE, THE NIGHT HAD TURNED COLD, AND ALPHONSE had pulled his coat high on his neck as he slipped from the church down Second. Disjointed thoughts tromped through his brain—the joy of Zach's basketball game, fear that his plan was only wishful thinking, hope that time would erase his hatred and the hideous details of what he knew to be true, the sinking, helpless feeling that the Monsignor would again escape.

He'd just turned onto the brick street of Pierce when he first heard the footsteps. There was no mistaking it; someone was following him. Pausing and cocking his ear, his senses searched the blackness, but there was nothing but silence.

Continuing on again, wary, the footfalls at his back returned instantly.

He quickened his pace. He ducked down an alley. Had the Monsignor seen him at the church? Would he actually be following him to try and catch him off guard? Alphonse peered around the corner, his heart pounding.

A silhouette paused at the intersection, then turned his direction down the alley.

The footsteps came louder, closer.

He pressed his back flat against the rough siding of a garage, his mind catapulting from fear to igniting anger. "Make a stand and be done with it," he muttered to himself.

The figure passed silently.

Alphonse swallowed hard, stepped from the shadows, and shouted out, "Ya fuckin' bastard!"

Whirling around, the figure spread his arms wide while Alphonse moved to the center of the alley.

"Scared ain't ya, ya prick!" yelled Alphonse charging forward.

"Alphonse?" The reply was puzzled, almost timid.

Alphonse halted, sudden confusion riddling his face.

"Alphonse!" The voice shook. "It's me! Goodman! Jimmy Goodman!"

Long moments passed. "Goodman?"

"Jimmy Goodman."

Alphonse gradually lowered his arms and relaxed his fists, growling, "Hoboes should know better 'n ta sneak up on a fella." Still shaken, Alphonse approached cautiously.

"Wasn't sure it was you," Goodman said quickly. "Never expected ya to get a shave and a haircut."

"Christ, Goodman, ya scared the shit outta me."

"Went looking for ya at your shack."

"Was at the basketball game, whole town was."

"Think I was the boogeyman?"

"Worse . . ." Alphonse began shuffling toward the street light on Franklin. "Ya comin'? . . . blacker 'n the inside of a dog out here."

Goodman kept pace alongside.

"What the hell ya doin' back here? What happened ta Californie?"

"Changed my mind. Headin' ta Birmingham. Hankerin' to hole up there fer the winter."

Alphonse nodded, smiling at a memory. "Did 'er the same when I was hoboin'."

"Thought ya might wanna tag along."

"Why would I wanna do that?"

"First of all, I gotta say you take the cake, Alphonse. A hobo watchin' basketball in a gym full of screamin' people . . . damn." Goodman chuckled. "But she was clear as a bell the other day. You're still a hobo."

"That was a long time ago, Goodman. I've grown crotchety."

"Just crotchety?"

"Could be a damn murderer, fer all ya know."

"Yeah, yeah, yeah, so could I." Had there been a moon, Goodman's gigantic smile would've eclipsed it. They briefly stood still, both marinating in the thought of Birmingham.

"Ya lookin' fer a place ta sleep?"

"We hoboes can sleep pert near anyplace, you know that."

"Jesus Christ, Goodman!" Alphonse smiled and shook his head. "It's Jimmy, ain't it?"

"Yep."

"I'm askin' ya, Jimmy, do ya want my hospitality. Sleep at my spot before ya hightail it to Birmingham."

"Like inside?"

"Gotta porch 'n got me a picnic table."

"Much obliged." He laughed. "Gives me time to convince ya to head south."

SITTING ON THE STEPS OF the rickety porch, Goodman and Alphonse gabbed far into the night.

"It's like this, Alphonse. Ridin' the rails these days, lotsa things've changed."

"Some things don't," Alphonse said. "Ya still got the kettle in the jungles. Ya got the smells and sounds a just sittin' in a boxcar . . . and the folks."

"That may be, but nowadays ain't many of us left."

"S'pose not."

"All I ever wanted was to ride alone, take care of my own self," Goodman mused. "But anymore, Alphonse, I've been thinking it'd be damn nice ridin' with another fella. Look out for each other, see the same shit together. Hell, never thought I'd hear myself saying that, but getting older, reckon I could get used to the company."

Alphonse peered in the blackness, watching and feeling the quiet.

"We could head on down to Birmingham like two peas in a pod. Watcha think, Alphonse?"

His mind far away, Alphonse mustered a smile. "Been remembering one time when me 'n Mitts were trippin' back north from Florida. Damn freight loaded ta the gills— every damn car crammed with cargo. Can't recall why we were in such a blame hurry, but we did 'er just the same 'n we got seasoned damn fast."

Alphonse worked the nubbin of his stogie hard as he spoke.

"So me 'n Mitts got this hair-brained idea we were

gonna ride that cannon-baller anyway. We hopped in a damn reefer . . ."

"Not a reefer . . . a reefer?"

"Damn straight it was. We'd no sooner made room by some crates a oranges before that door was slammed shut. We knew we were inta it when we heard the damn yard bull pound a stake inta the handle. The son-a-bitch sealed us in. And there we were, headin' north locked in a damn reefer."

"Christ, how long were ya trapped?"

"Better part a two days. Longest two days a my life. Wasn't hardly any light 'cause they kept them reefers sealed pretty tight, but Mitts could see enough ta try 'n light a fire with the scraps a cardboard we found. Wasn't no use. All the crap stacked ta the ceiling was ice cold, the deck 'n everythin' frosty white . . . I still can see Mitts huddled down shiverin' with breath like smoke . . ."

"What'd ya do?"

"Only thing we could. We started rippin' the cardboard offa the crates. Then the damn cabbages started rollin' like rocks all over the deck. Finally, we got enough big sheets so we could roll ourselves in the cardboard. Damn near two days we rode cocooned together like a couple caterpillars."

"But you made it."

"Got me some awful achy toes from time ta time. Mitts lost three fingers."

"Lucky ya didn't freeze to death."

"Damn lucky, but the best part about the whole shebang . . ."

"There's a best part, Alphonse?"

"When they unlocked us in Chicago, we musta looked like a couple popsicles. Ya shoulda seen the railroaders' faces. After them boys unwound us, they helped us out. We didn't hurt anymore. Had sun on our faces . . . Mitt's hand bad like it was—he still ripped off his shirt, skin white as fish belly. God, that wonderful warm sun . . ." Alphonse savored the memory and closed his eyes. "Mitts did a little jig in the sun. We couldn't stop grinnin' at each other. Never'll forget Mitts' face 'n his eyes . . . never will."

"Alphonse, you're a damn hobo!" said Goodman coming alive. "It's still runnin' through yer blood."

Alphonse sagged a little, as if he'd talked himself empty.

"Won't soon forget the moral of your story, Alphonse."

"Moral?"

"Never ride in a damn reefer."

"That wasn't what I was drivin' at."

Goodman thought for a moment, saying finally with an understanding smile, "I get your point."

"Only a hobo would."

"Looks to me like you've been standin' still in this place a long time."

"That I have," Alphonse said somberly, staring off into the night.

"So what's holding ya here?"

"Right now Jimmy, feel too feeble ta do anythin'." He flipped away the chewed bit of stogie. "Always thought I'd like ridin' again, but . . . there's some things I can't shake clear of."

"Set your mind to Birmingham. Ya know ya don't need much."

Alphonse twisted around, taking stock of his shack, the picnic table, the worn trail to his outhouse.

Jimmy thought he saw a glimmer. "We could head out lickity split!"

Alphonse flattened his hands against the floor and pushed hard as if he never wanted to move from his porch, as if he never wanted to move from that moment with Goodman.

"Need ta talk ta Edgar."

"Who?"

"My friend."

"Friends are hard ta come by."

"Ain't that the truth." Alphonse suddenly paused, his face clouding. He winced and lowered his head to his hands.

"Alphonse, what's wrong?"

"Just got an awful screwy fright, Jimmy." He looked up, quickly wiped his face, the lines in his face deepening, the clarity of his eyes now gone.

"It's scary ta think you'll miss hatin' somethin'. Without Brennon and that church ta hate, I'm not sure how I'll fill the space. Hatin' him's been like my rudder."

CHAPTER THIRTY-THREE

The Deal

BENEATH A LOOMING, LEAD SKY, ALPHONSE WOKE WITH A
start on his porch. It was a little past eight the next morning, but the low clouds and gray drizzle made it feel much
earlier. He knuckled the sleep from his eyes and noted the
spare blanket neatly folded by the door. Shrugging, he
tossed it inside. His short hair was smashed flat from his
sleep, and the drizzle, light but steady, moistened and made
it glisten as he hobbled past Butch's grave and climbed the
stony rail bed. The rails, like bands of silver, narrowed,
pointing south toward Vandellia. He turned and peered
northward then, but Goodman was nowhere in sight. He
knew he'd gone, but he searched anyway. Giving up, he lowered in stages to sit on the rail and rested an arm atop his
knees, the other propping his head.

And there he sat. On either side the rails faded away;
ahead was the rest of Indiana and a thousand choices, and
back was the path past his outhouse where he lived, where
for fourteen years he tried scratching meaning from his
meager life. Though old, his body brittle, he sat as if abandoned like an orphaned boy, like a refugee stranded with no

one, not knowing which direction to turn. The cement sky blended into hazy faraway distance, and he sat quietly in his gray world where he noted only the occasional moist leaf sparkle briefly in the heavy air. Slumped down, filled with bone weariness, he again tilted his head north then south at the vacant rails, and he felt neither anger nor guilt as he shook his head slowly from side to side. What he felt instead was a crushing regret, a loss of precious time weighing him down, bowing his back and clouding his mind. He sat alone on the rail in the drizzle, musing that at one time he'd lived like Goodman, that back then he didn't appreciate fully the luxury of choice.

A sudden forboding he couldn't explain compelled him to shake his mind clear of its spiraling descent, to get up on his wobbly legs and connect again with his futile life. Down the rail bed across the way, he could hear the wind build and rattle lightly his tin roof, and he heard it ripple the tar papered sides of his shack. In a thousand years, he never could have predicted it, but there he was.

The sudden sight of the Monsignor approaching his porch seared into his brain and instantly twisted the fibers of his body into coils.

His eyes had been fixed on the Monsignor, and so engrossed had Alphonse been on the unfolding scene, he was unclear as to how he'd found his way to be standing alongside his picnic table. Like a raven landing and folding its inky feathers, the Monsignor settled on the porch, the stiffening wind flapping and billowing his cassock and coat, his beady black eyes cold and detached. Beneath the bent awning, its Tri-County Hardware sign squeaking occasionally, the Monsignor stood pillar straight and motionless on the sagging porch. To Alphonse, everything about him, his black cassock, his coat, his dark eyes half hidden by a hat, made it feel as if he'd simply materialized from the dismal gray sky.

The wide brim of his black fedora was raked down low, almost hiding the purplish eye that was swollen nearly shut. The Monsignor's long arms stretched out of sight behind his back.

For a long while, each could only stare at the other, and neither moved.

As the Monsignor shifted his weight slightly, something in his face, the scar, his cold dark eyes in the dingy light, reminded Alphonse of that night fourteen years ago in Cleveland's jungle, when he was still Jimmie from the South, reminded him of Brennon staring hungrily while Sheeter and Stubbs did what they did, and how after, when they'd left him bleeding and nearly unconscious, Brennon had crept close from his hiding and said, his voice low and unmistakable, "You stranded me in this shithole, it's your own damn fault," then kicked dirt in his face before disappearing silently back into the night.

Alphonse raked his hand across his face and blinked rapidly trying to clear away those long ago images. He dug out a stogie and considered it. After sucking in a huge breath, finally all set, he sneered, "So, Brennon, what the hell brings ya ta my piece a paradise?"

For the moment, the Monsignor held motionless. He was only a voice. "I'm here to make you an offer."

"Arrogant asshole. What makes ya think ya got somethin' I'd want?"

"Look around." The Monsignor gestured toward the shack. "You have no house, no car . . . nothing worth any-thing. I could change that. I'm prepared to make possible what every man wants when they get to be your age."

"Ya wanna bribe me ta ferget what ya did?"

"To forget your lies!"

Alphonse savored his stogie. "Why? Ya already said no-body with half a brain would ever believe me."

"They won't. You know that as well as I do. But Edgar . . ."

"Edgar's a whole 'nother story, ain't he."

The Monsignor moved to step from the porch but hesi-tated. Still elevated, he tilted his chin higher, his open eye knifing and steady.

"It'd be in Edgar's best interest if you'd use your influ-ence to . . . keep him quiet about his . . . misunderstanding."

"Why ya so damn jacked up, if it's just a mis-under-stan-ding," Alphonse said, punctuating the syllables with his stogie.

"There's no telling where an idiotic story like this could lead. Even the tiniest crumb could mushroom into some-one's truth."

"Now let me get this straight, padre. You wanna give me cash, which I don't give a crap about, ta keep Edgar quiet about a 'story' ya claim ain't nothin' but crap?"

"Then perhaps you'll care about this." The Monsignor stepped from the porch and approached quickly. He with-drew a folded sheet of paper from the breast pocket of his coat and smirked as he handed it to Alphonse.

Alphonse unfolded the paper. It was written on formal church letterhead and signed by the Monsignor. He scanned it quickly, then refocused on the top and read it carefully. As his eyes slowly tracked the message, his weathered face grew ashen and his hand shook, rattling the paper lightly.

In the deathly stillness, Alphonse suddenly exploded. "How dare you! Edgar's done none a these things. He never disrespected a soul. He's done every shit thin' ya ever asked him ta do! This is all a goddamn lie!"

"Father Kimmit has been appointed as my replacement." The Monsignor spoke calmly, enjoying his words. "He's an intelligent young man . . . devoted . . . and we've gotten to know each other well since he's been here."

"No honest priest would ever believe that bullshit!"

"He wants to start off on a good foot and has asked me for advice in all things concerning this parish. Counsel from a bishop would be hard for a priest to ignore."

"This . . ." Alphonse wadded up the paper and pitched it to the ground. "This horseshit if I don't persuade Edgar ta ferget the sick shit ya done?"

The Monsignor's expression dripped arrogance, confidence. "I'm not sure how Edgar'd get by in this town without work. You know, being nearly blind, a wife . . . and his boys . . . well, they probably could adjust in time."

The shake in Alphonse's legs was steady as his face creased dark with fear and desperation. It took several long moments before he was finally able to retaliate, and said, "Well, padre, maybe the photos I took might set a few things straight fer ya."

The Monsignor held up a small paper bag, then with a glib smile, tossed it on the table where several burnt flashbulbs slipped out and skidded across the top. "Did you honestly think I would believe you took pictures?"

His eyes quivering, Alphonse finally responded through tight lips, "See ya found my message."

"Stupid little man. You could never afford a camera," jeered the Monsignor.

"Army surplus. Damn cheap!" responded Alphonse instantly. "Ain't but a short freight ride ta Fort Wayne." He stared straight at the Monsignor. "They got all kinds a gadgets, cameras included."

The Monsignor studied Alphonse for a long beat, then finally said, "How could someone like you ever know how to operate a camera?"

"Remember Newman, drives the camera for the *Herald*? Nice kid. Showed me all the tricks, how she works." He mimed holding up a camera and pressing the shutter. "Easy as pie."

"Bull!"

"Maybe it is." He tried on a coy smile. "Maybe it ain't."

"Edgar's job is on the line!"

"Yers, too!"

The Monsignor rattled out quickly, "Convince Edgar to be quiet. I have money."

"Pile a jack from Sunday's offerings, no doubt." Alphonse took a long draw on his stogie, the fire in his eyes growing stronger. "Ya'd buy me a car?"

The Monsignor was about to contest, but held back, and spit out like a single word, "I could make it happen."

"A shiny car just ta push Edgar ta forget the sick shit ya done?"

"Say it however you want, but yes!"

"Ya been right all along, padre, I ain't got nothin' ta lose." Alphonse scanned his shack, the path to the back where his stuff was stacked, then briefly beyond the Monsignor to the freight tracks up the hill from his dog's grave. "But my life don't require much." He focused back on Brennon. "Now Edgar . . . ya been promising Edgar a decent wage fer years, and ya ain't ever paid 'im squat."

"I'm in no position now to affect Edgar's salary."

"Here's a lesson outta yer own shit book. Edgar did bust yer face, but ya gotta learn ta forgive. I'm thinkin' that good man deserves a bonus."

"You have the audacity . . ."

"Yer damn right, I do!"

The Monsignor slammed his fist against the table. "I want those photographs!"

Rubbing his stubbled chin, Alphonse said calmly, "An' probably a generous bonus ta boot." He nodded to himself. "An' ya wouldn't want Edgar ta think he was sellin' his son, now, would you—so you set 'er up like a gift, anonymous, maybe from some generous soul who died 'n left it ta the church."

"You pathetic little man."

"Pathetic's probably close, but with pictures showin' ya in all yer glory . . . well . . ."

The Monsignor spun on his heels, never looked back, and stormed off.

Alphonse watched until the black silhouette disappeared into the gloom, then sank down to his picnic table, using his trembling hand to mindlessly play with the sack of flashbulbs.

At last, he moved slowly to his feet and climbed the gray cindered rail bed. The drizzle had become rain again. He locked his eyes to the hazy distance, never feeling the wind rippling his face, and headed toward Vandellia in the now slanting rain.

CHAPTER THIRTY-FOUR

The Blue Cat

IN LESS THAN A MONTH AFTER ZACH'S FIRST GAME, COOLER weather and changing colors signaled that summer was finally over. It'd been an autumn Saturday, when Alphonse and Francis settled under the broad and sheltering elm at The End, where, they both agreed, a monster catfish by now must surely rule.

The sky was clean, robin-egg blue, and sunlight sparkled through the yellow and rust colored leaves, winking shadows on the ground. A molasses box packed with sandwiches and a Mason jar of water waited in the shade. Alphonse wedged the stub of a stogie in the corner of his mouth, resting his back against the wizened elm, and watched intently as Francis pushed the prop into the soft bank, then carefully threaded a worm onto the hook of his new spinning rod. He briefly admired the rod and the shiny reel with its green striped line, then winged his bait far out into the canal.

"Alphonse," he said, adjusting the rod in the prop. "Say again how you came by the new spinning rod."

"Straight up bought it."

"But it's new." His face puzzled, Francis turned around and said, "How could—"

"It's yers now, 'cause I'm a noodler, ya know."

"I mean—Alphonse, I know you don't have much money."

"Never needed money."

"So how'd you buy the rod?"

"Ya know old man Gilespie—lives close ta me down by the marsh?"

"He's a grump."

"That's him. A while back he corners me on my way home from work. He says, 'Ain't no secret ya make squat bein' Edgar's flunky.' That Gillespie's one helluva feisty bastard, 'n hell Francis, I didn't know what he was drivin' at . . ."

"Does it always have ta be so complicated?"

"Ya wanna hear this?"

Francis sighed and nodded.

"Wanted ta know if I needed some extra money, says he could use somebody ta shovel his walks this winter. Not too keen on the idea, I says, and then he offers ta buy me whatever I want—a trade off sorta deal, like barterin'. And bingo, I got myself a brand spankin' new spinnin' rod."

"And now ya hafta shovel his sidewalks all winter?"

Alphonse smiled. "Just on the days it snows."

"For a spinning rod?"

"Hell, who knows?" Alphonse grinned, his eyes reflecting the sparkling morning. "Yer spinnin' rod could be the start a my new prosperity."

For some time both were quiet, every so often eyeing

the cork bobbing serenely in the canal's murky water. Alphonse rose slowly, exaggerated his stretch, then settled again on the ground at the base of the elm.

"Don't look like yer fish 'r playin' today."

Francis reeled in his line and showed Alphonse the empty hook. "Something stole my bait."

"Carp are sneaky bastards."

"Carp are hogs." Francis threaded on another worm. "It woulda swallowed the hook. We were yappin' and whatever it was got my worm fair and square." He launched his fresh bait back to the water. "Guess I wasn't paying attention, but I wasn't daydreamin' like I used ta."

"Mighta been that cat, Francis."

"I wish. Haven't caught a catfish since the derby."

"It'd be a son-a-bitch ta pry the smile from my face if ya caught yer cat here 'n now."

Carefully, Francis placed the rod in the prop and sat down cross-legged beside it.

"Ya say, not much daydreamin' these days?"

"Been a long time since I did that."

"Damn . . . that's music ta my hairy ears."

"I gotta tell ya, Alphonse," Francis stared out at the brown, peaceful waters. "Things are getting real weird 'round the house."

"Do tell."

"Mom 'n Dad . . . they keep whispering to each other and giggling. It's weird."

"Gigglin'? The two of 'em? Jesus H. Christ, them two gigglin' is damn weird."

"Mom gotta new dryer, but I don't think that's it.

And—this'll really knock ya on your butt, Alphonse—after work on Thursday, they walked down to Raabe's."

"The car place?"

"Yep . . . Raabe's used cars."

Alphonse scrunched his eyes tightly and pumped a fist against his chest.

Francis eyed him. "Why'd that get ya all fired up?"

Alphonse beamed a wide toothy smile. "A car, Francis. Think yer dad's gonna buy a car?"

"Heck if I know. Mom would have to drive 'cause of Dad's eyes. Zach says he won't talk about it because he doesn't wanna jinx the deal."

"Betcha it'd be neat ridin' 'round in a car."

"S'pose so."

"S'pose so?"

"You're not gettin' what I'm sayin'. Feels like a lot of things are different now. Lately, Dad's been watching me. All the time askin' me stuff about school 'n all."

"Hell, that sounds like a damn improvement ta me."

"It's just that before, Dad never had the time to pay much attention. Mom, too."

"Well . . . I'll be go ta . . ." A sudden movement caught Alphonse's eye. He pointed his gnarly finger at the bobber moving sideways.

Francis spun around and waited. His bobber again began twitching.

"We gotta nibble, Alphonse!"

Francis scrambled to his feet, grabbed the rod and reeled down to tighten his line. Waiting, waiting; the cork finally dipped beneath the surface. Putting his entire body into the effort, Francis yanked back aggressively to set the hook—and his entire rig, line, sinker, and fish zinged up, out, and back through the air. Alphonse's look of anticipation flashed to utter surprise, his eyebrows raised high and his mouth a perfect "Oh"—and he dodged sideways just in time to miss the tiny blue gill flying straight toward his head. In a flash then, he and Francis rummaged in the weeds and finally located the little bugger a dozen yards beyond the bank.

Alphonse simply couldn't contain himself as he bent over double with an uncontrollable belly laugh. "Can ya imagine what was goin' through that poor fish's brain when he looked 'round 'n found himself airborne, starin' eyeball ta eyeball with me?"

"Lay off." His face scarlet, Francis sank to his haunches to toss the blue gill back.

Still amused, Alphonse stood, looking over Francis's shoulder.

"With that set, ya probably coulda sent a twenty-pound carp wingin' my way."

"Very funny." Francis undid the mess he'd made of his tackle and tossed his rig back to the drink and said with more than a little annoyance, "You wait, Alphonse. The day ain't over."

Alphonse wiped his eyes, then took his bowler off, turning it around and around, still grinning. "At least ya didn't slime my hat."

Francis scowled and refused to look at Alphonse.

"Put a lot a miles on this hat." Alphonse pointed to an ancient stain. "Now this here spot . . ." he began.

Francis began chuckling and couldn't stop, his chuckles escalating to a full-fledged belly laugh of his own.

Alphonse raised his eyebrows in mock surprise. "Now ya laugh?"

"Your face," Francis gasped, "Shoulda seen your face when my fish was flyin' your way."

Alphonse gave him a good-natured swat with his bowler and plopped back down on the bank.

"So, Francis," he teased. "Ya still seein' that good lookin' babe?"

"What're you talking about?"

"Ya know, the one you was talkin' ta after Zach's game."

"Her? She's not a babe!" Francis blushed. "She's just a girl in my class."

"That may be, but I know women."

"Dangit! She wasn't a woman!"

Alphonse exaggerated a wink. "I always say, there ain't nothin' wrong with a little romance after a big game."

Francis rolled his eyes and bit his lip.

"Holy hell, Francis!" Alphonse suddenly jabbed out a finger and scrambled to his feet. "Yer cork's gone!"

"This could be our fish!" Francis grabbed up his spinner, waited, and felt the line. "Feels different. This ain't no blue gill, Alphonse!"

Francis reeled down, waited until his line was straight and his rod tip bent slightly. He focused on where the line disappeared in the water, then jerked his rod up sharply to set the hook.

The mystery was hooked soundly and drove to the opposite bank where the water was deeper, stirring up the gunk from the bottom. Alphonse knelt at the edge of the bank, tracking where the line zipped through the canal. Francis held the rod tip high. The line cut left, then sliced close to the near bank and finally ripped back toward the deep. After an eternity, Alphonse yelped, "Got our cork back!"

"For now . . ." The rod pulsed, yet Francis held it steady. "He ain't near ready."

"Looks powerful, Francis!"

"Is."

"Ya can't just let 'im swim circles all afternoon. Start crankin'!"

"It's my fish!"

"Not yet it ain't."

Far out, the line carved a slow turn. Finally, the fish rolled finning to the top.

"Damn," Alphonse whispered. "See 'im now."

"It's a blue cat!" Francis tightened his grip on the rod. "Better 'n a ten pounder!"

"Three, maybe four," said Alphonse reverently. "It's a son-a-bitchin' nice cat . . . bring 'im in close."

"It's still got fight!" Francis said, carefully cranking the reel. "Wish we had a net."

"Don't need no stinkin' net." Alphonse kicked off his boots and tossed his socks up the bank. He shoved his pants to his knees, then with his feet in the water, he made ready.

"Bring 'im ta papa." He tongued his stogie and hunched far over. "Work 'im in close 'n I'll handle the rest."

"I'm not so sure, Alphonse."

"Me 'n fishin' go way back. We got this baby."

"Might still run!"

As Francis gradually worked the fish closer to the bank, he memorized the gulping mouth, the tail swishing slowly from side to side, the shape of its smooth broad head, and the bluish color of its four-inch whiskers.

Alphonse leaned way out, straining to grab the gills. When his bowler accidentally slipped from his head and splatted against the water, the fish spooked and ripped back to the deep.

"Damn, Alphonse!"

"Ain't my fault!" Alphonse snagged his hat and threw it up the bank.

Reeling it in close again, Francis suddenly yelped in panic, "Alphonse! We only got 'im by the whisker!"

"Go slow!" Alphonse spread his legs wide. "Slower 'n a cat sniffin' fer fish heads."

"Gonna be slippery—"

"Been noodlin' fish since before you were—"

"Alphonse!"

A few feet away, just beyond Alphonse's knees, the fish slowly finned. No longer needing to crank, Francis gently leaned the rod sideways toward the bank. "Ya ready?"

"We got 'im."

"Watch out for his stinger!"

Alphonse deftly lifted the exhausted catfish by its gill plate and dropped it on the bank. An equally exhausted Francis wilted to his knees while Alphonse yanked out the hook and stoned the fish.

"Biggest fish I ever caught, Alphonse," Francis said just above a whisper. He stared open-mouthed at their cat. "Never woulda got 'im if I was using my old cane pole."

Alphonse dangled his feet in the water. His eyes sparkled excitement, his face giddy, as he said emphatically, "Progress, Francis, progress."

Francis looked long into the old wrinkled face. "Thanks for the spinning rod, Alphonse."

"Well, Francis," Alphonse gave Francis a warm pat on the back. "Ya broke 'er in just fine."

Francis suddenly kicked off his sneakers and whipped his socks over his shoulder. He pushed his jeans up to his knees and plunged his feet in the canal, lifting his wiggling toes above the surface. "Been forever since I did this."

Alphonse nodded. "My pappy always said it was the best part a fishin'."

They sat for the longest time, silently watching their feet share the canal. And while Francis couldn't come up with anything to say just then, he savored the peace at The End, and the contented smile resting on his friend's old weathered face.

III

FRANCIS: MAY, 1964

———

CHAPTER THIRTY-FIVE

Going Home: St. Joseph, Indiana

THERE'S NOT MUCH MORE TO TELL YOU ABOUT THAT
summer long ago. There were those in town who swore it'd
been the hottest on record, and most felt that with the great
pigeon scare behind them and with the Monsignor's swift
departure, they would finally be able to relish the late start
of autumn. In those crisp autumn weeks, well before Hal-
loween, there returned to St. Joseph an equilibrium of
sorts, parishioners becoming encouraged with their new
pastor while settling back into life, like lacing up a pair of
familiar boots.

For me, I'd pushed out of sight that dreadful summer. I
couldn't put it into words, but especially then, I'd become
enthralled with the changing of the season. I savored the
clean sky suspending motionless the soft lazy clouds, loved
watching the leaves swirl and rattle down the brick streets,
and I never seemed to tire of the smell of brittle leaves
burning alongside the curbs, the light crackling sound and
cloudy smoke pausing just above the smoldering fires. On
the surface, it looked like I'd survived my horrific summer,
yet there remained locked away the mystery and questions

surrounding Alphonse and my Dad whenever they spoke of the Monsignor and the bell tower. Though those questions often sparked my mind, they could never be called a haunting. Instead, those mysteries remained half buried, only faraway noise as I stumbled into the monotonous rut of my school year.

Yet so insidious had the bell tower been, I never had an inkling of how thoroughly it had infused my thoughts, keeping unfocused my tattered mind, and how decisively it had molded my perception of myself. Separated from Zach that entire summer, I was not aware of my overpowering drive to be like my brother, to have those pats on the back from friends, to delve headlong into basketball where maybe I could sit next to him on the bench at a tournament game.

This intense need never weakened throughout my last year of grade school, and in fact, grew to near obsession as I plowed into my four years of high school. Despite my consistent vigil watching Zach and Rupert, I was never able to catch up to my brother. While I'd made the team my sophomore year, I was unable to pull alongside Zach and strut with him into the gym together.

Partly because I was growing older, but mostly due to my desperate need to become something I was not, those warm and confiding moments with Alphonse grew further and further apart. Alphonse would stand back and bide his time, and in retrospect, I suspect he often wondered if he could've done more to help during that scalding summer, and I'm sure he struggled to find creative ways to convince me that I had wonderful qualities that not even my brother possessed.

What the hell am I doin'? I'd agonize. *I'm scared to even go in the damn game.* The jeering and cat calls when my nerves made it impossible for me to make even the easiest of uncontested lay-ups became too much, and near the end of my junior year, without consulting anyone, I quit the team. It was then that I folded completely into my private world of self-doubt and self-deprecation, and I muddled through the rest of high school without making a wave, without ever being seen. Sometimes I'd wander to the Friday night dance, climb high up the bleachers and sit in the dark to listen to the music; some Saturdays I moseyed down to the Choo-Choo and played pinball if my brother and Rupe weren't there, but always I kept my eyes averted and listened. I'd become the kid with a pleasant enough face, the kid who never seemed to mind watching alone from the back.

As my senior year began winding down, I became convinced that after I graduated, I'd follow my brother and head to Indiana State University. Never weighing the pros and cons, without any hesitation or consulting anyone, I was off to college simply because that's what all the really cools kids did. Maybe there, I'd often think, the change in scenery might help me blend in . . . maybe there I might meet a friend like Rupe.

But after I left St. Joseph, the change in scenery clarified nothing, and on most evenings my freshman year, I sat for hours on the back porch of my rooming house staring out, watching students gab and joke as they meandered down the alley.

I said there wasn't much more to tell you, but that's not

exactly accurate. I've skirted the last few details because they're painful, but with you coming along this far, I need to tell you about the day I can never forget, the day that, in hindsight, pivoted me and redirected my world. I remember it clear as day even now after all these years, and how I heard the news still grooves my brain.

It was the end of my first year at ISU, after I'd taken my finals. I was on a bench outside of Arps Hall, hunched over a paper I was scrambling to finish for desperately needed extra credit, when Zach found me. His face was dark, and for what seemed an eternity, he said nothing.

I waited for him to spit it out, clicking my pen so hard it sounded like a cap gun. Hell, I hadn't seen him more than a dozen times the whole semester, and I was getting damned annoyed by his weird interruption. I tapped the open notebook in my lap.

"Zach, I gotta get this done by noon."

He checked his watch, did some mysterious calculation in his head, and said flatly, "You'll have ta scoot."

"Right, Zach. So—?"

He sat on the edge of the bench, fiddling with his slide rule. After a few moments, he shoved it back in its holster, then propped his elbows on his knees. He kept his head down. When he finally spoke, his voice was barely audible. "Mom called this morning."

"But we'll be home on Friday."

"Plans have changed." Zach stalled, looking like he had more to say. He stared at his clenched hands.

"What?" I demanded, drumming my pen against my notebook.

"Francis, this is fuckin' shitty . . ."

I snapped my notebook closed. "It's Dad ain't it?"

"Alphonse."

"Alphonse?" I searched his face.

He scrubbed his face with both hands and sat up straight, then turned toward me. After several long, deep breaths he finally said, "Alphonse is dead, Francis."

I couldn't talk. I couldn't even look at him. I slammed my eyes shut.

My voice finally peeped, "How?"

"Mom only said he was killed last week in Vandellia."

"What!" I winged my pen somewhere. "Last week? Jesus fuckin' Christ!"

"Mom's been trying to get a hold of us. What with finals and all . . . the phones in the dorm . . . she tried, Francis."

"Not damn hard enough!" I yelled, jumping to my feet.

Zach left to change our bus tickets so we could head home early. In truth, he understood that I needed to be left alone.

While the shock percolated, gaining strength by the second, the sketchy news consuming every cell in my body, I began recalling all those times when I could've shared more time with Alphonse, but didn't; when I could've walked together with the man, but made excuses, believing I'd outgrown the need for his comfort.

Suddenly, standing there in front of Arps Hall, the blunt facts crashed into me as if I'd been hit by a runaway train.

I knew I had had no business being on that team bench, that Zach had the talent not me, and I thought about all those basketball games where Alphonse and I could've sat together cheering for Zach. With all my energy focused on being like my brother, I'd left Alphonse alone to cheer by himself. I got to wondering if I was the reason Alphonse gave up going to the games altogether my junior year, after Dad had his stroke.

For the three hours on the bus back home, Zach and I spoke little. I understood that his mocking Alphonse whenever he could in high school, joining in the chorus that Alphonse was just a crazy old fool, wasn't really Zach, that he had his own sorrows for the man who helped him into the world. But on the bus I couldn't talk to him about Alphonse —I wasn't ready to talk to anybody about that.

When we finally made it back home, Zach walked straight in through the front door. I stalled outside.

Ever since Dad was found unconscious on the boiler room's floor, I'd had a hard time visiting with him. He could still walk okay, but since he was no longer able to work, he seldom got up from his chair and he never watched the TV they'd bought. He existed by grumbling his needs to Mom who understood, but to me he barely said a thing.

I was scared to see him. I was scared that Alphonse's passing had plunged the Dad I knew further out of sight.

When I finally came in, Dad wasn't slouching like usual. Instead, he sat oddly upright in his faded lounger, but his head hung low to his chest. Engulfed in silence, barricaded far away, he stared down at the wet hankie his big hand was wadding in his lap.

Zach sat with Mom at the kitchen table. I just stood in the doorway, struggling to find anything concrete, anything that wasn't erratically whirling past. I guess I had that look, the fragile look saying that anything could instantly send me to some faraway abyss, because it took forever for Mom to look my way. Eventually, she motioned for me to join them at the table, but even after she patted the seat for me to sit, I didn't budge. I couldn't relax, couldn't yell; I couldn't make sense of anything. The house was stifling.

"Francis," she'd said gently. "Join us?"

I fumbled for words. "Thanks, but . . . think I'd like to go for a walk."

"You go right ahead, Francis. Dinner's at five."

I nodded and backed out of the kitchen and onto the porch.

Everything seemed different and the same at the same time. No noise rattled from the laundry room, no clothes hung drying on the line out back, and in the alley, I noted the Ford collecting dust. It was as if everything had paused, everything held in suspension, as if the entire world was waiting for me before life could begin spinning again. Even on the porch, I felt like I couldn't breathe and needed to move. So with jittery, unfocused eyes seeing nothing, I slowly walked away, allowing my legs to automatically carry me toward my old hideaway, The End.

Maybe I was marching faster than I thought, maybe it was shorter than I remembered, but in no time, I was cutting from the dirt road to the now overgrown path.

Ahead was the elm marking where the canal joined the Little Auglaize; ahead were the nooks where I sat for hours eyeing my cork, and ahead was where Alphonse helped me land the blue cat of my childhood dreams. But I was afraid and could go no further. Then, as if a dense fog had suddenly lifted, I realized that to go forward would stain my memory, would dilute what I needed to preserve. The trees needed to always dangle my bobbers, the confluence must always stink, and in the autumn, the blue cats should forever spark the fantasy of boys. I got to thinking that I'd like some day to return to The End as an old man, where I could recall that early summer fun—Zach and Rupe playing basketball, the tiny blue gill my brother ignored, our bike ride home through that wicked storm. Right then, I needed The End to remain unchanged, so that even in a hundred years it could enthrall boys and mesmerize old men. Christ . . . sounds like I'm talking about that pigeon child I'd found.

I never made it all the way back to The End, and I suppose it's just as well. Not yet ready for home, certainly not ready to hear the details about Alphonse that my mind clamored for, I ambled along the canal, following it through town, eventually settling down on the culvert by Third Street. The sun burned hot through my shirt, yet I barely noticed. I sat stunned, watching a thousand miniature catfish swirling close by the cement for comfort. For a brief time I felt safe, remembering how Alphonse had always kept an eye out for me. I recalled him giddy when he yelled, "Bring 'im ta papa!"; I recalled our feet dangling in the water, him sitting content and smiling like a little boy in a bowler.

I sat on that culvert, the sun beating down, sifting through my memories of the old hobo—his stories about his days riding the rails with Mitts, how they had to stand all afternoon waiting for a sandwich at the "salivation army," how he described the baseball finale at the end of the season, "The World Serious," and we both understood that he knew exactly what he was saying.

A cold nose nudging my shoulder startled me: someone's dog out on a lark of its own. I watched it lope away. The shadows were growing long, the culvert cooling, and the school of infant catfish had vanished. The sky had become opaque, and far away, thunder rolled among the gathering clouds, and I knew then that I'd delayed long enough.

Heading home down Second past the church, I dared not eye the steeple and the bell tower where I'd spent those Friday evenings summers ago. I knew that I should be done with it, but I wasn't. While I'd grown to understand the gross facts of what happened, the details of why and how remained a mystery. With Dad the way he was . . . and now with Alphonse gone, I would never know how they dealt with the immensity of it all. I had it easy, I escaped and was never really there; they had nowhere to hide and had to live it.

Suddenly, I needed to know the details of what happened to Alphonse, and I picked up my pace.

"Francis!" I spun around at the sound of an old familiar voice.

And there he was, Father Yossarian, as beet-red in the face as I remembered, wearing a tremendously wide smile. I grinned back and jogged to meet him on the rectory porch.

"Father Yossarian! You found your way back."

"Yes, yes," he beamed, arms wide in welcome. "How are you, Francis?"

"S'pose I'm doin' all right."

"How about a cup of coffee?"

"Never liked the taste. But I wouldn't mind the visit."

The rectory was different from how I remembered it. There were no plaques or antiques on the tables, and a sense of casual living, a degree of untidiness had replaced the austere, brittle feel of the past. Muddy boots sat outside the Father's office door. Inside, the office was spacious yet spartan, and there were places on the walls where time had outlined the pictures and awards that had once hung there.

The only vestige of that other time was the huge ornate mahogany desk.

The office smelled of coffee. Father Yossarian offered me a seat and leaned against the desk.

"I was so sorry to hear about Alphonse," he said quietly. "I know what he meant to you."

I couldn't look at him, didn't know what to say.

"Your mom tells me you're now a college boy."

"Well, I'm in college, 'n that's about it." I shifted restlessly in the chair.

"Zach wants to be an engineer?"

I nodded. "That's Zach."

"You?"

"Still gettin' my feet on the ground. Maybe English."

The Father grinned. "You'd make a wonderful teacher, Francis."

I shook my head. "Never thought you'd be back here."

"I needed to come back to St. Joseph."

"Needed?"

"Yes. I didn't leave on good terms with myself or my

Lord." The Father stood abruptly. "I'm having coffee." He retrieved two mugs from the end of the counter. "And you're going to have some cocoa while we chat." He disappeared through the door beyond the counter and quickly returned. He handed me a mug, and I wrapped my hands around its warmth.

"Things have a way of working out, don't they?" He perched on his desk and blew softly at his steaming coffee. "Apparently, Father Kimmit wasn't a good fit. I was finally able to get reassigned here last fall, just after you and your brother left for Indianapolis." He smiled, but it seemed to me to be a sad smile. "With Monsignor Brennon gone—"

I cut him off. "He's still a bishop?"

"Archbishop." The Father sighed, his usually cheerful face troubled. "They say he's making wonderful changes in the diocese. I'm not sure," he said, shrugging. "He's thriving on one level at least."

He sipped his coffee, and when I didn't say anything, he said, "Your parents seem to be doing remarkably well. I try and get by your house at least once a week."

"With the way Dad is now, I bet Mom really appreciates it."

"She says the doctors are very encouraged about your father's improvement. He may never work the boiler room again, but it could've been devastating. And every day his speech is getting better. He's even started to joke."

I raised my eyebrows. "We're talking about my dad, right?"

"Yes." The Father chuckled. "And we both know that's one heck of an improvement."

I took a big swallow of cocoa, and it was good.

"Your mother's an incredibly strong woman."

"She gets things done, all right."

Father Yossarian set his coffee on the desk and leaned forward. "Francis, if it hadn't been for your mother, Alphonse wouldn't have been buried in our cemetery. I officiated, and Alphonse was finally welcomed inside the church with open arms. Your mother arranged everything and paid for his burial."

"I missed his funeral!" I blurted out, staring at my cocoa, turning the mug around and around.

"Alphonse would've understood," the Father said, his voice low and soft.

Ignoring his comment, I began, "Do you remember the bell tower?"

The Father nodded.

"The baby pigeon I found that last night? Dead a hundred years and still looked almost alive?"

"I do."

"When you took it away," I swirled the last of my cocoa in the bottom of the mug. "You scared me."

"What you found scared me. It was all wrong." He lowered his eyes. "Right then, it struck me like an omen—an evil one."

"An omen of what?"

"I'd suspected it early that summer, the way the Monsignor watched you from the sacristy, the way his eyes tracked whatever you were doing. I should've at least said something to your father."

"You couldn't have known, not really. And besides, you left town—you weren't even here."

"I thought I'd still have a chance." The Father swiped his forehead. "But by then, my hands were tied with my sacred vows to secrecy."

"What—"

The Father's face grew dark. "Certainly you remember from second grade catechism: no matter how horrendous or evil, a priest can never divulge what he hears in the confessional. We all took that sacred vow. Unfortunately for me, one of the last things I did before leaving was hear the Monsignor's confession."

I searched the Father's face. "So, then you knew for sure, but then you couldn't say anything?"

He nodded.

It took a while for that to sink in, but then I suddenly wanted an answer. "Tell me. Did God forgive the Monsignor?"

He shook his head. "I don't know, Francis. I like to believe that God forgives all who are truly penitent."

I thought the Father's answer was rote and weak, just a repeat of what had been drilled into his head in seminary. I was too tired to press further, but at least the Father seemed to be sincere.

"Alphonse tried to help, I know that now," I said. "But I still can't get over missing his funeral."

Father Yossarian asked with a gentle smile, "Are you one of those guys?"

"What guys?"

"Wishing you could go back and change what can't be changed, making yourself miserable with regret in the process." He took a last swallow from his mug and grinned. "If I could figure out how to rewrite my own script, I'd be one heck of a bored fellow."

"Bored?"

He nodded. "If you worked out everything perfectly all the time, there'd be no surprises. I like being surprised even if I am shocked by my own stupidity from time to time."

I'm sure I looked beyond bewildered, but the Father just smiled at me, then leaned close as if sharing a secret. "Alphonse loved you and your brother like his own sons."

I heard the words, rolled them around and around in my head. My nose must've been running because what I asked came out sloppy.

"Father . . . how did it happen?"

"He'd broken his neck. A couple railroaders found him by the rails at the Vandellia train yard. They figured he must've slipped trying to pull himself into a boxcar."

My voice shook as I asked, "How did they even know who he was?"

"He had a bindle, a hobo bindle. In it, they found a picture of your mother and father with your brother when he was an infant."

Something within me suddenly changed. I couldn't put my finger on it, but something not completely horrible began germinating.

"Then . . . he died a hobo?"

"He always was."

I remember little of what the Father said next, and I'm unclear as to how I found myself walking steadily toward Alphonse's old shack. Standing by his picnic table, I studied the shack, then recalled the Father's words about letting guilt and regret screw up the present. I quickly realized that I didn't need to go inside—for those snow days playing checkers, those times were gone.

I passed Butch's grave and climbed the rise to the rail bed. The brooding storm had moved off, and the sky hinted blue while juvenile frogs squeaked in the distance.

Ahead down the tracks lay where it happened. My eyes searched the hazy distance, and I finally understood that I didn't need to go there either.

For a long time, I stood on the rails that silvered south toward Vandellia. The marsh lay before me unchanged, and I was sure that after all this time, the three-legged rats had long since disappeared. I couldn't help but laugh out loud as I recalled Alphonse's reassuring words, that rats won't ever learn to count.

A twenty-minute walk would take me home where my family awaited. I wasn't exactly sure how I frittered away the entire afternoon. I'd promised Mom I'd be home for dinner by five. I'd be late, but then I always was.

THE END.

ACKNOWLEDGMENTS

I don't fully understand this business of publishing, the myriad details necessary to put my story on the printed page. "El Autor Camina Solo" may describe other writers, but this adage could never serve for my journey.

To my son, Devin, whose bottomless energy pushed me forward, and to my daughter, Stephanie, whose calm, reassuring voice kept me heading in the right direction, a simple Thank You can never say enough.

It's impossible to calculate the value of the good folks at SparkPress: Crystal Patriarche, with her unbounded enthusiasm; Brooke Warner and her ability to forgive my mistakes; Lauren Wise, whose steady, gentle push kept me on track; Kelly Bowen, who nudged me into publicity when I preferred to hide; and to the rest of my publication team at SparkPress, I owe you enormous thanks.

To my brother, Mark, whose careful hand and keen eyes supported me in my daily life, you have my heartfelt appreciation. To my editor and writing guru, Judy Fort Brenneman, a wonderful writer in her own right, a master in the art of storytelling, a communicator of composition, thank you—and thanks for being my friend. Without your endurance and unworldly patience, the story of "Alphonse" would have never been told.

And to my best friend and unwavering partner in life, Juanita Kerven, I can never express accurately my gratitude for your loyalty and perseverance as we both saw this story through to the end. During all these years, as I plugged along on a serious and often dark story, you've given me what I've needed most: your infectious enthusiasm for life each and every day, your easy and gentle smile I can never live without.

ABOUT THE AUTHOR

CARL SEVER began writing fiction in part because of his
interest in the 1930s Dust Bowl, hobo culture and lore, and
small-town midwestern life, especially in areas dominated
by the Roman Catholic Church. His writing has also been
an important part of recovery from a traumatic brain injury
he suffered in a car accident in 1990. Carl has been a
teacher, a journalist, and nature photographer. He has also
been a businessman and co-owner of an exclusive wholesale
photo lab. He's an avid outdoorsman, passionate fly-
fisherman, and adventurer who has explored the mountains
of Colorado, Montana, Canada, and Alaska. His travels
have taken him to Costa Rica and Panama, reinforcing his
study of Spanish as a second language. He's a lifelong
learner, with studies ranging from screenwriting and sculp-
ture to nature photography. *Alphonse* is his first novel.

SELECTED TITLES FROM SPARKPRESS

SparkPress is an independent boutique publisher delivering high-quality, entertaining, and engaging content that enhances readers' lives, with a special focus on female-driven work. Visit us at www.gosparkpress.com

The Half-Life of Remorse, by Grant Jarrett, $16.95, 978-1-943006-14-4. Two tattered mendicants, Sam and Chic, meet on the streets, both unaware that their paths crossed years before. Meanwhile, Sam's daughter Claire, who Sam doesn't even know is alive, is still unable to give up hope that her vanished father might someday reappear. When these three lives converge thirty years after the brutal crime that shattered their lives, the puzzle of the past gradually falls together, but the truth commands a high price.

Rooville, by Julie Long. $17, 978-1-94071-660-2. Even after thirteen years in California, TV weatherman Owen Martin can feel the corners of his squareness still evident. When he's fired from his job, he heads home to Iowa—but in his absence, Martinville has become the center of the Transcendental Meditation movement. With old customs and open-mindedness clashing like warm and cold fronts, Owen gets caught in a veritable tornado.

The Rules of Half, by Jenna Patrick, $16.95, 978-1-943006-18-2. When an orphaned teen claims he's her biological father, Will Fletcher—a manic-depressant who's sworn to never be a parent again—must come to terms with his illness and his tragic past if he is to save her from the streets. The Rules of Half explores what it is to be an atypical family in a small town and to be mentally ill in the wake of a tragedy—and who has the right to determine both.

The Year of Necessary Lies, by Kris Radish. $17, 978-1-94071-651-0. A great-granddaughter discovers her ancestor's secrets—inspirational forays into forbidden love and the Florida Everglades at the turn of the last century.

About SparkPress

SparkPress is an independent, hybrid imprint focused on merging the best of the traditional publishing model with new and innovative strategies. We deliver high-quality, entertaining, and engaging content that enhances readers' lives. We are proud to bring to market a list of *New York Times* best-selling, award-winning, and debut authors who represent a wide array of genres, as well as our established, industry-wide reputation for creative, results-driven success in working with authors. SparkPress, a BookSparks imprint, is a division of SparkPoint Studio LLC.

Learn more at GoSparkPress.com